The Merchant's Tale

MORE BY THIS AUTHOR

Historical Fiction

The Testament of Mariam

This Rough Ocean

The Chronicles of Christoval Alvarez

The Secret World of Christoval Alvarez
The Enterprise of England
The Portuguese Affair
Bartholomew Fair
Suffer the Little Children
Voyage to Muscovy
The Play's the Thing
That Time May Cease

Oxford Medieval Mysteries

The Bookseller's Tale
The Novice's Tale
The Huntsman's Tale

The Fenland Series

Flood
Betrayal

Contemporary Fiction

The Anniversary
The Travellers
A Running Tide

The Merchant's Tale

Ann Swinfen

Shakenoak Press

Copyright © Ann Swinfen 2017

Shakenoak Press

ISBN 978-0-9932372-9-4

Ann Swinfen has asserted her moral right under the
Copyright, Designs and Patents Act, 1988, to be identified
as the author of this work.

All Rights reserved. No part of this publication may be reproduced,
copied, stored in a retrieval system, or transmitted, in any form or by
any means, without the prior written consent of the copyright holder,
nor be otherwise circulated in any form of binding or cover other than
that in which it is published and without a similar condition
being imposed on the subsequent purchaser.

Cover design by JD Smith www.jdsmith-design.co.uk

This one is for

All my lovely readers
who have taken
Nicholas & the others
to their hearts

Chapter One

Oxford, Autumn 1353

It was the fifth day of October, in this seven and twentieth year of our King Edward, third of that name, and not yet dawn when I felt my sister Margaret shaking me by the shoulder. I groaned and rolled away from her, but nothing short of a team of oxen will stop my sister when she is determined.

'Up, slug-abed!' she commanded. 'Have you forgot our early start?'

Cautiously, I opened one eye. She was holding up a rush-light, which cast its sallow beam over my tumbled bedclothes. She made as if to drag them off me, but I clutched at a handful of feather bed and looked at her piteously.

'Not as early as this? Surely?'

'I have already taken the bread from the oven,' she said austerely, 'and the children are dressing.'

The puppy Rowan planted her forepaws on the edge of the bed and licked my hand with enthusiasm. She had grown a good deal in the last month, and could easily extend her ablutions to my face if I did not take evasive measures.

'Very well, very well,' I grumbled. 'If the pair of you will but leave me in peace, I will dress.'

'Five minutes, Nicholas,' she said, turning toward the door of my bedchamber. 'It is sharpish this morning, and I have made porridge.'

A rare treat. Usually we broke our fast with little more than bread and small ale, with perhaps a slice of cheese. Porridge was reserved for bitter winter mornings.

As soon as they were gone, I ventured a foot to the floor, and winced. It was indeed sharpish. If it was this cold in October, did that presage a bad winter? It was almost impossible now to remember the long hot days of summer. The water in the bowl standing on my clothes chest was very cold, but not frozen, as it was sometimes in winter. After splashing a little on my face, I managed to shake off the rags of sleep, with its shadows of the dreams which still haunted me, ever since the days of the Pestilence. I chose warm woollen hose, one of my thicker shirts, and a long cotte, though I was sure that by the time we had climbed Headington Hill I should probably be wanting to shed it.

I had left one shutter half open during the night. Now I opened both wide enough to lean out and breathe deeply. My window faced north, over the garden, and the sky was still night black and strewn with the Creator's scattered armfuls of stars, but over to my right I could just make out a grey wash brushed across the horizon, promising dawn. It was the feast of St Placidus, I recalled, a disciple of St Benedict, founder of the Benedictine order of monks. An obscure saint, one I only remembered because of the name he shared with the Placidus who had experienced the vision of the white stag. After the deer hunt in Wychwood a few weeks before, I suppose my thoughts naturally turned to stags.

When I lived as a boy on my father's farm at Leighton-under-Wychwood, autumn had always seemed a melancholy time. Even if the harvest had been ample, providing for winter survival, all around there was evidence of the dying year – in the flushed tints amongst the slumbering trees, the tired grass in the meadows, the silent closing down of birdsong. With Michaelmas would come the slaughtering of all those beasts which could not be over wintered, and even though I was a farmer's son, who had lived through it every autumn of my life, I hated it. Beasts who had been cared for like children, some even fed by hand, would know the ultimate betrayal of the knife.

I had lived more than half my life on the farm, but since I had come to Oxford, I felt the autumn differently. Here, this was Janus time, the cyclic beginning of a fresh academic year. That first autumn, when I was just short of my fourteenth birthday, October had meant, in addition, the start of a fresh life for me.

Our parish priest, Sire Raymond, had declared me ready. He had even written a letter on my behalf, recommending me as a student to an old friend of his, who had remained here as a Regent Master when Sire Raymond had been ordained and taken up his parish duties. From time to time that day, as I made the journey to Oxford with the carter from our village, I would finger the letter in my scrip, as if it were some magic talisman, a passport to a different world.

And indeed a different world it looked, when the carter deposited me in the street in front of the Mitre inn. I had never seen so many people, almost twice as many on that day as now walk the streets, ever since the time of the Pestilence. Nor had I ever seen such fine stone buildings, though in the years since my arrival the colleges have built still more. Even the Pestilence could not halt it for more than a year or two.

Today, tomorrow, and all this week, other young boys would be arriving, filled with the same dreams and apprehensions, breathing the spring of new life into the autumn of the year, so that the season is turned upon its head, promising fresh beginnings.

That first day I had found my way to Tackley's Inn, on the other side of the High Street from the Mitre.

'You will do well to go up to Oxford betimes,' Sire Raymond said, 'so that you may secure a place at Tackley's Inn. It is comfortable, and will not cheat you. I lived there two years myself. The university halls change with every change of warden, and you had best look about you until you decide which you wish to join. Some wardens are lazy, some will take your money yet barely feed you, some, I fear, can be cruel. Stay at Tackley's, attend the lectures, and keep your ears open. You will soon discover the best of the halls, and apply to live in one of them next year.'

It was Sire Raymond, my teacher since I was four years old, who had filled me with the longing to go to Oxford. My elder brother, John, more than ten years my senior, would take over the farm when my father grew too old and stiff, so my father made no objection. As a yeoman of some wealth, he could afford to indulge my desires.

'Aye,' he said, 'there you will gain the learning you will need to become a man of law, away to London at the Inns of Court. And once trained, you may even find a place in the royal service. I shall be proud of you, lad!'

'Aye, Father,' I said, as he clapped me on the shoulder. By then the king had grown into his full powers and was busy reforming the court, the law, and the governing of the country. Many paths to a bright future were opening up for any young man prepared to work hard.

My mother, I knew, had different hopes for me. The night before I left home, she took me aside and pressed into my hand a silver cross studded with simple uncut gems. On its stepped base it stood about the height of my hand's length. It had been a gift to her on her marriage from her maternal grandmother, who had been born into the gentry. I glanced over my shoulder at it now, where it stood on the shelf where I kept a few of my own books.

She brushed a fallen lock of hair back from my forehead and smiled at me.

'I know your father hopes you will take to the law, and I would never oppose him, but should you prefer the priesthood . . . I shall pray for you, Nicholas, that you may find the right path.'

I nodded, but kept my thoughts to myself. I inclined more to my mother's view than my father's. I knew nothing of the law, except that my father and his friends often grumbled about it. However, there was no one in the world that I admired more than Sire Raymond. To be a priest, with no trammelling of worldly affairs or dependent family, to spend one's time amongst books and the writings of great men . . . that seemed to me the ideal life. So I arrived in Oxford prepared to study what I must of the law, in order to please my father, but secretly hoping to follow in the beloved footsteps of Sire Raymond.

I smiled now, at my boyish blindness. In truth, Sire Raymond spent most of his own days in the comfort and care of his parishioners, with little enough time left to indulge the love of books which he had instilled in me. The years of plague had taken a heavy toll on him, for he would leave no man nor woman nor child to die alone and unshriven. God's hand must have been over him, for surely no other had taken less care for himself, yet he emerged unscathed.

Outside Tackley's Inn, I had hesitated. Now that the moment had come when I must play the man, and the experienced traveller, I knew that I was no more than a clumsy boy. The innkeeper would recognise me at once for what I was, and either turn me away or demand an outrageous rent for lodgings.

Another boy stood hesitating, like me, at the foot of the shallow steps. Shabbily dressed, and hungry looking – could he possibly be another new student? He looked too poor. Sensing my eyes on him, he turned and gave me a smile of great sweetness. I felt myself flushing, hoping that my disparaging judgement had not been mirrored in my face.

'Are you hoping for lodgings here, too?' he said. There was a touch of the country in his voice (as indeed there was at that time in mine, to my shame), but he spoke with more confidence than I was feeling.

'Aye,' I said. 'My tutor, our parish priest, he lodged here when he was a student and suggested it.'

'Mine also!' the boy's smile widened. 'I think that is

a sign that we shall be friends.'

I could not forebear smiling at such an eager approach. I dropped the bundle I was carrying and held out my hand. 'My name is Nicholas Elyot.'

He bowed over my hand with the courtesy of a gentleman. 'Mine, I am afraid, is Jordain Brinkylsworth.'

My astonishment at a name of such grandeur attached to this scrawny and threadbare person must certainly have shown in my face, for he laughed, looking down ruefully at his dusty shoes, which were parting at the toes, his hose (much mended), and a cotte too large, yet faded from some other person's long use.

'We run to large families,' he said, 'and that has impoverished us. It is an article of faith with my mother that we were once landed gentry, but that I cannot quite believe. Yeomen, perhaps. Now we are but poor tenant farmers, and if I am to make my way here, I shall need to earn the chinks in order to live.'

He spoke with a frankness I found somewhat embarrassing, conscious of the heavy purse my father had given me, which I wore concealed under my shirt (my mother's wise precaution).

We were still standing doubtfully before the inn, when another boy ran up the flight of steps, then paused and looked down at us.

'Have you come for rooms at Tackley's? Best not hang about there like silly sheep, the beds are being taken fast. Come, I'll show you to the innkeeper. I'm John. John Wycliffe. I came up early, in the Trinity Term.'

We followed him obediently into the inn, where we were able to secure beds in a room with John and one other boy, Tom Winter. John's confident introduction ensured that we were charged no more than the normal student rent. By the time all was arranged satisfactorily, the bells were ringing for Vespers from a church across the way.

'St Mary's,' John said. 'Best attend on your first day, though it will not be expected every day. Supper is served here after Vespers.'

As we walked over to the church, Jordain said cheerfully, 'I have some bread and cheese left from my journey. I shall have that, rather than spend my pence on the inn's supper.'

By now I knew that he had walked to Oxford all the way from his home, and it had taken him four days. Shy but determined, I said, 'Let me buy you supper. I had rather sit down with a friend than alone.'

For a moment I thought I had offended him, then he said gravely, 'That is kind of you, Nicholas, but as soon as I have earned my first shilling, I shall treat you in return.'

And so he did.

There was an urgent tapping on my door, and then Alysoun stepped inside, looking important.

'Aunt Margaret says that if you do not come *this minute*, she will give your breakfast to Rowan.' She gave a mischievous grin. 'Rowan would dearly like it.'

'I am coming,' I said. 'She shall not waste my porridge on that greedy dog.'

Alysoun slipped her hand in mine.

'There's honey.'

'Then let us make haste. I shall not miss the chance of honey.'

Although both Alysoun and Rafe were excited to be on our way, they still took time to eat with enthusiasm the ample breakfast Margaret provided. The porridge was excellent, for my sister had brought back a sack of the oats we had harvested at the farm, and had them ground at Trill Mill.

'We shall want baskets and sacks,' I said, wiping my mouth and washing down the last of the porridge with a sip of ale.

'Teach your grand-dam,' Margaret said crisply. 'I had everything ready last evening before I went to my bed.'

'Why do we want sacks?' Alysoun asked. 'The blackberries would be squashed.'

'Baskets for the blackberries,' Margaret said. 'Sacks

for the hazelnuts.'

'And the bullaces,' I said, 'as long as they are not overripe.'

'There may be sloes as well,' Margaret said. 'And crab apples.'

'Some of our own apples are ready to pick.'

'Not today,' she said. 'I have already gathered the windfalls. Tomorrow,' she added graciously, 'you may pick the apples.'

I rolled my eyes, but knew enough not to point out that I had a business to run. Just as important as the field harvest on my cousin's farm was the free and abundant harvest to be found growing wild. Years ago, before Elizabeth and I were married, we had discovered a fine spot on Headington Hill, and every year since then it had provided for us, except in the plague years, when no one had felt any desire to gather the wild harvest, since no one expected to live long enough to eat it.

Elizabeth was gone, but I still took our children there every autumn, and this year we were to be a large party. Mistress Farringdon and her family would join us shortly, and on our way past Mistress Metford's cottage we would gather her up, as well as Philip Olney and their son. Philip had grown less cautious of late in his visits to his mistress – or his common law wife – and sometimes I worried for him, lest the university authorities should discover what he had been at pains so long to conceal.

As we were collecting up our supply of baskets and sacks, and a large hamper packed with food for our midday meal, there was a knock on the outer door of the shop. Rafe ran to answer it. Mistress Farringdon was there, with the girls Juliana and little Maysant, both flushed and eager. I kept my eyes averted, but behind them I had glimpsed Emma Thorgold. This morning she wore – as she often did in Oxford – one of her aunt Farringdon's homespun brown dresses, too large and cinched in at the waist with a simple cord girdle. Her hair had now grown enough to hang in two short plaits to her shoulders, like any young girl of the town. It was as if she wished to make a show of the fact that she was no more than Mistress Farringdon's niece, and not heir to her grandfather's substantial estate.

'We are ready,' Margaret said, shooing the children out in front of her. 'Shall you lock the shop, Nicholas?'

'Aye, Walter has a key.'

My journeyman scrivener would take charge of the bookshop today while I was gone, although I would have been glad to be here when the first rush of new students came seeking paper, ink, and quills. If there were one or two boys of means, they might even buy a secondhand book before they had spent all their coin on drink and gambling. Usually we went a-foraging earlier than this, during the last week in September, but Rafe had been laid up with a summer rheum, so Margaret had decreed we must delay.

'And here is Mary,' Margaret said as I locked the shop door.

I had forgot that Mary Coomber, Margaret's friend from the dairy, had said she would also join us. She had no family to provide for during the winter, and I was surprised she could spare a day away from her work, but now she came surging across the street, an ample woman, well fed on her own excellent cream and cheeses. She too must have risen early, to milk the small herd of cows she kept in the croft behind the dairy.

Margaret herded us, like a shepherd's dog with an unruly flock, and drove us down toward the East Gate out of the town. In front of the third cottage beyond the gate, Beatrice Metford was standing with Philip and Stephen, ready to join us. Philip stooped to take his son upon his shoulders and Beatrice picked up his crutch. During our time in the country, Stephen's legs had grown a little stronger, so that now he was able to manage with a single crutch, an achievement of which he was justifiably proud.

Our large party at last complete, we headed out over the East Bridge, and turned half left on the road to Headington village. It was a steep climb, partly through woodland, though there were small farms carved out of what had once been a southern arm of Wychwood. This part was now severed from the royal forest. Trees were giving way to pasture and – where the ground was level and not too difficult to plough – to arable.

The two dogs, Rowan and Emma's small white Jocosa, ran ahead eagerly, drunk on the rich brew of country smells. Despite her small size, Jocosa was a sturdy creature and made no demand to be carried, as I have noticed in the small pet dogs of my wealthier lady customers. Perhaps life at Godstow Abbey had taught her humility and self-reliance.

We did not need to venture as far as the village of Headington at the top of the hill, which was just as well, for the children soon began to tire, and Mary Coomber was puffing like a blacksmith's bellows by the time I said, 'Here. This is the spot.'

Most of the party subsided gratefully anywhere they could find a seat, on a fallen tree trunk or a tuft of grass. Philip lowered Stephen to the ground, handed him his crutch, and wiped the sweat from his forehead.

'I am the least tired,' Stephen said cheerfully, 'having ridden my sturdy mule all the way.'

'Mind your tongue, lad,' Philip said with mock severity, 'or your mule might prove too stubborn on the return journey.'

Alysoun sprang up again from the ground. 'There's lots of blackberries!'

To prove it, she began picking and eating fruits almost as large as my thumb.

'Leave some to take home,' Margaret said, 'or you will have a sore stomach and there will be no preserves for winter.'

'I think I can see bullaces,' Emma said, pointing. 'Through there.'

'But no nuts.' Maud Farringdon sounded disappointed.

'The hazels are a little further on,' I reassured her,

'off to the left. You cannot see them from here. And a large crab apple tree. It is old, and does not bear much fruit some years, but I came this way in the spring and it was full of blossom, so I think we shall be lucky.'

'Does not the Priory of St Frideswide own this land?' Philip said, sinking down to sit cross-legged on the ground at Beatrice's feet. She laid her hand on his shoulder and he leaned back against her knees.

'Not here,' I said. 'They hold the church of St Andrew in Headington, and all its glebe lands, and I think some of the messuages in the village. Here, we are in the remains of the old royal forest, where we have the right to pick the wild fruits, or so I've always believed. You are the lawyer, Philip, but no one has ever prevented.'

'Aye, so long as we do no damage, we should be in our rights.'

After the climb, no one but the children seemed in any hurry to start picking. Mary Coomber, having regained her breath, leaned forward, planting her strong, capable hands on her plump knees.

'I know you wondered why I wanted to come with you this year, Margaret.' She grinned. 'And halfway up this hill I began to wonder myself! But I've had an idea, and wanted to share it with you. And with Maud and Beatrice too.'

The women looked at her expectantly. Philip raised his eyebrows at me, but I shrugged. I knew nothing of this. Besides, my eyes were drawn to Emma, who had followed the children to the tangle of blackberry vines, which climbed well above her head. Unlike Alysoun, Rafe, and Stephen, and even little Maysant, she was putting blackberries into her basket, but there was a telltale purple stain on her lips. I turned my head toward Mary, to hide my smile.

'You mentioned the priory, Master Olney,' she said. 'Now, 'tis nobbut a fortnight until the priory's St Frideswide's Fair, when all of us will be obliged to shut up our shops for six days, and lose much custom by it, just when Oxford is flooded with merchants and buyers. All the rents and the tolls and such, they go to the priory. I may sell a small measure of my milk and cream to the townsfolk who are my regular customers, lest it go sour, but I may not sell my cheeses, neither the soft nor the hard.'

'That is very true,' Margaret said. 'Nicholas may not sell his books and other goods, when the students are just come to Oxford for the Michaelmas term. The busiest time for the shop. And the new lads will not know this and go away disappointed. It causes problems every year.'

'Well, I have decided that this year,' Mary said, 'I will take a stall at the fair. I think that the rent paid to the priory will soon be covered by what I may earn by selling my cheeses, but I have an even better plan.' She paused for effect. 'Why do you not join me?'

'Me?' Margaret looked startled. 'I am no shopkeeper. I have nothing to sell.'

Mary waved her arm at the blackberry bushes. 'You make the best preserves in Oxford. And you always make more than you need for the family. Why not sell what you do not need at the fair? And you, Beatrice. And Maud.'

The women looked at one another, in some astonishment. Then Maud Farringdon said cautiously, 'Apple butter and apple cheese should fetch buyers. It needs only windfalls, and Margaret says she has plenty. Even we have some, in the wilderness behind our cottage.'

'Did you say there are bullaces, Nicholas?' Beatrice turned to me. 'Emma thought she saw a tree. They make an excellent fruit cheese as well, though the stones are troublesome.'

'A coarse sieve,' Margaret said. 'Push the pulp through. Much easier than picking out the stones.'

'But do you not lose much of the pulp?'

I jerked my head at Philip and he got to his feet. I handed him a sack.

'Let us leave them to it,' I said. 'I will show you where the hazel nuts are to be found.'

'I will come with you,' Juliana said, taking a sack

from the pile I had laid on the grass.

I thought she would rather have joined in the women's plans, but wanted to prove she could be useful.

'And I.' Emma set down her basket of blackberries, which was already nearly full, and picked up another sack. Her sleeves were rolled up to the elbow, and I saw that her arms were badly scratched. 'The bullaces are over there, are they not? I will make a start on those. If we are to make fruit cheeses, we shall need a great many.'

'Aye,' I said. 'They will come to no harm in a sack unless they are overripe.'

'If they are, then I shall pick crab apples. But they will not be overripe yet. Not till the end of October.'

I smiled at her. 'You have blackberry juice on your nose,' I said.

By the time Margaret gave us permission to stop for our midday meal, we had filled several sacks with hazel nuts, two with crab apples, and two more with bullaces. The children had been discreetly persuaded to pick nuts, else there would have been far fewer of the blackberries, which Mary and Beatrice had piled high in their baskets. Without this precaution there would have been more than one child with a sore stomach before night.

'It is quite settled then,' Margaret said later, as she packed away the scant remnants of our picnic. 'We have decided that a simple stall will not be enough for all we have in mind. We shall rent one of the large booths the priory sets up on the fairground. Mary will arrange that tomorrow with the lay steward at the priory. She has already a good stock of cheeses in hand. The rest of us will set to and make our preserves. The fair begins on the nineteenth. We shall be busy until then, Beatrice and I, with Mary and Maud when they can be spared from the dairy.'

'I can help,' Juliana said. 'And Emma too.'

Emma and I exchanged a glance. Since our return from the country, she had been working hard to complete the book of hours ordered by Lady Amilia. She now shared a bedchamber in the Farringdon house with Juliana, and her aunt had moved little Maysant in with her, to allow the older girls more room. Emma worked on a small, unsteady table by the window, not the best for fine lettering and illumination, but despite her difficulties the book was nearly done.

She smiled at me and gave a small nod, whose meaning I was not able to guess.

'Certainly I can help. In the nunnery we spent part of our time working in the kitchens. I cannot claim to be a cook, but if I am told what to do, I can do it.'

'Then you may undertake the simple but tiresome task of separating the bullaces from their stones,' Margaret said serenely.

'I remember that there was a damson tree at my grandfather's house when I was a child, and the cook used to curse the stones, though William and Juliana and I always loved the damson cheese he made. Do you remember, Juliana?'

'Aye. But that tree blew down in a storm last year. I think bullaces are much the same. Just as sour.'

I had noticed lately that Emma spoke more and more of her childhood, when she had lived happily with her parents on her grandfather's manor. Perhaps the wound that marked her time as a virtual prisoner at the abbey was beginning to heal over. When she had mentioned the kitchen of the abbey her face no longer wore that bleak look which used to come over her whenever she spoke of Godstow. In time, perhaps only the good memories would remain – the music, her work in the scriptorium, the beauty of the place, and the friends she had made there, like Sister Mildred and John Barnes, the porter.

'Well, that is how we shall proceed,' Margaret said briskly, 'but for now we must gather our materials. Some of the best blackberries are too high for most of us to reach, so Philip . . .? And Stephen, I think you might use your crutch to knock down the nuts on the upper branches of the hazel trees. How useful that you have it! Then the girls may gather them up. Nicholas–'

'Never fear,' I said hastily, 'we have barely touched the crab apples. I shall find plenty to occupy me there.'

By the time our master of the hunt, my capable sister, finally called a halt to our foraging, we were all scratched, bloodied, tousled, and exhausted, but our harvest was almost more than we could carry, and involved tying sacks together in pairs, to be slung over our shoulders, like a pedlar's pack ponies. Maysant, who had fallen asleep, curled up on the grass, awoke groggily. Stephen, realising that his father was puzzling over how he might carry both his share of the sacks and his son, was quick to speak out.

'Do not worry, Father. I can walk back down the hill. And carry a sack as well.'

'Aye, lad,' Mary Coomber said comfortably. ''Tis far easier going down than coming up. You and I shall hold each other upright at the tail end of the company and take it slow. If I should fall, you may heave me to my feet again.'

At that we all laughed, for Stephen would be no more able to heave Mary Coomber to her feet than a mouse might topple St Mary's Church.

We made our way down toward Oxford, slumbering in its river valleys below us – slowly, for we were all tired. Emma and I brought up the rear, behind Mary and Stephen, since I was concerned lest either of them should stumble and fall, while Emma had lingered behind, clearly wishing to speak to me.

'I shall finish the book this evening,' she said quietly. 'The last of the colours will dry overnight, so I can bring it to you tomorrow when I come to help your sister in the kitchen.'

'You have done very well. I know it has not been easy for you, working on that little table in your bedchamber.'

My initial intention, that only Emma and I should know that she was acting as a scrivener for me, had of necessity proved quite impractical. She must do her scribing somewhere. It was not suitable for her to sit with my scriveners in the shop, so Maud and Juliana Farringdon had needed to be told, though the child Maysant took an interest only in the fact that she now shared a bedchamber with her grandmother, which was a larger room. Margaret had soon guessed what we were about, and I felt it only just to admit Walter and Roger to the secret – which was barely a secret any longer.

Walter was unperturbed. 'She will not be the first woman scribe, Nicholas,' he said, to my surprise. 'You know my father worked in London for a time, and his master's wife was a scrivener, though she could not draw, not beyond a foliage border. They sent out their pages to a studio of illuminators, and the wife of one of the artists there undertook the drawing and painting along with the men. He said she did excellent work on the miniature scenes within the capital letters. Sometimes she painted with a brush that had no more than a few hairs.'

Roger was less philosophical about my employment of Emma, accustomed to regarding himself as the artist in my establishment. Yet he was not lacking in integrity. He knew that Emma was the better artist, even if he could not quite conceal his jealousy. My solution was to provide him with a great deal of work, so that he should not think he was being replaced. The less time he had free to grumble, the sooner he would forget his grievances.

When we reached the High Street, we all made our way to the dairy. Mary had a number of cool, stone-built rooms, where our wild harvest could be kept fresh, until it was needed for the busy work in Margaret's kitchen. The dairy had been in Mary's family for three generations. When it was built, one of the many small streams which wander through this valley – to join either the Thames or the Cherwell – had been diverted to flow beneath the stone slabs of the dairy floor, so that it was kept cool even on the hottest of summer days.

We unloaded our burdens with relief, while Mary insisted that we should all sit down to dishes of blackberries and her thick cream before we made our separate ways home. Even while we were enjoying some of the best blackberries I ever remember eating, the cows were beginning to give voice in the back croft.

'We'll away,' Margaret said, 'and leave you to your milking. I will take one sack of crab apples and make a start this evening.'

The other women assured her that they would come to help, though it was clear they were all tired. Philip grinned at me as we left the dairy.

'I shall be glad to return to my peaceful books at Merton tomorrow.'

'You are fortunate,' I said. 'I am ordered to pick our own apples.'

He laughed. 'A formidable woman, your sister.'

'They all are. I'll wager not a man or woman will pass their booth at the fair without buying something.'

'It seems a new merchant company has been founded,' he said.

They were not to be the only merchants I would encounter that week, nor would I avoid more dealings with the Priory of St Frideswide. However, my first task, even before picking apples for Margaret, was a visit to the bookbinder, Henry Stalbroke. As she had promised, Emma delivered the gatherings of the book of hours the following morning. I turned over the pages with care and delight.

'It seems a pity to put this in the hands of a woman who cannot possibly appreciate its quality,' I said with regret.

She laughed at me. 'How can you run your business and feed your family, Nicholas, if you want to keep everything for yourself?'

'Not everything.'

'Well, I confess I am somewhat loath to part with it myself, but there will be other books, will there not?'

'Of course. We must decide what you will attempt next.'

'There will be no scribing until this famous fair is

over and done with.'

'Aye, Meg is like a horse who has seized the bit and run away from his master.'

'Oh, I think she is far too steady to compare with a runaway horse. Besides, it was Mistress Coomber who first brought forward the idea.'

'So it was. I will not keep you from your 'prentice duties in the kitchen, while I shall escape across the river to Bookbinder's Island before Meg catches me.'

Lady Amilia had ordered a binding in a leather dyed a rich purple, almost the colour of ecclesiastical vestments, and when I described it to Henry Stalbroke, he scratched his head as he looked about his workshop.

'I have nothing in that shade at present, Nicholas. It will need to be dyed specially for this customer of yours.'

'All the better,' I said. 'The lady will prize it all the more if she knows that no one else can match her. Here are the gatherings. I know I need not ask you to handle it carefully, but I think you will find that it is very finely done.'

He took the manuscript from me and began to turn over the pages. After a few moments, he looked up, puzzled.

'I know this handwriting, and I know this illuminator. Surely it is the same as the book of hours you bought, made by that novice at Godstow, the one who ran away?'

I saw that I could not contradict a man with such knowledge of books as Henry Stalbroke. How long before the whole of Oxford knew Emma's secret?

'It is indeed,' I said cautiously. 'She began the work at the abbey, and consented to finish the book for me, as it was already promised to the Lady Amilia.'

He gave me a knowing look. 'That was fortunate. I had heard that the maid is an heiress.'

'So she is.'

Henry Stalbroke was perfectly trustworthy, but I saw no need to enlarge on my agreement with Emma. He would learn the full story as I brought more of her books to him for binding.

I walked swiftly back across Oxford to the shop, for I knew that Margaret would be fretting over those apples. I had also remembered my promise to give a basket of them to Jonathan Baker and his father, who had no apple trees of their own, their only one having died. Perhaps I could persuade young Jonathan to help with the picking in return for that basket of apples.

When I reached my shop, I found that Walter and Roger were doing good business, so occupied with students and their demands for quills and ink and paper that they had been unable to accomplish any work of their own. I set Roger to scribing again. Told Walter to explain to the new students how the hire of *peciae* was managed, and took over the other customers myself. The apples would have to wait.

The crowd of students had thinned – and I had sold two secondhand books – when a familiar figure came hesitantly through the door. I had known Canon Francis Aubery ever since I had first come to work here for my future father-in-law, Humphrey Hadley. The canon was a passionate lover of books. So passionate, I believe he would have starved himself rather than part with any of his own small library. Both Philip and I share his passion, but we are not fanatics. At least, I hope we are not.

Under the previous prior, dead now of the plague, Canon Aubery had been allowed to build up quite a fine collection of books for St Frideswide's library, indulging his passion for expensive books which he could not have afforded himself, although when he could, he still bought books from me. Those of a censorious turn of mind may say: But surely members of the religious orders are not permitted to own personal property? This may be the Rule, but amongst the religious communities in Oxford, devoted as they are to scholarship and the advancement of knowledge, the Rule may be kept, but the rules may be slackened. Certainly amongst the Augustinian canons of St Frideswide, the rules had been, over many years, notoriously slackened, and in more serious ways than the mere ownership of books.

However, the priory had acquired a new head four years before, one Nicholas de Hungerford, and by all accounts he was an irreligious boor. How he ever achieved such a distinguished post is a mystery to which I do not know the answer. Perhaps the position was in the gift of some great man who favoured him, although how that could come about was also a mystery. Prior de Hungerford was, also by all accounts, greedy, jealous, and violent. Needless to say, Canon Aubery was no longer allowed funds to purchase books. Instead, he came regularly into my shop to finger the forbidden fruits and to grieve.

As soon as the students had left the shop, I smiled at the canon and took down from its high shelf Emma's first book of hours, which I had kept for my own.

'Was it this you wished to look at again, canon?' I asked.

'Indeed, indeed.'

He blinked at me with his short sighted eyes and took the book reverently. I pulled out a stool for him. He was elderly, and he would take some time turning over the pages, holding the tiny pictures close to his face so that he might enjoy every detail. There were not many people I would trust with Emma's book, but he was one of them. I sat down behind the table I used as both counter and desk.

'It is a pity you were not here earlier,' I said, 'for I have a new book written and illuminated by the same hand, but I have just delivered it to Henry Stalbroke for binding.'

'You will sell that one?' His voice was a mixture of hope and regret.

'It is already spoken for, I am afraid. But the scrivener is now working for me, so there will be more in the future.'

He sighed, running a delicate finger over the spine of the book.

'Alas, under Prior de Hungerford, there will be no more books for us. Instead–' He hesitated. 'I am worried,

Nicholas. Things . . . have been . . . disappearing from the priory. A silver gilt chalice. A pair of very ancient silver candlesticks from the altar of St Mary, the gift of one of our earliest benefactors.'

'Stolen?' I was alarmed. If there were thieves in Oxford daring enough to steal from a church within the priory precinct, no one was safe.

'It would not be so grievous, if it were thieves.' He paused. 'To begin with, he had little idea of the value of our books, but now I worry–'

'You do not mean the prior himself?' I guessed which 'he' was meant, and was shocked almost into silence. 'He would not sell the priory's books!'

'Would he not?'

'You think that *he* is responsible for the disappearance of the church silver?'

'I would not wish to accuse any man unjustly, but I am afraid . . . The man's eyes are fixed on wealth and worldly position. He courts the king's son. He has acquired a following amongst seculars in the town. Men not of good repute. He makes use of them, instead of our lay steward and his servants, to collect rents from our tenants. There are whispers of threats being made. Bullying. Extortion.'

'Whispers only?'

'People are afraid to speak out.' He sighed again and laid Emma's book gently on my table. 'I had occasion to visit the priory grange a few days ago. There were two very fine stallions stabled there which I had never seen before. This morning I watched Prior de Hungerford riding into town on one of them. And clad in secular clothes.'

I knew not how to respond to this. The priory had a chequered history, at least within the last half century or so. In Oxford relations between the town, the university, and the many religious houses are always somewhat uneasy. On more than one occasion violence has erupted between the students and the young men of the town, sometimes leading to deaths. Yet I also knew that, of the quarrels between the town and the religious houses, that with St Frideswide's was by far the worst, and the root of much of the trouble lay with the priory's right to hold the fair, a right it had possessed for more than two hundred years.

The main grievance was the one Mary had expressed – the loss of trade to the town during the fair, when so many people were drawn to Oxford, not just from the surrounding countryside, but from as far away as Wales and Flanders and France. Since the decline in the great fairs of Champagne, merchants had looked elsewhere, and convenient centres like Oxford had benefitted. Yet these benefits went all to the priory and not to the town. After the losses of the plague years and the decline in the town's own cloth production, the monies flowing solely into the priory left a bitter taste in the townsmen's mouths.

Had the Augustinian Canons of St Frideswide's had a reputation for great piety, it might have been less bitter, but over this last half century they had come to be known for their worldliness, neglect of their duties, and scorning of the Rule. Successive bishops had taken them to task, but to no effect. There still remained good, devout men, like Canon Aubery, amongst them, but, so common report held, they were in the minority. So outraged had the town become some seventeen years earlier, that a group of local ruffians – possibly with the foreknowledge and even the instigation of the Guild Merchant – had taken the prior and all his canons prisoner, using them with violence and threatening them with death unless they agreed to renounce all the privileges and monies of St Frideswide's Fair. Terrified for their lives, they had sworn the oath. Ever since it had been the subject of regular and at times violent dispute, the town maintaining that the priory had resigned its rights, the priory arguing that the oath had been forced from them under duress.

'But surely,' I said now, 'with the income from the fair, there is no need to sell your church silver or your library of books. By all the signs, it seems likely to be a successful fair this year. Already both buyers and merchants have begun to arrive in Oxford.'

For the last few years, as the world slowly tried to recover from the Death, all fairs had been poorly attended, but the world, like a man recovering from some near fatal disease, was gradually returning to health.

'Our affairs have been mismanaged for years,' Canon Aubrey said gloomily. 'We have carried debts forward from year to year, and even the income from our tenants, our manors and lands, and from St Frideswide's Fair, have failed to solve the problem. Our spending has ever been above our income. In the past, some of our priors have lavished money on the building and embellishment of our church, beyond all that was reasonable.'

I nodded. The church of St Frideswide was one of the most magnificent in Oxfordshire. I had some sympathy with those who had built so gloriously to honour our Heavenly Father, in the name of Oxford's own saint, even though it had been costly.

'But now–' He twisted his hands together. 'Now the church is starting to fall into disrepair, and the priory's income finds its way into one man's pockets instead.'

'I see.' I rested my chin on my fist. 'Prior de Hungerford would not make use of you to sell the library?'

'He knows I would not do it.'

'Well, if the books come in my way, or if I hear aught, then I shall tell you at once.'

'I thank you, Nicholas. Though whether we can prevent . . . Sub-prior Resham and I, and a few of the other canons, will oppose any sale, but with all these foreign merchants arriving, a sale may be made in secret, without our knowledge.'

'Indeed,' I said. 'Well, you may be sure that I will do what I may.'

And that would be little enough, I thought, as I saw him out of the shop. He walked away along the High, his shoulders stooped, discouragement written in every line of his body.

It was true that foreign merchants had begun to arrive in considerable numbers.

I had not thought then that I should find myself entangled so soon in their affairs.

Chapter Two

After Canon Aubery left, I managed to work in the shop until midday, when I was summoned to a meagre dinner eaten awkwardly off the end of the table in a kitchen thronging with women. The aromas were enticing, an intoxicating mixture of fruits and honey, but I soon found myself banished to the garden, with the dubious help of the children, including the youngest, Rafe and Maysant, who would be of little use in the picking of apples. Alysoun I sent to fetch Jonathan Baker, with the inducement of a basket of apples for him and his father. Juliana soon joined us.

'It is as hot as a blacksmith's forge in there,' she said. 'And there are so many of us that we are falling over each other. My mother agrees that I shall be of more use here with you, picking apples.'

I was glad of her help, and with Alysoun and Jonathan we picked steadily for about an hour. Stephen was determined to help, although he could not climb into the lower branches of the trees as they could. Jonathan, I suspected, enjoyed showing off his skill, but Stephen in his short life had learned a patient acceptance of his own limitations and did not seem to grudge the other boy his minor triumphs.

In our small orchard, as well as some fruit bushes, we have three good apple trees and two pears, but the pears had been gathered long since, some to be dried by Margaret, and some to be pickled. It was pleasant now in the garden, the autumn sun drawing spicy scents from the bed of herbs near the house, and the languorous murmur of bees declining toward their winter sleep. Because the shop occupied the width of two messuages, the garden was also double in size. Along our eastern boundary a narrow alleyway led in from the High Street, which I closed off with a stout oak gate, to keep out intruders. As I climbed into one of the apple trees and reached down to lay apples into the basket Juliana was holding up to me, I began to turn over in my mind whether it would be possible to build a small stable at the far inner end of this alley, large enough to accommodate a single horse. In the normal way of things, I should have no need of a horse, but my hire of Rufus over recent months had cost me near as much as keeping him.

'Master Elyot!' Roger's shout from the kitchen door came close to causing me to fall from my perch.

'Aye?' I said, regaining my balance and looking toward him somewhat sourly.

'There is a gentleman wishes to see you. A stranger. Foreign mebbe. Here for the fair.'

'I am coming.'

I lowered myself with some caution to the ground, and brushed the fragments of twigs and bark from my clothes.

'Can you carry on, Juliana?'

'Aye.' She grinned. 'You may want to run a comb through your hair.'

I ran my fingers through it instead and a small cascade of dead leaves and twigs fell to the ground.

'You have the right of it,' I said. 'Roger, tell the gentleman that I will be with him shortly.'

Dodging the culinary workhouse in the kitchen, I ran upstairs to my bedchamber, where I combed my hair and washed my hands in the bowl on my coffer, for the smoke from Oxford's chimneys lays a fine ash on the fruit in our garden, and my hands were far from clean.

In the shop I found the stranger talking to Walter,

who was showing him the book Roger had recently completed, consisting of a collection of traditional tales, each with a full page illumination at the start. I had commissioned Henry Stalbroke to bind it in natural leather of a soft tan hue, with elegant tooling of vine leaves about the title. I had decided the book needed a cover that was not too flamboyant, lest it detract from Roger's paintings within. As I came into the shop, Walter was explaining that the book was Roger's work, and my younger scrivener was blushing with pleasure. It was good for him not to be constantly measured against Emma's skill and found wanting.

'You wished to see me, sir?' I bowed. The stranger was clearly a man of both wealth and taste, for his gown was of rich cut velvet, in a sober dark red, while the lace which could be seen at the neck and sleeves of his shirt was fine, but restrained.

'You are a son of Humphrey Hadley?' he asked, bowing in his turn.

'He was my father-in-law. No longer in this world,' I said, crossing myself.

He, too, crossed himself, with more feeling, I thought, than a mere gesture of politeness.

'Alas, I feared it might be so. He was a fine man. So many good men and women robbed of life untimely.'

I nodded. It was difficult for me to speak of it.

'I am Nicholas Elyot,' I said. 'I inherited the business from him. How can I help you?'

'Peter Winchingham.' He bowed again. 'I am here for the fair.' He was looking about him as he spoke, picking up and setting down the books on display. 'I deal in Flemish cloth, and have come early to secure a good position on the fair ground, for I was not certain how it might be, after . . . why, it must be ten years, more, since last I was in Oxford! But I understand that all will go ahead as in the old days.'

He laughed. 'Though I have heard some talk over dinner at my inn that the old quarrels between the town and the priory are as bitter as ever.'

'They rumble on,' I said cautiously. I find it is wise not to favour one side or the other in these endless disputes.

Roger had thought the man foreign, and there *was* something foreign in the cut of his gown, but he seemed English to me.

'You live in Flanders?' I enquired politely.

'In Bruges, though I may return to England soon. I have been there more than twenty years, married a Flemish wife, God rest her.' Again we crossed ourselves. 'Now that the king has agreed in Parliament to establish the Staple in England, many of us who have lived abroad will be returning home. An English Staple, at last, for English wool.'

'Indeed,' I said. 'It has always seemed wasteful of time and coin to carry our fleeces to Flanders, only to carry them back at increased cost, before they can be spun and woven.'

'It made some sense in the past.' He had picked up Roger's book again and was turning over the pages. 'In the days when England produced the best wool, but the best weavers were in Flanders and France. Now, that is no longer true. English weavers have surpassed all others. We should keep everything in our own hands and export only our finished cloth, not our fleeces. I shall be glad to come home, now that concern for the happiness of my wife no longer holds me in Bruges. I shall leave my elder son there, to manage the business. He is to marry soon. Meanwhile I shall find myself a property somewhere in the Cotswolds, where I may run a few sheep of my own and buy my fleeces near at hand. I shall employ my own spinsters and weavers here in England. How much is this book?'

Startled by the question coming hot on the heels of his business plans, I named a price much higher than I had intended.

He nodded, unsurprised. 'I will buy it. My daughter takes after me in her love of books, and I know such a collection of tales will please her. Cloth is my living, but books are my joy. Shall you have a stall at the fair?'

I shook my head, handing the book to Walter to wrap in a piece of cloth for protection.

'Nay, I would not risk my books in the weather. October can be very changeable here in Oxford. I shall lose business for a week, but there is no help for it.'

'Then I shall visit you again on a day not taken up by the fair. I must go to the priory now, to bespeak my booth. My men are unloading my goods on the jetty.'

'You came by boat?'

'Aye, up the Thames from London.'

That would be the jetty owned by the priory, close by Trill Mill. Boats coming upriver from London could moor there for the duration of the fair – at the cost of a mooring paid to the priory. It was situated at the edge of the fair ground, providing easy access for unloading goods. The priory kept guards there during the days leading up to the fair and afterwards, in case there should be trouble with some of the wilder elements from the town. There was another jetty, down on the main branch of the Thames, but merchants must provide their own servants to guard their boats and goods there.

'You are come early,' I said, handing him the book of tales and stowing his coins away in the locked drawer of my table. Later, I would move them to my strongbox.

'I am not the only one.' His look was thoughtful. 'Once I have made my arrangements for renting a booth in a suitable position, I am off over toward Burford, where I have heard there is a manor lying vacant.'

I smiled at him. 'I come from those parts myself. You say there are other merchants already here?'

'Aye. Englishmen and Flemings. Even,' he paused meaningfully, 'a few Frenchmen.'

'There is peace at the moment.'

'A peace of sorts. I have some dealings in France. I would say that this is but a brief truce, while both sides draw breath and repair their losses.'

'I do not see how it can ever end, this scourge of warfare.'

'Nor I.' He turned to go. 'Does the Mitre still have horses for hire?'

'It does.'

He nodded his thanks, and I felt a brief pang of jealousy as I bowed him out and closed the door. I hoped he would not hire Rufus, for I had begun to think of him as my own horse.

'Well,' I said, turning back, 'that was a profitable sale.'

I opened the drawer and counted out some of the coins. 'That was more than I expected for the book of tales. You shall have half the extra, Roger, for making the book, and you the other half, Walter, for showing it to Master Winchingham.'

They both grinned at the unexpected bounty.

'And now,' I said, 'since I had a different customer in mind for that book, Roger, you had best set to and make another. Walter, you and I need to take an inventory of our student texts, to be sure we are short of nothing, now that the new term is upon us.'

The business of making preserves of every sort imaginable continued for several days. After I had picked the apples, I had hoped to be free of further demands on my time, for this was a busy period in the shop, as the older students, aware of the week's ban on trading during the fair, hurried to buy such stationery as they would need for the Michaelmas term. Although the most costly goods I sell are the books, it is the regular trade in the smaller items which is the major source of the shop's income, together with the hire of *peciae*, the sections from the set study texts which the students could borrow and copy for their own use.

However, the merchant venture afoot in our kitchen required not merely the goods to sell, but the containers in which to sell them. I was assigned the task of finding a potter who could produce a supply of cheap jars in three different sizes, to serve as containers for the softer preserves.

'The fruit cheeses,' Margaret said, 'will be firm enough that we need only wrap them in oiled paper. But we need sufficient jars in these three sizes.'

She had chosen three of her own pots to provide guidance, and instructed me to visit several potters, to find the best price.

'Aye, very well,' I said, prepared to order the pots and fetch them when they were ready, but not intending to spend hours exploring all the potters in Oxford. I knew a reliable man in Grandpont, so I took the commission to him.

'I am glad of the business, Master Elyot,' he said, 'for like you I shall lose trade during the fair.'

'You do not intend to take a stall yourself this year?' I knew he had done so in the past.

'Nay.' He shook his head and eyed me sideways. 'Have you not heard the whispers? There will be trouble this year. My goods are too easily smashed. I'll stay at home and keep all in safety.'

'Then I hope my sister and her friends may not suffer,' I said.

When I reported this news to Margaret that evening, she gave me a scornful look.

'We are not afraid of a few wild lads from the town, looking for trouble. They will not bother us. We will remind them all too clearly of their own wives and mothers. They will be seeking out bigger prey, and above all, the lay servants of the priory.'

'Perhaps. But promise me, if trouble comes your way, you will close up your booth and come home.'

'Certainly,' she said, but I saw from the look in her eye that she felt that she and her friends were a match for any loutish group of young men. I hoped she might be right.

When at last I had collected the pots for the preserves and was freed from further assistance at this new merchant venture, I went during the afternoon, three days before the fair, to seek out a skilled carpenter I knew who had premises down a small alleyway off Fish Street, a few doors beyond the Guildhall. The alley itself was narrow and unprepossessing, but opened, after a few yards, into a wide court, lined all about with several buildings – a storehouse for seasoned timber and one for green, a workshop with lathes and saws and other large tools of the carpenter's trade, and a hellishly hot shed where timbers could be steamed and bent round forms when curved pieces were needed. John Shippan's father had been a boat-builder, working on the Thames over near the castle, and he had first learned his trade from his father in the boat sheds there.

As well as these buildings surrounding the court, the Shippans had a home built over the storehouse, and a very rickety outside stair led up the side of the main workshop to another room above, where John did his finer work and kept his accounts. They say a cobbler's children are always the worst shod. The same might be said of that staircase, for whenever I climbed it, I held my breath for fear it might collapse beneath me. You would think a master carpenter would be shamed by such a travesty of a stair, built of rotting and ill-matched wood. I had never seen the inside of their home, but the state of those steps caused me to wonder whether Mistress Shippan had to endure furniture made up from the broken bits of boxes and warped timbers.

'Maister be in his office, sir,' one of the 'prentice lads told me. This was a successful business and Shippan employed two journeymen and four apprentices.

I took my life in my hands and climbed the stair.

'Master Elyot, God give 'ee good day. I'll be with you the minute this is dry.'

Shippan was gripping two small pieces of wood together in his hands, which were long and fine, but muscular.

'Too small for a clamp, see?'

Somehow Shippan always put me in mind of those elves and other strange beings who populate the old tales.

Although he was quite tall, he was twig thin, with a pointed face which might be any age from fifteen to sixty. His high, domed forehead was topped with a thatch of ginger curls, forever tangled with wood shavings and sawdust, and the ears which poked through them were certainly pointed.

I swept more shavings off a stool and sat down to wait. The carpenter had a small enclosed brazier here, on which a saucepan was heating, holding some sort of glue, for there was a powerful odour of boiling cow's feet mingling with the more pleasant aromas of beeswax and olive oil, which he used for polishing his finished pieces. I wondered whether any of Mistress Shippan's kitchen pots were safe from her husband. He was an artist in wood, and like most artists, he was obsessed.

'There.' He laid his bits of wood carefully down on a workbench, where his account books lay open, with small tools and samples of wood strewn carelessly on top of them, then he moved the glue pot off the heat. 'How may I help you, Master Elyot?'

'I need a new scrivener's desk,' I said, extracting from my scrip a careful drawing, over which I had laboured for several evenings.

'I need it to be adjustable, allowing the working surface either to be set at a slope for writing, or flat for illuminating, so that the inks will not run while they are drying. With an upright rack above it at the rear to hold the text being copied, and on either side of that a framework with a series of holes for the ink pots.'

He picked up a pair of spectacles from the workbench and fixed them to his nose, looping the tapes at either side over his ears.

'Let me see.'

He took the paper from me and scrutinised it. I had written in the measurements of the various parts, and was quite pleased with my drawing.

'Hmm.' He picked up a fine stick of charcoal, and began to amend the sketch. 'You will do better with sturdier legs. There will be a lot of weight in this, and the one thing you do not want is for it to be unstable. Like this.'

He drew in wider legs, with cross-pieces bracing them.

'It cannot be too wide,' I said. 'The room where it will be used is not very large.'

'Then we can brace the legs like this instead.' He rubbed out his first lines with his finger and made a fresh drawing. 'Oak, do you want?'

'Aye. The best quality you have. With a fine, smooth grain.'

'I have some good lengths, well seasoned, the right size for this. And you will want a pair of weights to hold the book open on the rack. I can affix the cords to the back, so when a single sheet is being copied, they are out of the way.'

I nodded. Shippan had made a scrivener's desk for me before, the one Roger now used, though this would be more elaborate. No doubt he also made them for the colleges and the religious houses. He would know best how to turn my drawing – which now seemed to me somewhat crude – into a fine desk.

'Last month I made a desk for Durham College,' he said, 'and designed a new device for it. The brother asked for a shelf where he might keep his box of gesso pellets and another of gold foil, separate from the inks. I will show you.'

He rummaged amongst the papers on his workbench, then handed me a grubby sheet of poor quality paper containing an exquisite drawing of a scrivener's desk, which made my attempt look like something Rafe might have drawn in a careless moment.

'You see?' He pointed with his stick of charcoal. 'I made this small shelf, with a lip all round it, so that nothing might roll off. It is on a swivel, so that it may be drawn forward close to the working surface when it is needed, then swung back out of the way when it is not.'

It was simple, but ingenious.

'Then let us include such a movable shelf on my desk,' I said. 'I can see that it would be most useful, especially when applying the gilding. That is done after the drawing is completed in outline, but before the coloured inks are applied.'

'I will calculate you a price.' He turned over the lovely drawing as if it were a useless scrap, and wrote rapidly on the back with his charcoal stick.

'Will that suit?'

The total came to one and a quarter marks. Considering all the materials and the work involved, it seemed a fair price.

I nodded. 'Aye, that will suit. I should like a few embellishments, perhaps some carving on the sides, and on the outer frame of the rack at the top. Could you add in the cost of that?'

He raised his eyebrows, no doubt wondering why I should want something so fine for a scrivener's work desk, but he made no comment. He rubbed his cheek with the end of the charcoal, leaving a black smear amongst the fine sprinkling of sawdust.

'Another shilling?'

I shook hands on it. He added the additional shilling to the account, and I made my way cautiously down the outer stair, with both drawings carefully tucked into my scrip. He followed me down, glancing aside to the main workshop, where I could see, through the open door, one of the men turning what was probably a chair leg on a lathe.

'Do you take a booth at the fair this year?' I asked.

'Aye, but only for small goods, bowls and platters and cups, and suchlike. I will take orders for large items, or tell customers that they may see them after the fair in my shop, but I'll not risk the better things at the fair itself. You've heard the rumour about possible trouble.'

I had heard none of these whispers myself, but both the potter and the carpenter would have more dealings with the ordinary townsfolk than I did. Most of my customers came from the university or the religious houses. Only the richer sort of townsmen, or their wives, bought books.

'Do you really think there will be trouble? And if there is, surely they will leave their fellow townsmen in peace?'

He shook his head. 'We are all the more to be hated. By taking part in the fair, we may be regarded as leaning to the priory's side in the dispute. But I cannot afford to lose the business. I always do a brisk trade in these smaller items, and my lads have been storing up a stock of them for several months now.'

I nodded. These would be apprentice pieces, made by the boys while they were learning their trade, leaving Shippan and his journeymen free to work on the more elaborate pieces.

'And when do you think you will be able to turn your hand to my desk?' I said, pausing at the mouth of the alley.

'I can make a start tomorrow,' he said, 'when I have finished what you saw me working on.' He rolled his eyes. Seeing my puzzled look, he laughed. 'A parrot stand, if you please! The wife of the present provost of the Guild Merchant has acquired a parrot, brought back for her from his last voyage, by that son of hers who goes trading with the ship his father harbours in London. A parrot stand! To be carved and gilded like a grand lady's bedposts! Have you ever heard the like? Aye, I'll start your desk tomorrow. That's honest work. Call round tomorrow sennight, and you may see how I am progressing.'

'I will do so.'

I looked at his spectacles, which he had left dangling precariously by the looped tape over one ear. 'Where did you buy your spectacles, Master Shippan? My journeyman has need of a pair for close work, but the goldsmith in Northgate Street who used to sell them has shut up shop.'

'Aye. He's away to London. Said there were not enough wealthy customers in Oxford to keep up his business here. I bought my own spectacles at the fair two years ago. There's a merchant comes most times, who imports them from Venice. They are costly, but I would not be without mine, for the fine carving. And for writing up my account books. As I've grown older, my sight is less use for close work.'

'I shall try there, then.' I raised my hand to him in farewell.

I left, heading up Fish Street past the Guildhall. Glancing aside at it, I hoped the provost's lady's parrot lived long enough to enjoy its perch. These foreign birds can be delicate, though 'tis said that, properly cared for, a parrot may live as long as a man, or even longer. As I passed the turn to St Mildred Street on my way home, I smiled to myself. It would not be long before I would carry the new desk up there, to take the place of that woefully shaky table.

Ahead of me, I caught sight of a familiar figure. 'Jordain!' I called, quickening my pace.

He paused, and looked round, smiling. His scholar's gown, I noticed, had another tear, ill cobbled together. I wrinkled my nose.

'You are a poor seamstress, Jordain,' I said. 'Margaret could stitch that up for you so that it would not show.'

'I could not presume to ask.'

'No presumption. You cannot lecture in the Schools in that gown. You know that Margaret regards you as a second young brother. I have never quite outgrown childhood in my sister's eyes, and you are no better. Besides, it will entice her away from her cookpots for a time.'

His puzzled glance reminded me that I had not seen him since before our foraging expedition to Headington Hill. At this time of year he was always busy settling new students into Hart Hall and preparing his own lectures, though I believe he could have delivered them in his sleep.

'Come,' I said, taking him by the elbow. 'I am sure you have a few minutes to spare and I can tell you about the new venture which is afoot, and which is coming near to turning my premises into a workshop of jam makers.'

We were nearly at the shop and I had reached the end of my explanation, when we came face to face with Edric Crowmer, vintner and town constable, stomping up the street, glowering.

'What's amiss, Edric?' I asked. 'You look as though you have lost your life savings.'

He grunted. 'I have just been having words with Hamo Belancer.' He sniffed contemptuously. 'I went only to remind him of the meeting in the Guildhall this evening, and have had my ear chewed off, *again*, about his French properties. Does not every living soul in Oxford know of his grievances? If he has a case, let him take it to the king. Perhaps His Grace will launch another campaign merely to recover Hamo's lands for him.'

Once again Jordain looked puzzled, but I realised that, being more gown than town, he might have escaped Hamo Belancer's complaints.

'Like Edric here,' I said, 'Hamo Belancer is a vintner. He deals mostly in ale now, and some of the poorer sorts of French wine, though he used to sell the finest quality.'

'No better than mine,' Edric said, jealously.

'I think I have passed his shop,' Jordain said, 'but never bought from him. Near Mary Coomber's dairy, is it not?'

'Aye, not far. Well, Hamo's father was a Frenchman, married an Oxford woman, but left her and the boy here alone much of the time, while he managed his large estate in Guyenne. A fine, wine-growing estate.'

'So he would have us believe,' Edric said, in tones of disbelief.

'Well,' I said, 'he used to sell excellent wines. I remember from my early days as a student. Whatever the case, the father died, Hamo inherited his French property, but left it in the charge of a manager, though he would visit it once or twice a year. Then, after the king's campaigning a year or two ago in France, and despite our successes, the French managed to annex some of England's lands in Guyenne, including Hamo's property. He has lost both his wines and the rents from his tenants there. From being one of the richest merchants in Oxford, he claims he is now impoverished. He thinks the king should fight to reclaim those lost lands, despite the current truce.'

'He could always do homage to French John,' Edric said sarcastically, 'since he prides himself that half his blood is French.'

'Perhaps he might find it difficult to remain as an English merchant in Oxford,' I said mildly. 'After such an act, at such a time of repeated warfare between our countries. Like as not King Edward will retake those lands sometime in the future.'

'Hmph,' Edric said, 'I wish you every success in persuading him of that.' And he walked off to his own shop.

'Both of them members of the Guild of Vintners,' I said to Jordain, as we went on down the street. 'That is probably the meeting of which he spoke. And no love lost between them, as you have seen. But every trade has its common interests. No doubt one of those interests tonight will be a shared complaint about loss of trade during the fair.'

'But might they not take a stall at the fair?' Jordain asked.

'Aye, certainly they might. But they will say: Why should they pay the priory for a stall or a booth, when they have better premises of their own, just a short distance away, here in the town? And their goods are heavy to move, whether they roll their barrels to the fair ground or trundle them in barrows or handcarts. Then there would be damage to the wines through being stirred up. It is a reasonable grievance, more reasonable than complaining to the king about the loss of lands to the French.'

'You sound as though you have some sympathy with them,' Jordain said.

'I have. Remember, I too am a merchant, though in a small way, no more than a shopkeeper. I too will lose trade to the fair.'

'I have not been to the fair for years,' he said. 'It comes at a bad time of the term for me. I do not remember any booksellers there.'

'The last two years there have been one or two. No great rivals to me, mainly selling rough little books for the pocket, the kind of thing carried by pedlars, but it is a straw in the wind. Nay, I am thinking more of the wealthy merchants who bring their business to the fair. With coin in their purses, they are the kind of men who might spend some of it on my better quality of books, perhaps as a present for a wife or daughter. I've had one such customer already, come early to the fair from Flanders.'

As I was telling him about the cloth merchant Peter Winchingham, we reached home.

Margaret, so it proved, was happy to leave the heat and steam of the kitchen and sit on our favourite bench under the pear tree to mend Jordain's gown with neat, invisible stitches, while we strolled about in the cool and the shade of the trees in shirt and hose. Although it was October, this was an unexpected day of lingering summer warmth. The other women soon joined us, all of them red from the heat, although Mary had shortly to leave for her evening milking. I stole a glance at Emma as she sat near Margaret, fanning herself with a large dock leaf. When she had lived as a novice at Godstow, she had been pale, perhaps because the diet was low. Now she was flushed and rosy from the heat, wispy curls breaking loose from her braided hair and gathering softly about her face. She looked even younger, hardly older than Juliana. I turned away, lest she catch me watching her. I wanted to tell her about the desk, but even more I wanted to surprise her with it when it was finished.

'I thank you, Margaret,' Jordain said, receiving the mended gown and bowing like a courtier. 'I am forever in your debt.'

She laughed, tidying away her needle and thread into her sewing case. 'It was something neglected by the founders of the university, in laying down celibacy for scholars. Who was to take the place of mothers and wives in caring for poor, helpless men?'

'A problem for all men of the cloth,' I said, thinking privately of Philip and Beatrice. 'And not only for the lack of seamstresses.'

'In the colleges there are servants,' said Jordain, slipping his arms into his gown. 'Even sometimes women servants, who can undertake such tasks. But in a small, poor hall like mine, there is no money for more than a cook and a man for rough work.'

'You could learn to wield a needle yourself,' she said, standing up and brushing off from her skirts a few dry leaves which had fallen while she was sitting.

Jordain laughed. 'I think I am unlikely to live long enough to learn to stitch as finely as you do.'

I turned to Maud Farringdon, who was sitting at the other end of the bench, while Beatrice and Emma sat on the grass at her feet.

'How goes the preparation for the fair?' I said.

'Finished,' she said. 'All but potting up the last of the preserves made today, and scrubbing down your kitchen. Every surface has somehow become sticky, even where we were not working.'

I raised my hands in protest. 'Never call it *my* kitchen in Margaret's hearing!' Nevertheless, I was glad to hear that my home would be returning to normal, although I would no longer encounter Emma coming every day to help. We must discuss the book she should start on next, though I supposed that she would be needed at the fair, before she could return to scribing. They would serve at their booth turnabout, two at a time. Apart from Mary Coomber, I suspected they did not realise how fatiguing it would be, although in truth they had all been on their feet in that hot kitchen for many hours without complaint.

On a sudden thought, I said, 'Why do we not all take our supper out tonight? The fellowship of jam brewers deserves a holiday from the kitchen. And Jordain deserves a good meal before weeks of boiled cabbage at Hart Hall.

My scriveners can celebrate a return to a bookshop smelling of ink and parchment instead of burnt jam.'

I saw that Maud and Beatrice looked doubtful, perhaps reckoning up their lack of coin.

'We *never* burned any jam, Nicholas!' Juliana protested, but Emma laughed at her.

'Pay him no mind. He said that only to provoke you.'

'I shall treat you all,' I said, suddenly, magnificently, despite the look of alarm on Margaret's face. I always felt rich in the chinks at the beginning of the academic year. Besides, I had the feeling I should manage a few more profitable sales to the merchant Peter Winchingham.

'I have heard that Tackley's food is good,' Margaret said with caution, eying me anxiously, 'and not too costly. Walter and Roger eat their dinner there most days.'

I knew what Tackley's food was like. Substantial but very dull. I had eaten enough of it as a student.

'Nay, the Mitre,' I said. 'It is not much further away. I shall send Roger to be sure they can accommodate us, for they will be much occupied with guests staying, now that it is but two days from this until the opening of the fair.'

Before any polite objections could be raised, I went through to the shop and announced my plan. The two men looked surprised and pleased.

'I need you to bespeak us room at the Mitre, Roger,' I said, 'and on your way back, stop in at the dairy to tell Mistress Coomber what's afoot. She should have finished the milking by then.'

I was gratified by the men's pleased looks, but I had a guilty feeling that I had made my grand gesture more from wanting to see the delight on Emma's face than from any true spirit of generosity. I could not spend the evening alone with her, but we could at least spend it in company.

Our supper at the Mitre proved memorable. It was a fine evening, so – as there was such a crowd of us – the innkeeper proposed a table in the garden. Grown reckless, I ordered a course of salmon seethed in cream, followed by goose roasted on a spit, with onions and carrots cooked in the fat dripping into the pan below, followed in its turned by a bowl of late salad greens (somewhat wilted and disappointing, now that it was October). There was French wine for the adults and small ale for the children, and, to finish, honey and fig cakes for any of us who had a little room left to eat them.

We took our supper early, because of the children and because the inn would be busy at the later supper hour with its many guests, more of whom were arriving as we ate. We were nearing the end of our meal, some of us picking at the honey cakes more from greed than hunger, when a group of three merchants came out to sit at another table in the garden. They were unmistakable from their rich garments and that indefinable air of poise and confidence which marks out the wealthy man who travels from country to country, dealing in large shipments of goods and substantial amounts of money. One of them was Master Winchingham. He saw me, bowed, spoke briefly to his companions, then approached our table.

'I do not wish to trouble you or disturb your meal, Master Elyot,' he said, bowing to the rest of our party, 'but I wonder whether I might speak to you briefly?'

'Certainly.'

I stood up, and we drew aside from the tables. Philip cast a curious glance in our direction, but the others were busy sharing out the last of the wine or trying to stop the children eating too many of the honey cakes.

'It is not for me,' Alysoun was protesting. 'If no one is going to eat the last of them, I want to take them back for Jonathan. He helped us with the apples, and he never has treats like this.'

'How can I be of service, Master Winchingham?' I said.

'We cannot discuss this more than briefly here,' he said, 'but will you be in your shop tomorrow's morn?'

'Indeed I shall.'

'I have been offered several books. Very fine. Exceptionally fine. But I did not care for the man who offered them. He admitted they were not his to sell, but that he was acting for the true owner.'

'He came to you here, at the inn?'

'Aye. I only returned yesterday, and I had mentioned here that I had a love of books. That was to the innkeeper, but there were others nearby. It was in the parlour of the inn. Anyone might have heard. Then this man seeks me out this afternoon.'

'Have you seen the books?'

'He brought two with him. A Latin Bible and a book of hours. As I say, they were of the very highest quality. He claims there are more, the gentleman owner is selling his entire library before travelling abroad.' He paused. 'I did not believe him.'

'Do you have the books still?'

'Aye, I said I would keep them until tomorrow noon. If I bring them to you, will you examine them, tell me what you think?'

'He is asking too high a price for them?'

He shook his head.

'Nay. He is asking too little. I fear they may be stolen.'

Chapter Three

The following morning, both house and shop seemed more peaceful than they had been since our foraging expedition to Headington Hill. Mary Coomber possessed a handcart, which she used for delivering her cheeses and her flagons of milk and cream about the town, and I helped her wheel it across the High Street and in through the gate to our garden.

'I have no need of help, Nicholas,' she said with a laugh, showing off her muscular arms, from which the sleeves had been rolled up. 'Milking cows, I've been, since I was not much older than your Alysoun, and turning the great wheels of cheese soon after. By the time I was twelve or thirteen, my Ma had me trundling this very cart through the town. So you save your breath and your fine hands.'

I was aware that, despite her kindly nature, Mary had a touch of scorn for a man who spent his life dealing in books. She, by contrast, had passed her own life barely able to read and write, save for simple accounting, and thought book-learning both a waste of time and a mystery to any sane person living a sensible life. She would sit and listen happily if Walter told one of the tales he had learned from his mother, but she could not understand anyone who might occupy his time 'ferreting about amongst bits of dried cow skin', as she so trenchantly put it.

'Nevertheless, Mary,' I said mildly, 'I will give you a hand, and also help you and the others wheel it down to the fair ground. It will be heavier then, loaded up with all your goods. Let us hope you will have sold everything before you must wheel it up the hill again after the fair.'

She gave a scornful snort, but in spite of this I think she was glad of the help. She must be nearing fifty, and the cart was heavy.

Soon after I had left the women to loading their goods on to the cart, Master Winchingham arrived at the shop. By then we were busy, as usual on these last days before the fair and before most of the university lectures had begun, although Jordain was already at work in the Schools. There was no hope of a quiet discussion in the shop, so I led the merchant through the kitchen to the small parlour which opened off it and overlooked the garden. Master Hadley's wife had made it her own, but I never met her, for she had died before ever I came to Oxford. My Elizabeth had inherited the chamber for her own, but rarely used it, for she was generally too busy working in the shop, first with her father and then with me. Margaret had always preferred the kitchen. The room had a slightly forlorn appearance, although Margaret always kept it clean and aired. At least here we could be quiet and private.

'Now, Master Winchingham,' I said, drawing a chair for him close to the window and placing a candle table beside it. 'Will you take some refreshment?'

'Nay, I thank you.' He sat down and placed a leather scrip on the table. 'I am sorry to trouble you with this, and my suspicions may be quite unfounded, but I should be glad of your opinion.'

He began to unbuckle the straps of the scrip.

'As I mentioned when we met before, it is ten years or more since I was last in Oxford, although I have been in and out of London every two years or so. My business takes me to many countries. France, as I told you. Spain. The German states. I have twice visited Poland. Therefore, although I have bought books here in the past – from your father-in-law – I do not know how prices stand nowadays, not since the Pestilence. The prices asked for these books are considerably lower than they would have been when last I was here. Perhaps matters are very different now. Perhaps books are no longer so highly valued.'

'On the contrary,' I said slowly. 'Because there were great losses amongst scribes and illuminators, books have been hard to come by in these late years. There are still enough wealthy men – and women especially – to keep the prices high. I never lack for customers.'

'Well then, tell me what you think.'

He drew out from his scrip two books and laid them on the table. The Bible was quarto size, with an elaborately jewelled cover, fastened with clasps of gold. A volume which would hold an honoured place in a nobleman's library, or form a treasured centrepiece for some abbey's collection of religious works. The book of hours was small, duodecimo, like many designed to fit comfortably in the palm of the hand, or to be carried always by a lady or gentleman to consult for a daily round of prayers, anywhere, at any time.

I tried not to show on my face what I was thinking.

First, I examined the Bible. It would be about fifty years old, I guessed. Well read, but carefully. Parchment pages take on a sort of sheen from much handling, but there was no wear, no fraying, no loosening of the spine. It had been used regularly, but with reverence.

'How much is the seller asking for this?' I said.

He named a figure and I shook my head. 'Too little.'

Then I picked up the book of hours, which nestled in my hand with all the familiarity of an old friend. I turned over the pages, although I had no need to do so.

'And this one?

Again, too little.

I laid down the book of hours next to the Bible and looked up at Master Winchingham.

'I have never seen this Bible before, but as you are aware, it is exceptionally fine. You were told that the owner was selling up his library before going abroad?'

He nodded.

I picked up the Bible again, raised it to my face and

sniffed. I smiled at the merchant's startled look as I placed it back on the table.

'Incense,' I said. 'Unmistakable. This is a Bible which has spent much time in a church during services. It has absorbed the scent of incense into its very pages.'

'So, not a gentleman's library.'

I nodded. 'Not a gentleman's library.'

I picked up the smaller book.

'As for this, I can tell you where this has come from. Or at least, I can tell you where it *was*. I sold this book of hours myself. It must be nearly six years ago now. I had married Master Hadley's daughter and been taken by him into the business. He put me through all the stages he would expect of a journeyman scrivener, though in a shorter time than a true journeyman would spend. I learned about parchment making and book binding. I was trained in keeping accounts. I even worked at copying *peciae*. My penmanship is good enough for that, and even for the less important books, though I have not the hand of a true scribe. When he felt I knew enough of the business, Master Hadley allowed me to join him in the buying and selling of books.'

I ran my fingertips over the little book. It was nowhere near as fine as Emma's work, but it had a particular place in my life.

'I bought this book from a gentleman's son. He had inherited a few books from his father, but his tastes ran to horses and hunting dogs, so he was turning the books into coin, one by one. This was the first book I bought myself, and the first I sold.'

Master Winchingham had drawn a deep breath.

'Six years ago, you say. Do you remember to whom you sold it?'

'Aye, indeed. To a man I know well, who was in my shop just days ago. Canon Francis Aubery, of the Priory of St Frideswide.

The silence between us stretched out.

'Do you believe this canon is selling the priory's books? Through this somewhat disreputable fellow who approached me?'

'Nay, that I do not believe. Canon Aubery would cut off his right hand first. This book he bought not for himself, but for the library at St Frideswide's. He would never have sold it. Someone else at the priory, however, may be doing so.'

'Or else they have been stolen from the priory. As I said to you, I feared they might be stolen. The low prices . . . perhaps asked by someone who did not know their true value. At this time of the fair, there are many people in and out of the priory, which would not happen in the ordinary way of things.'

'That is certainly possible.' For the moment I was reluctant to share my own suspicions, which might be quite without foundation. 'Did you say this fellow told you there were more books?'

'Aye, he did. Though he did not say how many, nor what they are.' He pinched the bridge of his nose between thumb and forefinger. 'A thief might steal one or two books, but could a thief steal a great quantity without being noticed?'

'It seems very unlikely,' I said.

I turned the matter over in my mind. From the garden came the muted cries of the children and the over-excited barking of dogs. Jonathan Baker must be here with his dog, Digger, Rowan's litter mate.

'Exactly how have you left the business with this man who offered you the books?' I asked.

'He is to come to the Mitre tomorrow,' the merchant said, 'the day before the fair, when I said I would give him my answer.'

'Can you delay your answer? Play him like a fish? You are too much occupied with the business of the fair? You must attend to other matters in Oxford? Also, you wish to examine whatever he might have to offer, before you make a decision, and will wait to see how profitable your dealings may be at the fair. If you do well, you might be interested in more books.'

Master Winchingham threw back his head and laughed.

'You say that you are but an Oxford bookseller, Master Elyot, but I think you have the head for a merchant's trade, employing your skills at outwitting the Hanseatic League.'

I joined in his laughter. 'I have not the taste for it, I fear, but in this affair I think we must proceed by cunning, do you agree?'

'I do. I shall play the fish as you suggest. And tell him to return . . . not after the fair, that would not suit him, for if I refuse to purchase he will want to try his hand with others who have come to the fair from elsewhere. Too risky to try to sell to someone local who, like you, might recognise the books.'

I did not believe that would be a great risk, except with the other two booksellers, but I agreed with his reasoning. 'Perhaps he should come to you – what? – five days from tomorrow? There will still be two days left of the fair by then, but that will also give me time to make enquiries. Canon Aubery may be able to learn what is afoot.'

'That is agreed then.' He returned the Bible and the book of hours to his scrip and buckled it. 'For the moment it is probably best if I am not seen too much about your shop, despite my interest in purchasing books. I will come again in a few days' time, to hear whether you have managed to discover anything.'

'Aye, that would be best. Come in the evening on the second day of the fair, after Vespers. Come to sup with us, and we will put together what else we have both learned.'

I escorted him back through the shop and out the door on to the street. Walter and Roger looked at me curiously, but said nothing.

'A matter of business,' I explained, as I came back into the shop.

It might be necessary to take them into my confidence later, but at the moment there was little enough to tell, although Walter would probably remember that book of hours – I had been proud of the profit I had made on my first sale, and boasted of it. I had been, after all, but a boy of nineteen, even though I was newly a father.

The rest of that day and most of the next were taken up with much business in the shop and – when I could spare the time – helping to convey the cheeses and preserves to the booth at the fair which Mary had hired.

Traders could sell their wares in one of three ways. A few poorer folk, or country women coming into town with farm goods to sell – a basket of eggs or some jars of honey or a couple of laying hens – would pay a penny or two for the right to spread a cloth on the ground and lay out their wares. For them the fair meant little more than Oxford's weekly market. Next came the folding stalls. These were hired from the priory and consisted of a broad counter mounted on legs, with a canvas awning, somewhat like a boatman's tilt cloth. The whole thing could be folded up and stacked away at the end of the fair, to be stowed in one of the priory's barns. During the fair, the stallholder could fold it up and remove his goods for the night, or he could roll himself in a blanket and sleep under the stall to keep a watch over them. If the weather was fine, this was what most chose to do.

The booths were another matter entirely. Almost as substantial as the poorest houses in Oxford, like those in the derelict area just north of the church of St-Peter-in-the-East, they were small buildings with wooden walls and roofs, a shutter which could be lowered in front like the counter of a permanent shop, and a solid door with a lock. The lay servants of the priory had been busy erecting them from their separate parts for the last week. These were rented by the wealthier merchants, or those whose goods were either valuable or fragile. Master Winchingham would have hired one of these – probably one of the largest – and Mary Coomber had secured one for our partnership of preserve makers.

Success at the fair also depended upon where the booth or stall was placed, and the priory charged a higher rent for those in the most favoured positions, mostly those nearest the entrance to the fairground, which lay just beyond the South Gate of the town. There were also a few popular spots close to the largest booths selling food and drink. Some of these rivalled the town's hostelries. Indeed, some were even set up by the better ones like the Cross and the Mitre. Since they must lose their regular trade, except for those guests staying in their inns, they would make up for their losses as best they could.

Mary, it seemed, was a friend of the senior lay steward's wife, a connection which had stood her in good stead. The booth she had rented stood just half a dozen places in from the entrance, and faced north, so the direct sun would not spoil the goods. It also meant less work for us in transporting everything there and setting all out on the shelves inside. Although the booth could be securely locked, and there was little likelihood of a thief breaking in to steal a cheese or a pot of jam, the women had planned at first to take it turnabout to sleep in the booth. For once, I overruled my sister.

'This is mere folly,' I said firmly. 'You shall not, any of you, run the risk of staying in your booth overnight. There has been a great deal of talk in the town about possible trouble at the fair, and it is likely to happen at night. I am going to hire a watchman to guard your goods for you.'

Margaret protested, as I knew she would, but I think she was secretly relieved. It would not have been a pleasant experience for a woman alone, or even if two stayed together. As it turned out, I had no need to hire some stranger, for Roger offered to serve as watchman, although I insisted that he should be paid.

As Master Winchingham had told me, the merchants attending this year's fair were more varied than we had seen since before the Pestilence. Indeed, I believe I had never seen a greater gathering. The decline in some of the famous fairs of Europe was proving of benefit to our smaller English ones, even those like Oxford's, with its uncomfortable history of disputes between the town and the priory. It seemed the great merchants were untroubled by this reputation, or at any rate merely took the precaution of bringing more servants with them. The crowds milling about the fairground on the day before the opening of the fair included not only substantial numbers of wealthy men, but an unusually large number of their servants, all of whom were wearing daggers and taking no risks.

Not merely the cut of the strangers' clothes, but the Babel of tongues revealed their nationalities. Englishmen from every shire, with every dialect, were to be expected, as were the Welsh and a few Scots and Irish. The increase in numbers from other countries, however, was what most caught my attention. There were Flemings. Some, like Master Winchingham, were clearly Englishmen who had been drawn there by the Wool Staple, speaking English amongst their fellows, and Flemish to their servants, but others were themselves Flemish, mostly square built and shorter than Englishmen, with broad cheekbones and round, well fleshed faces. There were plenty of Germans, big men with dark hair and loud voices. Others, whose language I could not place, were perhaps Poles. Winchingham had said he had traded in Poland, but I had certainly never seen Polish men in Oxford, although I knew scholars who had travelled to their distant land.

The particular group of merchants which I eyed carefully, and listened to covertly, were the Frenchmen. Although there had been a nominal peace with France since the battles the previous year – small encounters, but bloody – everyone knew that it was no more than a temporary truce. King Edward would not so readily give up his claim to the French throne which, by English law, should have come to him. According to some obscure law, the French asserted that the crown could not descend through a woman. As a result, they had made a mere count's son their king, whereas our king, not only son of the king of England, but grandson through his mother of a king of France, was the rightful heir.

The wars in France had drained England of money in taxes, and even worse, the Pestilence had denuded the country of men of fighting age. Although – God willing! – the plague seemed to have died out these last four years, it would take longer than that to rebuild our fighting strength. We seemed always to be victorious in France, when it came to battles, but it is difficult to hold your victories secure in a foreign land, unless you have men enough to man your garrisons there. So our garrisons were weak and vulnerable, like those in Guyenne, where the French king had been nibbling away at English possessions, like those of the Oxford vintner, Hamo Belancer.

As though he had been conjured up by my own thoughts, there he was, the half French vintner, as I emerged from the booth, ready to push Mary's hand cart back up into the town. I saw that he was sauntering away from a group of those same Frenchmen, with a curious expression on his face, part complacency, part excitement. On catching sight of me, he assumed his usual discontented frown.

'So-ho, Nicholas!' His lips curled in a sneer. 'You are driven by these damnable canons to taking a booth at their fair! I would not sully my hands, nor give them the satisfaction of charging me rent and tolls.'

'Nay,' I said mildly. 'I do not plan to trade here. I have been helping friends to move their wares.'

Resolutely turning my shoulder to him, I lifted the handles of the cart and began to manoeuvre it round the stacks of goods and the busy traders who blocked the way through to the street, but Balancer took up his position beside me. Like a leech, he would cling to me until we regained the High Street. Inwardly I sighed, determined to shut my ears to yet one more recitation of his woes over his lost French properties.

Yet he kept his silence until we were free of the worst

of the crowds and passing through the South Gate into Fish Street.

'Even the French merchants have come to the fair this year,' he said. 'Now that there is peace.'

'Aye.' I waited for the usual tirade, but it did not come.

'Aye,' he echoed. 'With peace between our countries, perhaps justice will be done at last. I hope for restoration of what is mine.'

'You do?' My surprise made me incautious of speech.

He gave an unpleasant smirk.

'Aye.'

'You think the king will negotiate the return of those parts of Guyenne seized by the French?' I shook my head. 'He is more likely to seize them again by force. That is the only way to deal with the French. They break every treaty.'

'So it is your belief, Nicholas, that he will send his son with armed force into France again? I think not.' He grinned again, as if he were hugging some private joke to his chest.

I had no answer to his arrogantly provocative remarks, and continued to trundle the cart over the cobbles. It was easier now it was empty, but one of the wheels was out of true, and tended to set the cart heading off determinedly to the right. Constantly hauling it back to a straight path, I had little breath to waste on Balancer.

'And speaking of Edward of Woodstock,' he said, as though we had indeed been discussing the king's eldest son, 'it seems he arrives in Oxford this very day, on his way from the palace at Woodstock to his castle at Wallingford. He is to spend some nights at the priory. I understand that de Hungerford has his ear and is always ready to make the most of it.'

This was indeed news. If Prince Edward, the king's heir and greatest commander in the field, was coming to Oxford, it was surprising it had not thrown the town into an excited frenzy. Ever since his victories in battle as a mere boy barely sixteen, he had been venerated as a hero by every Englishman. He was a year or two younger than I, yet he held so many offices and had so much experience in the wider world, I felt like a child by comparison.

'You had not heard?' Balancer said, reading my expression correctly. 'One of those French merchants is a vintner like myself. He is to supply some of his finest wines to the priory while the prince is their guest.'

'I am surprised,' I said dryly, 'that you would wish to speak to the French merchants, particularly vintners. May they not be stealing the vintage from your very lands?'

He flushed at the provocation, but answered steadily. 'We must make allies where we may. I have had dealing with this man in the past. He has heard that the prince does not want to make a great show of his visit. He comes quietly, with a few attendants, like a simple nobleman. Nevertheless, the priory will wish to serve him wine of the very best quality.'

We had reached the High Street. Balancer gave me a curt nod and headed off in the direction of his own shop, having had the satisfaction of displaying to me his greater knowledge of affairs. As I proceeded more slowly, I wondered what he had been doing at the fairground, if he was not planning to trade there. Certainly there were always a few curious individuals wandering about, getting in the way of those trying to set up their stalls, but Balancer would not so demean himself. I had also noticed a few well known troublemakers from amongst the youth of the town. They had stayed quiet enough, but that might only mean that they were spying out where best to launch an attack once the fair was under way. I hoped the priory had made ample provision in the way of stewards and guards, to protect both merchants and buyers against danger.

Had Balancer taken that trouble to tell me about Prince Edward for some other purpose than lording it over my ignorance? Did he hope that I would spread the word in the town? That I would not do, though I would probably tell Margaret, who had a great admiration for the prince.

The presence of royalty might make the town louts all the more eager to stir up trouble.

And that was the second time that I had heard Prior de Hungerford mentioned in connection with the prince. I hoped Edward of Woodstock was a better judge of men than to be taken in by him. From all I knew of the two of them, they seemed to have nothing in common.

I need not have been concerned about whether or not I should keep my lips sealed about the prince's visit to Oxford. An hour or two before Vespers he rode into town, with very little show, but his arrival was like a stone dropped into a pond. Word of it rippled outward from Northgate Street as he rode down toward the priory, and I swear it took no more than a quarter of an hour to pass along the High to the East Gate. Margaret and Mary arrived back from the fairground with Alysoun and Rafe, all of them glowing with excitement.

'I have seen Prince Edward!' Alysoun exclaimed. 'The king's son! The hero of Crécy!'

Her tone was so excited that it set the puppy Rowan into an ecstatic dance, for she had been left behind all day, with only Roger and Walter for company.

I laughed, fending off the dog before she ripped my cotte. 'The prince is as great a warrior as Julius Caesar, do you think, my pet?'

'Much, much greater! Julius Caesar had a bigger army than the people of Gaul. Or at least he had a *proper* army, and they didn't. Prince Edward defeated the French with a much smaller army than theirs.'

Rafe tugged at my hand. He looked worried.

'He wasn't wearing armour.'

'Nay, he would not need armour in Oxford, my little man,' I said, hoisting him up on to my shoulders. 'No one here would hurt him, would they? And armour is very hot, even in the autumn. He is not going into battle now. Princes, like other men, may enjoy their leisure.'

I soon left the family to rest after the hard work of the day and made my way to the Priory of St Frideswide. There would be a special service at Vespers in the priory church to bless the opening of the fair the next morning. Canon Aubery would be there and I might be able to speak to him about the books which had been offered to Master Winchingham. The sale could be quite legitimate, approved by the canons in Chapter, although that did not explain the unrealistically low prices being asked. If the sale was not legitimate, then he should be warned of it. In the past, Canon Aubery had held the position of *librarius* in the Priory, but Prior de Hungerford believed in moving the canons about, so that no single man remained long in the same occupation. Even the most senior of the *obedientiaries* were moved, a practice which did not augur well for the already shaky finances of the Priory. But perhaps that was what de Hungerford wanted. If no one but himself knew the true state of finance, church repair, provisions, properties – aye, and the holdings of books and other treasures – then he had complete control of them in his own hands.

All who were trading at the fair were invited to join in the service of blessing, gathering below the rood screen, in the portion of the nave open to the secular congregation, and it was clear that many of them were making their way to the church. Perhaps, like me, they might also have the thought that the prince himself would be present. I admit I was curious. Strictly speaking, I was not one of the traders, but after the assistance I had provided for the last two days, I felt I had a right to be present. As I had closed the shop before leaving, I had felt the same twinge of annoyance as every other shopkeeper in the town, at the thought of the lost business during the following days. There were, I observed, a number of grim-faced townsmen also making their way toward the priory. I hoped that they did not intend to disrupt the service, and shame the town before the royal visitor.

Before leaving home, I had taken Walter aside. 'Tomorrow morning,' I said, 'I will meet you in front of the

Guildhall, and we will go together to search for the merchant of spectacles.'

He frowned. 'You should not waste your money.'

'Well, we shall see whether they are of any use to you. If they are not, then we shall forget the matter.'

The church of St Frideswide was magnificent. Larger even than the university church of St Mary the Virgin, its splendid nave stretched away between pillared side aisles, with a soaring roof that would not shame a cathedral. Even the side chapels were as large as some parish churches, and all of them exquisitely furnished with gilded statues, rich hangings, and silver vessels. Yet, when I looked more closely, I thought that there was a slightly neglected air about the place. And surely there were fewer rich lamps and candlesticks than I remembered from previous visits. I wondered whether Canon Aubery was right, that some of the Priory's treasures were being spirited away, and turned into coin. I noticed also that a crack had opened up in the east wall of the south transept, close to the corner where it intersected the nave. It was made more visible by a long streak of damp. There had been no rain for more than a week, so this must have accumulated over time.

I managed to find a place near the front, close to the rood screen, where I had a good view of the canons' stalls, and the separate thrones for the prior and sub-prior. St Frideswide's had not taken up the new fashion of pews for the common folk like me, so we must stand, while the canons took their places in the stalls of carved oak, comfortably provided, I saw, with velvet cushions.

The canons filed in, two by two, chanting the opening prayers of the service, and followed by Sub-Prior Resham carrying a gold cross as tall as himself. Last of all came Prior de Hungerford, obsequiously escorting a slender young man I took to be Edward of Woodstock. Compared with the prior's costly vestments, he was modestly dressed for a royal prince, even for a nobleman. His gown was of fine blue woollen cloth, generously cut, but without ornamentation. The borders of its wide sleeves were trimmed with white satin, but not cloth of gold, and he was quite without any gems, except for a single heavy ring on his right hand.

From his expression, I thought he was faintly amused at Prior de Hungerford's deference, but he hid it well and accepted the prior's own throne with a polite bow, while the prior seated himself in the sub-prior's place. Resham was obliged to squeeze in at the end of the stalls for the lesser canons.

The service was relatively short, the blessing of the fair merely being added to the normal service for Vespers. The priory was known for not dwelling over long on its acts of worship. My attention, I am afraid, was not devoted to my prayers, as it should have been, but divided about equally between the royal prince and the unpopular prior. I found myself liking the prince simply from the modest way he conducted himself. Anyone seeing this young man – for he was just three and twenty – and not knowing his identity, would never take him for a prince of the blood, heir to the English crown and to great lands in France, and the most successful commander of an army then living – outdoing, it was said, even the fame of his great-grandfather at the height of his powers. As for the prior, there was about him a shiftiness of the eyes, combined with a falsity of expression when praising God that stuck in my throat like piece of bone. No wonder Canon Aubery distrusted him.

My plan to speak to the canon came to nothing, for the brotherhood of the priory moved swiftly out of the church through their private door and were gone before any of us who were packed together in the large congregation could move. Besides, I thought, no doubt there is to be a magnificent meal served to Prince Edward, including those fine French wines mentioned by Hamo Belancer. I would not want Francis Aubery to miss that. I doubted whether the ordinary canons of a priory deeply in debt would normally dine so well, though meals in the prior's own lodgings might be a different matter. My discussion about the books Master Winchingham had shown me must wait for the morrow. I would surely be able to find the canon once the fair was safely under way.

The following morning I made my way down to the Guildhall early, for the fair would be declared open immediately after the service of Prime at the priory, and I wanted to seek out the merchant who sold spectacles before the crowds grew too large. Walter was already waiting for me, looking resigned. His own lodgings were nearby, a room over a fruit merchant's shop. After he had lost his wife and child to the plague, he had given up his cottage down Great Bailey, near the castle, and moved in here, where the goodwife gave him his evening meal. He claimed he needed nothing more.

'Good morrow, Walter,' I said cheerfully, ignoring his glum expression. 'If we walk smartly, we should be in time to hear the fair officially opened.'

He fell into step beside me.

'No sign of any trouble yet, then.'

'Not that I have heard,' I said, 'though I would not be too confident that it will not be brewing. I fear the presence of Prince Edward in the town may provoke some of the wilder elements into thinking that they may persuade him – and hence the king – to alter the terms of the fair's charter in favour of the town, either by allowing our shops to remain open or diverting the fair's tolls and rents into Oxford's coffers.'

Walter shook his head. 'Then they are like to be disappointed. A man who has faced a great French army and routed it is unlikely to heed the mischief of a handful of young miscreants.'

'I agree, but I doubt if there are many cool heads amongst them.'

We reached the entrance of the fairground and joined the crowd awaiting admittance. Margaret and Mary would already be inside, ready to open their booth for business, but as mere customers, we must stay until the temporary gates were opened. Craning over the heads of those in front, I could just make out the party emerging from the small postern gate leading through the town wall from the priory to this stretch of open meadow, which served as a fairground for one week in the year, but as grazing for sheep and cattle the rest of the time. Prior de Hungerford was clad in a magnificent robe, outshining the modest figure of the prince, who must have been persuaded into accompanying him. They were surrounded by a large group of lay servants, the senior lay steward, and a few of the canons. Not Canon Aubery, I noticed.

We were too far away to hear what was said, but it was mercifully brief. Then two of the lay servants raised trumpets to their lips and blew a fanfare. The crowd around us pressed forward, as the group from the priory withdrew. It took some minutes for the servants on the gate to collect the required ha'penny from each of us, some of the older people grumbling loudly that in the past they had come and gone to the fair without being expected to pay.

'Never miss a chance to line their pockets,' someone said loudly. 'True men o'God they be, these holy canons.'

He earned a scattered burst of rueful laughter. For myself, I thought it a short-sighted policy. I would never charge people to enter my shop, and that was the nature of a fair – a great, glorious, many-coloured shop, filled with exotic goods that would never be found in the ordinary course of the day in Oxford, as well as more mundane wares. Mix that with a sprinkling of foreign faces and strange tongues, a chance to gape and gossip, and it was little wonder that folk came even if they did not intend to buy, or had not the means to do so. Later in the day there would be entertainments too: juggling and acrobats, singers and dancers, perhaps even a brief, crude play with a moral or mystical message. The town might complain about the loss of coin, but that did not prevent all the good burgesses from enjoying the sense of holiday due to a pause in employment and the colourful spectacle before us.

'Now,' I said, 'let us search out the man who sells

spectacles and see what he can offer us.'

Walter looked at me glumly. 'If you say I must come with you, Master, I will come, but I cannot see how such heathenish devices can serve any purpose.'

It was a bad sign when Walter took to calling me 'Master'.

'What do you mean, "heathenish"? The Venetians who make these spectacles are no heathens. They are as good Christians as you or I.'

He shrugged. 'They live cheek by jowl with the Musselmen, do they not?'

'Even our own merchants trade with the Musselmen. That does not make them heathens.' I could see that I was being diverted from the true subject. 'Come. It will do no harm to see what is on offer.'

We found the booth in the first row without difficulty, for a large sign hung outside, depicting a pair of spectacles fit for a giant. The merchant was neither Musselman nor Venetian but a soberly clad Londoner, who looked more like an apothecary than a merchant.

'My journeyman scrivener here,' I said, 'is having some difficulty seeing his letters of late. What do you have that might serve to help him?'

Walter glowered at me, but would not look at the merchant. The man eyed him thoughtfully.

'This is a new problem? You have not had difficulty seeing the letters in the past?'

'Never.'

I wondered. I did not think this had come on Walter suddenly, I had noticed him straining to see for some months now, and the struggle had caused him to hunch his back, leading to discomfort and then pain.

'Forgive me, sir,' the merchant said, with almost exaggerated politeness, 'but your age would be . . .?'

'I shall reach my half century next year.'

The man nodded. 'Will you please turn your face to the sun?'

Walter looked more than ever suspicious, but obliged.

The merchant held him gently beneath the chin and carefully studied his face.

'Good,' he said. 'I see no problem there. You have no disease of the eyes, no sign of a veil growing over them, as may sometimes happen. 'Tis no more than the effects of years, which must come to us all.'

I noticed the lines of tension in Walter's face relax somewhat, and suddenly remembered what I had been a fool to forget. Walter's father, also a scrivener, had suffered from failing eyesight, and in the end had gone nearly blind. All this time Walter must have been worrying that the same fate was befalling him. His refusal to consider spectacles was an attempt to shut away his own fears.

The merchant opened a wide, flat box and laid it on the counter. It contained rows of spectacles, framed in wood, some with quite thin lenses, others as thick as the bottom of an ale flask, . He selected a pair from the thinner end and handed them to Walter, together with a sheet of parchment written all over in a small script.

'Try to read this, with and without the spectacles.'

Walter took both gingerly. He held the parchment close to his face at first, then further away, clearly having some difficulty in making it out. Then he balanced the spectacles on his nose, where they began to slip down. Gripping the nose piece against his face, he held up the parchment. I watched his face clear, and take on a kind of wonder.

'Aye,' he said grudgingly. 'I can see it better.'

'Try these.' The merchant exchanged the first pair for another, with slightly thicker glass.

'Better.' Walter said, with grudging admiration. 'Aye, I can read it fine now, but I could never work, holding these on my nose with one hand. I need both my hands to my work.'

'Never fear.' The merchant took the second pair back. 'The bridge of your nose is slender. The spectacles must be made large enough for every nose, but see these small holes in the outside of each frame?' He reached a box down from a shelf and opened it to display lengths of narrow ribbon and tape in varied colours. 'I will thread a ribbon through each side. Then you may tie them behind your head to keep the spectacles in place, or some people prefer to loop them over their ears.'

'Aye,' I said, 'that is what I saw John Shippan do. He keeps the loops ready tied, to pass over his ears. Like you, Walter, he needs the use of both hands.'

I could see that Walter was loath to admit that both the merchant and I were right, that he needed the spectacles, but there was a spark of eagerness now in his eyes, which had not been there before.

'Which colour of ribbon, Walter?' I said. 'I think you will not choose the scarlet.'

In spite of himself, he allowed me a small smile. 'Black.'

I turned to the merchant. 'We will take them. How much?'

The price he named was staggering, but after a brief discussion he agreed to lower it very slightly. 'They are the finest Venetian glass,' he said firmly, 'and have travelled all the miles here by sea and land. Many are broken on the way. I make little enough profit, sir.'

I forbore to say that he looked very well on it, and paid over the coin. If it improved both Walter's work and his back pains, it would be worth every silver penny. And besides, he would be unburdened of the fear that he was going blind like his father. I was a fool not to have suspected that before.

The merchant presented Walter with a large silk handkerchief in which to wrap the spectacles, and he placed them carefully in his scrip.

As he bowed us out of his booth, the merchant said, 'In two years or so, you may find that you need a thicker pair. That should not cause you concern. As we grow older, our eyes grow tired and lazy. I shall be here with the fair each year, and can provide.'

I hoped that it would be more than two years before

new spectacles would be needed, else this would become a drain on the shop's profits. For now, however, I smiled at Walter and he – reconciled to the heathenish devices – smiled readily back.

'Now,' I said, 'like the rest of Oxford, you are on holiday. Unless you need me for aught, I shall see you the day after the fair finishes. Although, if you care to come to the shop, we have tasks we can undertake.'

He nodded. 'Aye. Roger and I both feel we would be better to work part of the day, even during the fair, that we may not get behindhand.' Then, hesitantly, he said, 'I thank you, Nicholas. I was a fool. These will make the close work much easier.'

I clapped him on the shoulder. 'Good. Now go and enjoy the fair.'

Before we could both be embarrassed, I turned away, and we soon lost each other in the crowd, which was growing more dense by the minute. First, I paid a visit to Margaret and Mary at their booth, but seeing that they were doing a brisk business, I withdrew quietly without catching their attention. As I did so, I collided with someone, stumbled, then murmured a hasty apology.

'My fault as much as yours, Master Elyot. I wished to speak to you.'

She was little changed in face and manner, since I had last seen her, but dressed in quite a different fashion. Instead of the elegant but discreet gown of waiting lady to a gentlewoman, she now appeared to be a merchant's wife. Or perhaps even a merchant in her own right, as one or two widows have become. A gown of the very finest woollen cloth, dyed a rich but sober mulberry colour and trimmed with modest, pure white coney fur, it was a silent reproof to the extravagance of ladies like the one she had formerly served. It spoke of wealth but restraint, good sense reproving greed.

'Mistress Walsea!' I exclaimed, astonished but pleased to find her, quite unexpected, here in an Oxford fair. 'What do you here?'

She gave her small, contained smile. 'I am about my employer's business, Master Elyot. And I think you may be able to help me.'

'Anything I can do, mistress, I am at your service.'

Unconsciously I found myself glancing over my shoulder. Nothing to be seen but a cheerful throng busy spending silver pence they probably could not afford.

Her employer's son was at this moment on the other side of the town wall, in the Priory of St Frideswide. For her employer was the king.

Chapter four

I had last seen Alice Walsea two months before, when she had ridden away from Leighton-under-Wychwood, escorted by my cousin's son James to Burford, before she could become entangled further in the events surrounding the murders of Gilbert Mordon and her own cousin, Reginald Le Soten. Having heard nothing further of her, I assumed that she had managed to reach the king's court and make her report. Why she was now here in Oxford, in the guise of a wealthy merchant's wife, I could not know. I could but guess that it somehow concerned her covert occupation as an intelligencer for the king.

'You wished to speak to me, Mistress Walsea? Here we are somewhat too public, I fear. There is a booth belonging to the Crown Inn at the far end of this row. They will serve a reasonable cup of ale. Let us make our way there.'

She nodded her compliance, but instead of heading straight to the place I indicated, she strolled along, stopping to buy some sweetmeats at one stall and to admire some fine fabrics laid out enticingly by Master Winchingham's journeyman. The merchant raised his eyebrows and smiled, seeing me in company with the lady, but I gave him a blank stare, with a slight shake of my head. Mistress Walsea fingered the cloth and spoke knowledgably about it to the journeyman. For all I knew, her knowledge of good cloth was quite genuine.

When we reached the Cross Inn's temporary stall, she

seated herself at one of the trestle tables set out on the grass, choosing a stool with its back close to the town wall, which here formed the northern boundary of the fair ground. I sent the pot boy for two cups and a flask of their best ale and took another stool, facing back the way we had come, where the rows of stalls and booths formed a kind of street, giving a curious illusion of permanence. It was strange to think that in a few days' time there would be nothing left but yellowed patches in the grass, discarded rubbish blowing about until rain and frost devoured it, and a flock of sheep wandering where the noisy crowds now gathered.

When the pot boy had brought our ale and left, I turned to Mistress Walsea.

'I was glad to see that you managed your departure from Leighton in good order, mistress. I trust the rest of your journey was safely accomplished?'

I poured us both ale and raised my cup to her.

'I had no problems, save that the second carter's horse went lame with a cast shoe, which delayed us. Nay, it was all quite peaceful.'

She took a sip of her wine.

'It is not still the affairs of Gilbert Mordon which bring you here?'

'Not at all. They are in other hands now.'

'And nothing is heard of his lady, or her lover?'

'Nothing.' She took another sip. 'I am here on quite another matter.'

I smiled. 'You have come to trade at St Frideswide's Fair?'

'Indeed I have. You will find that I have a stall selling ribbons and laces. Over there.' She waved toward the lower end of the fairground, nearer to Trill Mill stream, where the pitches were less costly.

'I have left my girl to mind it. She knows nothing of . . . my other work.'

'And that is what you wish to speak to me about? Your other work? Could it be that you are concerned with the possible trouble there may be at the fair? Trouble stirred up by the young men of the town?'

'Oh, I am quite sure your town authorities, and your deputy sheriff, are more than competent enough to deal with any such trouble. I understand that Cedric Walden is considerably more able than High Sheriff de Alveton. My business is with something quite different, although I am afraid I have very little to guide me. It is hardly more than a whisper.'

She drummed her fingers on the table, and frowned.

'Word has been sent from one of our garrisons in Normandy, that a man known to them had plans to come to St Frideswide's Fair posing as a merchant, but his business is not trade.'

'And his business is . . . ?'

'Provided the payment is sufficient, whatever you may wish. Theft, arson, kidnapping, murder.'

'A man of many talents,' I said dryly.

'Indeed. And since it was the merest whisper picked up in Normandy, we have little else to go on. Although it may be that he is meeting someone here in Oxford. There is no better place, for the casual meeting of men who mean ill to others, than at one of these bustling fairs, a place of shifting crowds from many nations, lasting but a few days, then vanished like some passing vision.'

She smiled. 'As I knew you already, and have seen your nose for a puzzle, I thought I would seek you out and ask you to keep your eyes open. Nothing more than that. Eyes, and ears also.'

'I might serve you, and your . . . master . . . better, if I knew what I should keep them open for. Can you describe the man? I shall need somewhat more to go on, in the midst of all this.' I indicated the people milling about, drifting down from the first street of the fair, where most of the expensive goods were to be found, and sauntering along the other less pretentious streets of stalls.

'That I am afraid I cannot do, nor could those who informed us of the rumour. I cannot tell you anything of his appearance. It may indeed be no more than a rumour, so I do not ask you to waste your time unduly. The man is clever. Although he is known to have been guilty of a number of crimes, he has always managed to escape justice. He can pass himself off in many guises.'

'Like a merchant of ribbons and laces? I asked.

She laughed. 'Aye, even as that, though I suspect he would choose a grander trade. He is known for arrogance. It is to be hoped that one day his arrogance will betray him.'

'But he *is* French?'

'Oh, aye, he is French.'

'Then unless he is also able to pass himself off as Flemish or German, that will narrow the search considerably.' I rubbed my chin. I had been in a hurry this morning, and I could feel the bristles coming. 'There are certainly Frenchmen here. I noticed quite a large group yesterday, although I have not seen them today. One is the vintner who supplied the wine to the priory for the prince's dinner last night. One of the vintners here in Oxford knows him.'

'If he is a merchant well established in his trade, he is probably not the man we seek, but the man we seek might be in his company. Or it may be that he uses a genuine trade as cover for his crimes.'

I nodded. 'They seemed to stay together, the Frenchmen, in a group. It could be that they do not feel altogether safe in England, even if the profits to be made at the fair are a temptation.'

'I must return to my stall,' she said, getting up, 'else I shall cease to be credible as a true merchant. I should be keeping a close eye on my own profits.' She inclined her head. 'I thank you for the ale, Master Elyot. Your sister is well?'

'Aye, she and her friends are selling preserves and cheeses here at the fair. They have developed a recent taste for the merchant's calling.'

'It can hide much,' she said seriously, 'and is an

excellent excuse for travel. Give you good day, Master Elyot.'

'And you, Mistress Walsea. Should I hear or see anything suspicious, I will bring you word. Where do you stay at night?'

She had already taken her first steps away from the table, but glanced over her shoulder. 'At Tackley's Inn. In the High Street.'

I supposed it was a compliment to me that Mistress Walsea thought I might be of some assistance to her in this quest for an unknown French criminal, but I felt ill equipped to be an intelligencer for the king. I had forgot to mention the presence of Prince Edward in Oxford, but she was almost certain to know of it, for she had not appeared surprised when I mentioned the dinner at the priory. The prince had been visible to all at the opening of the fair, yet Mistress Walsea might well have known in advance that he was to come this way. I wondered how long he planned to stay. A fair could have little attraction for a royal prince, who could summon merchants to come to him whenever he chose.

Having paid for the ale, I walked slowly back past the stalls and booths until I reached the one manned by my sister. Mary was busy cutting a quarter round from one of her large cheeses, while Margaret was offering a sample of her damson cheese to a burly Fleming who looked as if he would drive a hard bargain. I was about to turn away and head home when I saw Emma coming toward me, carrying her little dog. I stopped where I was and smiled at her.

'I would guess that amongst the crowds here is no place for Jocosa,' I said. 'She will be trodden on.'

'I do not usually carry her. She is not one of those ladies' dogs who are no more than an ornament, but you are right, she is hardly safe here. However, during these last busy days, she has formed a bad habit of chewing anything left about in my aunt's house, so I might not leave her there. And I wanted to see the fair, before it comes to my turn behind the counter.'

'And have you seen much?'

'Enough, for the moment.'

'Then why do we not walk out beyond the fairground? There is a stretch of open meadow beyond, and we can cross a branch of Trill Mill Stream and then Shire Lake Stream by footbridges, and even walk as far as the Thames.'

'I should like that. And Jocosa can run about. All this mischief comes from being shut away in the house.'

We walked companionably out past the last of the stalls, where the unsullied grass of the meadow lay enclosed by the curve of the stream. There were two of the priory's lay servants here, to prevent anyone stealing into the fair from this side without paying, but they recognised me and nodded when I said we were going to walk in the meadow.

Once clear of the fair, Emma set Jocosa on her own feet, and the fluffy white bundle raced ahead of us to the first stream, where she planted her feet firmly in the soft mud and lapped at the water as if she had not drunk for days.

'I hope she will not fall in,' I said.

'She has more sense. More sense than I, at any rate. It was not she who fell into the river at Godstow.'

'Here is the footbridge.' I pointed ahead, where a narrow plank bridge with no handrail provided a crossing, so that one might reach the lower meadow. 'Can you manage it?'

'Certainly,' she said scornfully, stepping out confidently ahead of me, closely followed by Jocosa.

The bridge over the second stream was sturdier and even possessed a wobbly handrail. Emma displayed her scorn of it by not even laying her hand on the rail. When we reached the wider, rushing waters of the Thames, we looked for somewhere to sit.

'This fallen branch of the willow will serve,' Emma said, sitting down with no heed to her dress. Today she wore something a little finer than one of Maud

Farringdon's work gowns, but it was hardly suitable for the heiress to Sir Anthony Thorgold.

'I have been wanting to talk to you about the next book I should undertake,' she said.

'And I. But there has been little chance, with all of you steeped in blackberries and crab apples up to your eyebrows.'

'Aye, it has been hard work, but I thought it such an excellent enterprise. I am so glad that my aunt has been making friends and starting a new life for herself and the girls here in Oxford. It has been very hard for her, since William's death.'

I nodded. I realised for the first time what I had not considered before, that Emma's decision to come back to Oxford might not be simply for her own sake, and certainly not for mine, but out of care for her aunt, who had shown great fortitude since her son's murder, though his death so soon after her husband's had left her poor and vulnerable.

'I think Meg and Mary are glad to befriend her,' I said. 'And Beatrice too needs friends, for her position is a very difficult one.'

'Aye. It is very well for Philip Olney to live comfortably as a Fellow at Merton College, but it demands very much of her.' Emma smiled a little bitterly. 'She must be shunned and vilified by many. Why does he not do the honest thing, and marry her?'

'She has refused him,' I said. 'She knows how much the life of scholarship means to him, and will not be the means of robbing him of it.'

She bent down to stroke Jocosa, who had curled up at our feet. Without looking up, she said, 'You chose to give it up, to marry your wife.'

I plaited my fingers together and looked out over the river. A boat was being rowed up the river, heavily laden with goods. A latecomer to the fair.

'I was much younger, having just been awarded my Master's degree. I had not yet taken up a position in the university. Philip did not know Beatrice until he was older, already established as a Fellow and *librarius* in the college. It was different for him. Besides, I am probably not a true scholar.'

She looked at me slantwise, still bending over the dog. 'You might have been.'

'Perhaps. But I am very content as a bookseller. And I have my children.'

'And Philip has Stephen. The boy needs more than an occasional father.'

I found that I was somewhat annoyed at this.

'Philip is an excellent father. He spends more time with him than many a married man in the town.'

'Well, let us not quarrel about it, Nicholas.' She sat back and laid her hand on my arm. 'Let us talk about books.'

As always, the touch of her hand sent a shiver through me, and instantly I regretted the sharpness of my last remark.

'Aye. Have you thought what you would like to make next?'

'I have. While we were cooking, Margaret mentioned that Walter has been writing down the stories his mother used to tell him. She says he is an excellent teller of tales.'

'He is.'

'Does he plan to scribe the book himself? Or Roger? Or do you think he would let me do it, and illuminate it? I should dearly love to, for it would be a fine change after holy books. But I would not want to offend him, if he plans to make it himself.'

'I will speak to him.' I was relieved after those few awkward moments that we could speak of books again. 'Walter greatly admires your artistry, he has spoken of it often. I think he would be pleased.'

'But perhaps he would wish to scribe the words himself?'

'He might. You could share the work between you. Only the other day he told me that was how matters were managed when his father was a scrivener in London.'

'So his father followed the same trade?'

'Aye, until he went blind. I have just realised that was preying on Walter's mind.'

I told her about Walter's recent difficulties with his sight, and his reluctance to try spectacles.

'But he is reconciled now?' she said.

'It seems so. When the merchant assured him that his problem was no more than age, and when he found that the lenses transformed what he could see, I think he believed at last that it was not incipient blindness.'

She plucked a tall seed head from the grass and began to tease the seeds from the stem, so that they flew off, borne by the breeze which was picking up here in the open meadow by the river.

'How clever they are, these spectacles. It seems like magic, but it is no more than a piece of curved glass, is it not?'

'Aye, and I think the shape of the curve makes a difference, but I do not understand it. Something the Italians invented, for they have clever ways with glass.'

'I expect it came about quite by accident.' She smiled. 'Someone broke a curved cup or a bottle and it fell on top of a piece of writing. "God be praised!" he cried, "It is magic! The words have been made larger!" Everyone thought he was crazed.'

'Aye, I expect that is how it happened.' I smiled back at her. Suddenly she reminded me of Alysoun, who always wanted to know how and why everything had come about.

I shivered, and turned up the collar of my cotte. 'Come, this wind is reminding us that it is October. Let us return to the fair and find something to eat. I fear Margaret will not be cooking dinner today.'

'Where are the children?' She stood up, shaking the fallen grass seeds from her skirts.

'With John Baker. He has had to close his shop, so he said they could help him scrub out his ovens now that they have been left to go cold. They will be kept busy, and come home grubby.'

She took my arm as we walked back to the fair, the little dog circling round us. The fair seemed more than ever like one of those magical cities Walter described in his stories, seemingly permanent, but illusory. The warmth of her arm against mine reassured me that no permanent harm had been done by that brief clash over the matter of Philip's unmarried state.

'Before we met near our booth,' she said, 'I saw you talking to a woman.'

I felt a small stab of gratification that she was curious enough to ask.

'Mistress Alice Walsea,' I said. 'We met at Leighton.'

She raised an enquiring eyebrow. 'Was that the lady who was fleeing from the manor, after the murder of her cousin?'

'The same.'

'And why is she here? I thought she was attached to the court.'

'Only in a manner of speaking.' It occurred to me that while Emma was serving preserves, she might have more opportunity than I would of observing any Frenchmen at the fair. Mistress Walsea, I was sure, would not mind another pair of sharp eyes keeping watch, so I explained to Emma what I had been asked to look out for.

She paused on the far side of the footbridge over Trill Mill Stream and frowned.

'There is very little to go on.'

'Mistress Walsea knows no more. The man may not even mean any mischief here in Oxford, although he may be meeting someone here.'

'Well, I shall, like you, keep my eyes and ears open, though for what, I am not sure. Come, Jocosa, time to carry you safely away from all those heedless feet.'

When we had eaten a simple meal at the booth run by the Cross Inn, Emma went to help Meg, so that Mary could return to her cows before late afternoon, and I made my way home. Although the shop must remain closed, there is always work to be done. Walter and I had not completed our inventory of the *peciae*, and I am always behindhand in writing up my accounts. It was very quiet in the shop, with Meg away at the fair and the children with John Baker, so I was able to finish the inventory and even wrote a whole page in my account book.

The October dusk was drawing in as I went into the garden to feed the hens and shut them away for the night, as my sister had asked me to do when I told her I was returning home. The last of the silly creatures caught and stuffed firmly into the hen house before she could rush off again, I sat down on the bench and pondered the problem of the books which had been offered to Master Winchingham. I had hoped that I might see Canon Aubery today at the fair, but there had been no sign of him. He had not even been with the small group attending Prior de Hungerford at the opening. I supposed it was not surprising. The noise and roughness of the fair would not be to Canon Aubery's taste, nor would he care much for the profits it might bring to the priory, since such a large portion seemed destined to find its way into the prior's pockets instead of into the priory's coffers to pay for the much needed repairs to the church.

The book of hours which Master Winchingham had shown me, I knew, without question, belonged to the priory. Canon Aubery had bought it from me for their library, and I saw no reason why it should have left there. The Bible was unfamiliar, but it had clearly spent many hours in a church during services. Since it now appeared in company with the book of hours, it seemed reasonable to assume that it, also, belonged to St Frideswide's.

The books were being sold by some nondescript fellow whose appearance suggested to Master Winchingham that they might be stolen, but since the man claimed that he had a whole gentleman's library to dispose of, our conclusion that he could not have stolen so many books from the priory seemed justified. Therefore, someone at the priory was selling the books, using this man as his agent. Canon Aubery had already told me that he suspected Prior de Hungerford was stealing the priory's gold and silver treasures, which meant he was the man most likely to be behind the sale of the books.

It was a crime, and should be stopped. The books belonged to St Frideswide's, not to the current prior. However, the crime involved the Church, which always closes in upon itself to protect its own. Reporting my suspicions to the deputy sheriff would be useless. Moreover, with a royal prince now staying at the priory, any interference by a layman like me would be all the more rigorously resisted. It seemed there was little I could do, except to warn Canon Aubery, and the other canons who were not of de Hungerford's faction, about the theft of the books.

Tomorrow I would send him a message.

Tomorrow evening also, I recalled, Master Winchingham was to dine with us. I would be able to report at least some action on my part.

We were all tired that evening, even the children, although they had enjoyed the messy task of scraping and scrubbing the remains of old fires from John's bread ovens.

'You see,' Alysoun said, 'it is best to allow the ashes to build up for a little while, Jonathan's father says. It adds more flavour to the bread. But if it goes on too long, it gives his loaves a bitter taste.'

I saw that Margaret rolled her eyes at this nugget of information. She scoured her small bread oven every day.

I nodded sagely. 'So the rich folk, who only eat the upper crust of the loaf, and give the bottom, with its ashes, to their servants or poor beggars, are depriving themselves of the best portion?'

'Aye,' Alysoun said. 'I like the bottom crust best.'

So she did. But then she only ever ate Margaret's bread. The bottom crust, fresh every morning, was crisp and delicious.

I turned to my sister. 'And how fared your trading

today?' I asked.

Margaret was sitting by the small fire I had lit, not for cooking, since we had eaten a cold supper, but to stave off the autumnal bite in the air. She looked weary and had prized off her shoes.

'Very well indeed. Better than we had hoped. But it is a wearisome business. I am glad I need not carry on beyond this week of the fair.'

'It has been worth all the labour, then?'

'Aye, I think so. And not just for the chinks earned.'

I nodded. Like me, Margaret had seen how the companionship had been a benefit to both Maud Farringdon and Beatrice Metford. Even Mary Coomber, for all her sturdy independence, was glad of it.

'And now,' Margaret said, getting a little stiffly to her feet, 'as soon as I have put tomorrow's dough to prove, I am going to bed. Off with you, children. Perhaps Papa will see to you.'

'By the time I have counted to a hundred,' I said, 'you must be undressed and in bed. After that, I'm for bed myself.'

I had not had such a tiring day as Margaret, but the disruption to my normal work and the noise of the fair had wearied even me.

As it turned out, it was not a peaceful night. I had fallen asleep as soon as I stretched out in bed, but I think I cannot have slept long when something woke me. I lay awake, my eyes staring into the dark, my ears stretched for the sound that had disturbed my sleep. At first I could hear nothing, then it came again, very distant, a muddled sound I could not place.

I sat up and groped for my strike-a-light and tinder box on the candle table beside my bed. Feeling about in the dark, I knocked the box on the floor. By the time I had retrieved it and managed to light my candle, the noise had grown louder. It seemed to be coming from the southern part of the town, but as my bed chamber faced the back of the house, I could not be sure.

Perhaps I should investigate, and make sure the shop was safely barred. Every night I barred the street door and the shutters, but I had been tired – could I have forgotten? I dressed clumsily and in haste. By the time I reached the top of the stairs, Meg was already there, also carrying a candle, but still in her night shift, though with a blanket round her shoulders.

'Trouble,' she said grimly.

'Is there anything to be seen from your room?'

'Plenty to hear.'

She led me into her bedchamber, which was over the shop. I opened the shutters and leaned out, looking up and down the High Street. Here and there a few lights glimmered, as our neighbours, also woken, looked out.

'It is coming from the fair, I think,' I said, struggling to make out anything in the dark. The sky was overcast, with nothing but a sliver of moon showing occasionally as the clouds moved overhead with the high winds of heaven.

'If they destroy our booth,' Margaret said, 'and Roger sleeping there alone–'

We were both thinking of the rumours that there would be trouble from the town at this year's fair.

'They are more likely to attack the priory servants left there on guard,' I said. 'Their quarrel is with the priory, not the merchants.' I was trying to convince myself. 'I am going out to find out what is afoot.'

'There is no need for that. Do not be foolish, Nicholas!' She grabbed my arm.

'I will stay away from trouble, but if no one has alerted the castle, then someone must do so.'

'It need not be you.'

'I will be careful.'

I patted her arm gently and extricated myself. In the kitchen I took down a lantern from the shelf where we always kept a few ready, and lit the candle from the one I had brought from my bed chamber.

'Bolt the shop door after me,' I said, 'but stay in the

shop so you can open it for me in a hurry if need be.'

'I wish you would not go.'

She followed me through into the shop. We could hear running footsteps in the street.

'I will be careful,' I said again, as I slid back the bolts, took up the lantern, and stepped outside. I waited just long enough to be sure she had bolted the door behind me.

There were already a few others about – one of the junior fellows from St Edmund Hall, William Rushington, came running up behind me. The night porter from Queen's College was hurrying ahead of us toward Carfax.

'The constables are out,' Rushington said.

'Aye.' I could see that Edric Crowmer had been joined by half a dozen constables from other parishes. They were also heading for Carfax.

'It must be fighting down at the fair.' Rushington quickened his pace. 'Everyone has been saying there would be trouble.'

'Have you any idea who is behind it?'

He shook his head. 'The usual mischief-makers, probably. I suppose we should be glad they aren't attacking students for once.' He broke off and gave a nervous laugh. 'I forget that you are no longer of the university, Nicholas. You are a townsman now.'

'I take no side in these endless, stupid quarrels,' I said, somewhat breathless from the speed we were making, 'but one of my scriveners is keeping night watch for my sister and her friends. I hope he is not in danger.'

By now we were in Fish Street and more people were hurrying down toward the South Gate and beyond it to the fairground.

Suddenly the crenellations of the city gate sprang more clearly into view as light flared up behind it.

'Mother of God!' I said. 'Fire!'

We began to run faster, but before we could reach the gate we were thrust aside by a body of horsemen. Soldiers, riding from the castle, under the command of Cedric Walden.

'Fire!' The cry went up all about us. Although it was outside the city wall, there was a wind blowing, stronger than it had been earlier in the day. It would take no more than a gust of spark-laden wind, carried over the wall, to set alight the wooden houses at the lower end of Fish Street. By the time we were level with St Aldate's church the crowd was almost too dense to allow us through, but at last the soldiers were herding people into some kind of order.

Frightened householders poured out of the nearby houses, bringing buckets, bowls, anything that could hold water, and there were willing hands to dip them in Trill Mill stream, beyond the gate, and pass them, man to man, back to soak the thatched roofs, the most vulnerable part of the houses.

Rushington joined the line to help, but I shook my head. 'I am going to see whether my man is in danger. There are enough people here.'

As soon as I reached the entrance to the fair, it was clear where the fire had been started. The wooden entrance gate, set up for the duration of the fair, was ablaze, though the soldiers were dousing it and already the flames were dying down. It was a blessing that the stream ran so close. If the fire had once spread to the town, half the houses in Oxford would have been destroyed, and many of the college buildings too.

Cedric Walden was directing his men, his face smeared with smuts from the fire, and as he turned around he collided with me.

'Nicholas Elyot! What are you doing here?'

'My younger scrivener is acting as night watchman at one of the booths, just within. Has the fire spread beyond the gatehouse?'

'Scorched the two nearest booths, but no great damage done. Luckily someone in Fish Street spotted it quickly and sent word to us.'

'May I go through?'

The worst of the fire was out now, but the timbers still smouldered, and here and there a spark would flare up, until a bucket of water was thrown over it. Further along the street a man was lying stretched out on the ground.

'Someone hurt?' It was not Roger. Too burly.

'The priory's watchman. They hauled him out and struck him over the head. He will survive, but turns groggy when he stands up. We've left him to lie until his wits are less shaken. He may be able to tell us who did this. At least they pulled him out before they started the fire. Otherwise he would have had no chance.'

Walden was starting away, so I caught him by the sleeve and repeated my question. 'May I go through? I want to see whether my man is unhurt.'

In the light from the soldiers' torches we could all see anxious faces peering out at us from beyond the charred gateway – the night-watchmen and the stallholders who had slept here.

The deputy sheriff shrugged. 'It's risky. Take care your clothes do not touch the timbers. They are still hot enough to set you alight.'

I nodded. 'I shall take care. I've no wish to be a human torch.'

I drew my cotte close around my body and plunged through the burnt remains of the gate. The stench of half charred wood caught in my throat, but I was through. Almost at once, I caught sight of Roger in the cluster of worried and frightened men. His face, like Walden's, was blotched with the black smears of soot, and wore an expression of fear mixed with excitement. I drew him aside.

'Are you hurt, Roger?'

He shook his head. 'Nay, they came storming in, shouting that the priory had no right to the rents and tolls of the fair, and they punched a few of us, and got some punches back. I gave one of them a bloody nose, he's journeyman to that butcher in St Mildred Street. Saw him clear as day. They were carrying torches.'

His words came tumbling out in a rush. He was still in a high fever of excitement.

'You should have stayed well clear. Someone might have drawn steel on you.'

'Nay, they were not interested in us, just wanted to affright us, keep us clear of their real business, which was with the priory, but it only had one man here, fellow in the gatehouse. I thought they usually had lay servants here at night. Why should we pay the priory rent, if they leave us unguarded?'

I could see that he was half in sympathy with the townsmen.

He drew a long breath. 'Fellow in the gatehouse, is he hurt?'

'A blow to the head, I'm told, and somewhat addled in his wits, but he will recover.'

'That's a relief. We tried to go to his aid, but they were too many for us.' He glanced across at the group still gathered on the near side of the burnt out gatehouse. 'Most of the servants of the rich merchants, they're armed, but they stayed guarding their own booths and did not join us.'

I could see that the other men, like Roger, were peaceable local citizens, probably mostly with small stalls and their own modest goods.

'Margaret's booth was not attacked?'

He shook his head. 'I think they were after any money that might be in the gatehouse, but those canons are no fools. It will have been taken away to the priory when the fair closed last night. Then they set fire to the gatehouse. Dry timber, it flared up at once. Either because they were angry they hadn't found any money, or they'd intended to do that all along, make trouble for running the fair.'

'I do not suppose it will make a difference. They will contrive something, and still demand a ha'penny to enter. Now, let me see you back to the booth. We both need what sleep we can get in what is left of the night.'

Before I left Roger, I asked whether he had recognised any of the other attackers, but he had only been able to see the one man clearly.

Back in the street, I sought out Cedric Walden.

'My man recognised one of the villains,' I said. 'He's journeyman to the butcher in St Mildred Street.'

Walden grimaced. 'I know the fellow. He's been in trouble before. I have one other name, from someone in Fish Street who saw them running back into town, and I hope that fellow over there may be able to tell me more.' He jerked his head toward the gatekeeper, who was now sitting up, being given a cup of ale. 'Your man unhurt?'

'Aye. No harm done. It seems a group of them tried to fight back, but they were outnumbered.'

'You'd best get back to your bed. I can see that we'll have a night of it here, but I'll leave men on guard from now on, till the end of the fair.' He made a face. 'We do not want this kind of trouble when we have a royal visitor in Oxford.'

I laughed. 'I suspect Prince Edward has seen far worse than this. God give you good night, sheriff, what is left of it.'

Back at the shop, I knocked loudly and heard Margaret draw back the bolts to let me in.

'It was trouble at the fair, wasn't it? Are you all right, Nicholas? Why are you so dirty? And is Roger safe?'

As we walked through to the kitchen, I gave her a brief account of what had happened, and reassured her that both Roger and her booth had come to no harm.

'What fools!' she said. 'More than fools. Wicked. That fire could have spread right through the town. People would have been killed. All for a grudge against the priory.'

'Fortunately the castle was alerted in time, and no serious damage was done. But you are right. It is time an end was put to this quarrel, but it seems impossible, like the hostility between the town and the university. That is quiet for now, but I fear it will break out again.'

'Let us hope not yet. One war at a time is enough for a small town. Best we try to get what rest we can for what is left of the night.'

'Aye. God give you good night, Meg.'

I kissed the top of her head and trudged wearily up the stairs. I carried with me the smell of the fire on my clothes and in my hair.

The next morning it was the turn of Beatrice and Maud to open the booth, for which Margaret was grateful, after our broken night, but Emma, Juliana, and Maysant were soon on our doorstep, even before we had finished breaking our fast.

'Such a to-do early this morning!' Juliana said, flushed and excited. 'Soldiers came marching into our street and knocked up the butcher, demanding his journeyman, but his journeyman never came home last night. They say he was one of those who tried to set fire to Oxford!'

'Not quite to Oxford,' I said. 'They burned down the gatehouse to the fairground. But if the fire had not been put out quickly, it could easily have spread to the town.'

'You were there?' Emma said.

'Only after the fire was reported to the castle. The deputy sheriff and his men had nearly put it out by the time I reached the fairground. I went to see whether Roger was unhurt.'

'And he is?'

'Nothing but bruised knuckles from punching your butcher's journeyman on the nose. The fair will carry on today. Sheriff Walden will see to it that there is no more trouble.'

Roger arrived on the heels of the girls, having stopped hastily at his lodgings to clean himself of the detritus of the fire. I left him to the cosseting of the women and joined Walter in the shop, where I put Emma's suggestion to him, about the collection of his mother's stories. He was experimenting with the tapes attached to the sides of the spectacles, unhooking the loops from his ears and tying the tapes instead behind his head. Raising his face, he looked at me owlishly through the disks of glass.

'Very odd, this,' He said, lifting the spectacles above his eyes, then letting them drop back on to the bridge of his nose. 'They make my writing larger and clearer, but when I look at you, everything is blurred, a sort of fog.'

I shrugged. 'Don't ask me to explain it. Ask the Venetians. What do you say to Emma's suggestion?'

He smiled shyly. 'If the lady wants to make a book of my stories, then I say aye. She will make a fine job of it. I should like to see how she will draw Hob-by-the-Fire and some of the other creatures. I haven't finished it, mind, but she could make a start on what I have written.' He looked suddenly anxious. 'Do you think it good enough to make a book?'

We had had this conversation before, and as before I reassured him, for he had the true storyteller's gift. All he lacked was the confidence to put himself forward amongst the writers of books whose work he had spent all his life copying. One benefit if Emma were to have the scribing of it: she could take the stories away from him firmly, and he could no longer tinker with them, as he was wont to do.

Walter settled to the repetitive but essential tasks of copying out more *peciae*, referring to our inventory to check which were most needed, and exclaiming from time to time about the improvement the spectacles made to his sight. I told him he might take a holiday, as I had suggested, but he shook his head, saying that he would rather be busy. I found a small, clean piece of parchment, and began my letter to Canon Aubery.

To the reverend Canon Aubery of the Priory of St Frideswide, from Nicholas Elyot, Master of Arts, greetings in God.

It has been brought to my notice by a merchant visiting the present fair that a person of name unknown has offered to sell him two books, with further to be shown. These books I have seen and examined. One is a Bible of fine quality, in a jewelled and clasped binding, clearly used in church services. The other is the book of hours you purchased from me some six years since.

In view of our recent conversation and your fears for the priory's treasures, I write to warn you and the other canons that the library may also be at risk of similar plundering. I suggest, therefore, that you take measures to protect the priory's collection of books as well as your other treasures. As this is a matter for Church discipline, I fear there can be no intervention by the secular authority. However, you might consider an approach to the bishop.

If I may assist you in any way, please do not hesitate to call upon me.

I am your friend and servant in Christ, Nicholas Elyot.

By the time I had finished the letter, folded, sealed, and addressed it, Roger had joined us in the shop. There were crumbs of pastry on the front of his cotte.

'Ah, Roger,' I said, 'before you make a start on your work – if, like Walter, you are here to work – I would like you to take this to Canon Aubery at St Frideswide's. It must be put into his own hands. Do not leave it with anyone else. If you cannot find him, or if he is occupied about church services, wait, however long it takes. This must be delivered into no other hands but his. Is that clear?'

Roger looked at me in some surprise at the tone of my instructions to him. 'Quite clear. And if I do not find him before dinner?'

'Stay until you find him. If it comes to Compline and he still cannot be found, then you may return here, bringing the letter back with you.'

He took the letter and went out, looking baffled. Walter looked across from his desk, peering, this time, over the top of his spectacles.

'This is the matter of the books the merchant Master Winchingham brought?'

I could not remember discussing it with him, but perhaps the merchant and I had still been talking when we came through the shop after our meeting in the small parlour.

'Aye,' I said. 'Something is afoot at the priory. I do not like the smell of it.'

Chapter five

Unfortunately, with all the confusion of the last few days, I had forgotten to warn Margaret that I had invited the merchant Master Winchingham to sup with us that evening, only calling it to mind during our midday dinner. When I broached the subject, my sister gazed upon me with an expression which conveyed, more clearly than any words, what she thought of me and my failure to consider all that was entailed.

'I am to understand,' she said, dangerously quiet, 'that this is a wealthy gentleman, a merchant of Bruges trading throughout the cities of Europe. A merchant, moreover, who has in hand the purchase of a manor here in Oxfordshire? You have invited him to sup with us? Here in the kitchen? With a bare afternoon to prepare?'

I nodded, guiltily. I was aware, also, that she still looked tired after yesterday's long day at the fair, playing the part of shopkeeper (to which she was unaccustomed), then followed by a disturbed night.

'He does not seem to me a man who makes much of . . .' I was not sure how to express my sense of Peter Winchingham. 'He is a plain-spoken man. Despite the fact that he trades in fine cloth, he dresses soberly. He is not one of those newly enriched merchants who ape the courtiers,' I searched my mind. 'He is poles apart from a man like Gilbert Mordon.'

'So I devoutly hope.'

'There are many of the great merchants here at the

fair who carry that air of superiority, and gaze down their long noses at people like us. That group of French merchants, for example. But Master Winchingham could not be further from them. I think he would despise such pretensions.'

She sniffed. 'Nevertheless, I have my own pride. I cannot entertain such a man in my kitchen, amongst my greasy pots.'

I thought that she had never hesitated to do so before, not even when the Lady Emma Thorgold ate with us. Perhaps it made a difference that Master Winchingham was a man, and a stranger. And lived, exotically, in Bruges. I kept my tongue behind my teeth.

Alysoun had been listening to this exchange with a keen interest.

'Aunt Margaret,' she said, 'you could serve supper in the small parlour. I could help.'

Margaret looked at her thoughtfully. 'Aye. 'Tis not so convenient as the kitchen, but it could be done.'

She turned to me. 'And who else have you invited?'

I was startled. 'No one.'

'Then you had best put your mind to it. If we are to entertain this merchant, then you should provide him with more stimulating company than our small family. Invite Jordain and Philip for conversation, and Emma for quality.'

'But that will make more work for you.'

She shrugged. 'It will mean a great deal of work and little enough time to do it, in any case. No need to waste it on a single guest.'

'If you are sure?'

'I would not waste my breath, else.' She was truly annoyed with me.

'Is there aught I can do to help?' I asked humbly.

'Aye. You may go to the butcher in Great Bailey – the expensive one, just past Carfax – and fetch me a leg of mutton. I shall need to start it roasting slowly. Then ask Mary Coomber for a plate of those comfits which we have not yet taken to the fair. Alysoun, you shall help me make an apple and blackberry pie. It's fortunate I kept back some of the blackberry preserve. Rafe, take the dog into the garden and keep her there, out from under my feet.'

'It is cold in the garden today,' Rafe whispered.

'Then put on your thick cloak and capuchon,' she said. 'If you run about you will be warm enough.'

Margaret was in full battle mode. I mouthed my apologies to Rafe, who went off grumbling to himself, but Alysoun looked pleased and slightly smug, finding herself part of Margaret's armed forces against the incompetent world of men.

I set off for Great Bailey, stopping in St Mildred Street to extend the invitation to Emma, who was minding Maysant while her aunt and cousin took their turn at the fair. She raised her eyebrows when I explained the situation and apologised for the short notice.

'You are to be the ornament to the occasion,' I said, 'to raise the quality of the company above the mere shopkeeper level into something rather more grand, for this merchant from Bruges.'

'He is a widower, you say? Should I exercise my charms on him?'

'He is old enough to be your father,' I said, abruptly, and she laughed.

'I shall be there. And pass my sympathy to Margaret.'

Once I had bought the leg of mutton – at excessive cost – and carried it home, and fetched the comfits from Mary, I sent Walter to Merton with a message for Philip, and walked round to Hart Hall to see Jordain myself. As always at the start of term, he was so busy I had hardly seen him.

'Supper?' he said. 'I should be more than glad to come. I am afraid we are back again on a diet of bread, cabbage, and a sliver of hard cheese. Our cook seems to be unable to contrive anything else with the small allowance I am able to afford for food.'

'Well, tonight you will be able to enjoy the most expensive mutton in Oxford,' I said, still sore at the amount of coin I had handed over. 'And you will like Peter Winchingham. He is a great lover of books, and does not put on the airs and graces of so many great merchants.'

Walter had already returned from Merton when I reached the shop.

'Master Olney thanks you, and will be pleased to come,' he said. 'And we have had a message from Master Stalbroke that Lady Amilia's book is ready.'

'Good.' At least, I thought, with these increased numbers I should be protected from any frostiness on Margaret's part. If all went well, she would have forgotten her annoyance by the time the meal was over. And I was certain that she too would like Peter Winchingham. I must make arrangements to collect the book from the binder.

Walter and I sat down at our desks to try to salvage what we could from the last of the day, but had barely started when Roger finally returned.

'You managed to see Canon Aubery?' I said, for I saw that he was carrying a letter. He should still be waiting if he had not delivered mine.

'In the end. I had to kick my heels for a long while. The canons had a meeting in Chapter, which seemed to go on for several hours, and it was not a friendly one, I tell you. I heard shouting.'

'Perhaps they are worried by last night's attack,' Walter said.

'Aye, that might be it.' Roger laid the letter in front of me and sat down on his stool. He brightened. 'I saw the prince. Quite close. He nodded and smiled at me.'

'Good,' I said. 'And Canon Aubery?'

'I was able to speak to him at last. He took me to his chamber. Did you know that they do not have cells in a dortoir, like ordinary monks, but bed chambers, divided off, each man his own?'

'And?' I said.

'I gave him the letter, and he said that I had best wait in case he needed to send an answer. While he wrote it, he gave me wine and fig sweetmeats.' He grinned. 'I was hungry by then, you may be sure.'

'He is a very courteous man,' I said, picking up the letter Roger had brought and lifting the wax seal with the tip of my paper knife.

From Francis Aubery to his friend Nicholas Elyot, greetings in God.

Rather less formal a letter than mine, I thought, smiling.

Your warning comes most timely. I have been these three hours in Chapter where we discussed the matter of priory treasures which have gone missing, such as I told you of. As no one now holds the position of librarius, volumes missing from our library had not, before this, been noted. Our debate concerned the safe-keeping of the priory's remaining treasures, lest they fall victim to thieves. It was a matter of bitter dispute, but in the end the voice of the majority prevailed. All treasures will be removed to the choir of the church, close by the high altar, in so sacred a place that even the most nefarious of robbers would not dare to set foot there, nor lay hand on objects under divine protection. Now that I have received your warning about missing books, I shall undertake to move the library to the same sanctuary. In this we are supported by all my brothers of good will, and by Sub-Prior Resham, but not, I regret, by the prior.

Your friend and servant in Christ, Francis Aubery

I folded the letter and looked up. 'Thank you, Roger. A most interesting reply.'

So the canons were making a stand against Prior de Hungerford at last. Francis Aubery did not say whether they would report him to the bishop, but that seemed the most logical next step. The religious houses of Oxford, as well as the parish churches, and to some extent the university itself, came under the general jurisdiction of the Bishop of Lincoln. It was a jurisdiction lightly exercised, but a case of serious misconduct would certainly be investigated by the bishop. At the moment, it seemed there was no definite proof against de Hungerford, but his opposition to the canons' plan to preserve the treasures, combined with the known ostentation of his recently acquired wealth, certainly laid the grounds for suspicion. I hoped the canons would write to the bishop, for he would have the means and the authority to investigate.

During the meal this evening I would explain to Jordain and Philip the problem Peter Winchingham had brought to me, and assure the merchant that matters had now been taken in hand by those who could best deal with them.

I told Roger that on the morrow he should collect Lady Amilia's book from Bookbinder's Island before coming to the shop, and gave him a purse to pay for it. After the scriveners had left – early, since the shop was closed to customers – I helped Margaret move sufficient chairs and stools into the small parlour to accommodate our company for supper. The children would eat early, in the kitchen, but Alysoun would be permitted to help with the serving of the meal. Her contained excitement gave a sparkle to her eyes, and she had insisted upon arranging a few late roses in a jug to stand upon the coffer against the wall.

'Is Roger not wary of spending tonight as watchman?' Margaret asked, laying out our best pewter plates. 'After last night's trouble? With this meal to prepare I have not even been able to learn how our business has fared today.'

I shook my head. 'Roger has asked a friend to go with him. Besides, Cedric Walden is leaving soldiers to guard the fairground. He thinks the provision of lay servants by the priory not able for the task.'

'He should have thought of that yesterday,' she said. ''Tis only by the grace of God that Oxford was spared the spreading of that fire.'

Privately, I agreed, but I respected Walden. He carried out the duties of a full sheriff with competence, something which could not be said of John de Alveton, High Sheriff of Oxfordshire and Berkshire. The care of two counties was a fine excuse for always being needed somewhere else.

'There had been nothing more than rumours,' I said, 'before the fair opened, and there are always rumours. Probably Cedric Walden expected nothing more than the usual fist fight. Some bruises and a few bloodied noses.'

'The strife between townsmen and priory has been growing more serious since de Hungerford came,' she said, shrewdly. 'He has raised the tolls and rents, as well as maintaining the priory's rights for all our shops to be closed.'

'That is a condition of the ancient charter,' I said reasonably. 'It is an annoyance that we must shut up shop, particularly for us just at the beginning of term, but it is their right. Prior de Hungerford could indeed use the town with more courtesy, but as his own canons detest him, he is unlikely to make the effort to woo the town.'

'Now, there you are mistaken, Nicholas.' She paused, tucking a stray lock of hair back into her wimple. Despite her annoyance at the lack of preparation time, it was clear that all was almost ready.

'What do you mean?'

'I have heard talk in the town – in the market, and yesterday, too, amongst the local people at the fair. Prior de Hungerford is not unpopular with *all* the townsmen. It seems he has a group of . . . perhaps one should not call them friends. Allies? Cronies? Men not particularly known for their honesty. Men of violence, too, some of them.'

'Curious company for a senior churchman.'

'Curious indeed,' she said. 'He drinks and dices with them, aye and goes hunting.'

'He is not the only churchman to hunt.'

'Perhaps. But they usually hunt on their own lands, or by permission of the king. It seems de Hungerford does not always seek permission.'

'Well.' I shrugged. 'It is not for us to worry about de

Hungerford. The deputy sheriff will keep a watch on disputes between town and priory. And I have just heard from Francis Aubery that the canons are taking a stand against the prior's possible stripping of the priory's valuables.'

Margaret opened her mouth, clearly wanting to know more of this, but we were interrupted by Alysoun dragging Jordain into the parlour to admire the preparations, and any further discussion of de Hungerford and his misdemeanours would need to await another occasion.

Philip and Emma arrived soon after, having met on their way along the High Street. I had intended to escort her here myself, but she had forestalled me, and would probably have poured scorn on my suggestion that she should not walk the streets of Oxford alone. It was a different matter in the summer, with its light evenings, but now October brought darkness with the onset of Vespers, and the dark streets of the town are no safe place for a woman alone. However much she might protest and assert her independence, I would not allow her to walk home without company.

Three of our four guests now having arrived, Margaret busied herself with some last minute touches to the food, while we stood about in the small parlour, a little awkward at first with the formality of the room, until I started to explain why Master Winchingham was coming, and how he had approached me about the books which had been offered for sale. While we talked, I sent Alysoun to look out for the merchant from the door of the shop.

Philip shook his head. 'It sounds like a bad business, Nicholas. From your description, that Bible must be worth a great deal, and the book of hours would command a fair price.'

'It is not as fine as some I have seen.' I gave Emma a sly sideways glance, which made her blush. 'Nevertheless, it is a pretty thing, and of course I was able to identify it beyond any doubt.'

'Bad luck on the thieves,' Jordain said.

'Aye,' I said, 'but I would know a fair number of the priory's books. When Canon Aubery had the monies for it, he purchased many books for their library, first from my father-in-law, and then from me. There was a good chance I might recognise one of the books from the collection. The man tried to pass them off as coming from a gentleman's library, but that was a blatant lie.'

Our talk moved on to the fire of the previous night, and I gave an account of all I had seen, though I had come too late to identify the fire raisers.

'Roger recognised one of them, though the fellow seems to have gone missing. No doubt Sheriff Walden will be able to round them up.'

'I wonder what their punishment will be,' Jordain said. 'It was a stupid, dangerous thing to do.'

Margaret joined us from the kitchen, looking worried. 'It is growing late, Nicholas. Vespers is long over. Should your Bruges merchant not be here by now? It is no distance to walk here from the Mitre.'

'He may have been overseeing his business at the fair,' I said. 'That might have delayed him.'

'But the fair is closed when the bell for Vespers rings from the Priory,' Philip objected.

'Could he have mistaken the day?' Emma said. 'You told me he is elderly.'

'Not that elderly.' I regretted having teased her about Winchingham's age. 'But you are right. Perhaps he was uncertain which day I meant. I will walk along to the Mitre and fetch him.'

'I will come with you,' Jordain said. 'If the town is restless, and you were seen amongst the traders at the fair, best you don't go alone.'

I demurred, but he was determined. Philip said he would remain to keep Emma company, and they both offered to give Margaret any assistance she needed. I could see that my sister had no very high opinion of any assistance from a university scholar, but she held her peace.

I peered over Alysoun's shoulder and out of the door.

'You bide inside, my pet. It is cold here. Go back to the kitchen. We are going to fetch Master Winchingham.'

Jordain and I donned warm cloaks and I lit a candle lantern, for it was full dark outside. Like the previous night it was overcast. The colleges and a few householders lit lanterns or torches before their doors in the early hours of the night, but these scattered patches of light only served to make the dark in between even more impenetrable.

Jordain and I picked our way slowly up the street. Some of the cobbles were uneven, and there were holes where a few of the more useful stones had been prised up and carried away by someone who needed to mend a wall. In better times, the High, one of the four major streets of the town, would have been repaired long ago, but ever since the deaths in the Pestilence labour was scarce. The town authorities, their own numbers cut down, had difficulty maintaining Oxford. This was a proud place, and would surely rise again, but at the moment, like so many other towns and villages, we were still licking our wounds. By day the broken surface of the street gave no problems. We had all learned to avoid the holes and the half loosened stones without giving it any thought, but at night it could be treacherous.

Jordain echoed my thoughts. 'This poor surface to the street – do you suppose the merchant might have missed his footing and fallen? He might be lying somewhere with a twisted ankle.'

'He can only have come this way,' I said, holding the lantern high, 'from the Mitre to us. If he is lying anywhere in this short stretch of road, we shall come across him, surely?'

To be certain, we cast our eyes back and forth all the way, but there was no sign of anyone lying in the street.

At the inn, we enquired from the innkeeper for Master Winchingham.

'The gentleman from Bruges, Master Elyot?' he said. 'Why, he set off to come to you more than an hour ago. He should surely be with you by now.'

'That he is not.' I was beginning to be worried. Would the townsmen's violence have been turned against a visiting merchant? Or more likely, in the expectation that he might carry a rich purse, had he been set upon by thieves?

'There was no sign of him betwixt here and my shop,' I said. 'Could he have gone roundabout?' I saw no reason why he should, but it was worth the asking.

'Aye.' One of the older pot boys was just passing with a tray of dishes for the inn's guests. 'Master Winchingham you be seeking? He did say as how he would fetch a flask of wine to bring with him to supper. He'll have gone there first.'

'Do you know where?' I asked.

'He did say summat about Hamo Belancer's vintner shop. Said as how he used to go there when he was in Oxford years ago. I warned him, 'tweren't the same now. Hamo don't have such quality wine, but he said he'd go anyhow, since he knew the place and none other in Oxford.'

He gave a sharp bark of laughter. 'Old Hamo is probably still chewing the merchant's ear about them properties he reckons he owns in France, what the French king stole from 'un.'

I felt a wave of relief. Hamo's shop, like every other one in Oxford, should be shut during the fair, but he was not above a little backdoor trading. Master Winchingham might not even be quite aware of how strictly the law was meant to be kept. If he had gained access to the vintner, he could still be there now. Hamo would relish a fresh ear to receive the tale of his woes.

Jordain and I turned back the way we had come and crossed the street. Just before Mary Coomber's dairy, on the corner of a narrow alley that wound south through a maze of mean shops and small houses, stood the vintner's shop owned by Hamo Belancer. To all outward signs it was closed, the shutters firmly bolted, but a narrow frame of light surrounded the drop counter on to the street. It was very dim, however. The light must come, not from within the shop itself, but further back. I had never been inside, but assumed that like most shops in the centre of Oxford it had living accommodation and storage space behind and above the shop itself.

We looked at each other.

'No sign of your merchant here,' Jordain said.

I nodded, but pointed down the alley. 'There is a back door down there, and I think I can see more light. I've no great wish to knock Hamo Belancer up, but I suppose he may be able to tell us whether Master Winchingham has been here. Or whether he is still here.'

'Aye, best we try,' Jordain said.

We began to pick our way down the alley, an unsavoury place to lie so close to a wine shop. It smelled of cat, and worse, and the unpaved ground underfoot had an unpleasant sticky feel to it. My lantern cast our shadows, grossly enlarged, on to the confining dirty walls, while the faint light further along provided no illumination for anything within the alley.

As I held the lantern, I was leading the way. Suddenly I stumbled over something, hit my shoulder against one of the greasy walls, and nearly dropped the lantern. Jordain reached out a hand to steady me.

'What's amiss?'

'There is something here,' I whispered, sure even before I looked. 'Something soft.'

I lowered the lantern and we both looked down. A man lay sprawled in the filth of the alley, face down. It needed no second look to identify the gown. It was Peter Winchingham. And there was blood on the back of his head. Even as we crouched down to look more closely, the sliver of light ahead of us went out.

'Is it?' Jordain asked.

'Aye. 'Tis Master Winchingham.'

Jordain began to get to his feet. 'I'll fetch Hamo Belancer to help.'

I put my hand on his arm.

'I think not.' I was not sure why I was so reluctant to draw in the vintner. 'It is not far to my shop. We can carry him that far between us, and Margaret will know best how to tend him. He is breathing, but that is a nasty blow to his head. Hamo would be little help. Let us get him somewhere warm and safe.'

I managed to turn the merchant over on to his back, afraid that the mud and slime of the alley might block his breathing, and with the sleeve of my cotte wiped his nose and mouth clear. I put down the lantern and eased my hands under his shoulders.

'If you will take his legs–' I said.

Jordain stooped to do so, gripping Winchingham about the knees.

'I will need to walk backwards,' I said, 'so you must direct me.'

'We'll have need of the lantern,' Jordain said, 'and neither of us has a hand free.'

In the end we balanced the lantern precariously on Winchingham's chest, and prayed it would not fall, casting us into darkness. Cautiously we began an awkward shuffle back along the alley to the street. It was a relief, when we reached it, to breathe the cleaner air, and to have the benefit of a few other lanterns, widely scattered though they were. The distance to the shop was mercifully short, but the merchant was a well-built man and we were both gasping by the time we reached the door. All the while our burden might have been a dead man, but for the faint movement of his nostrils.

I banged on the door awkwardly with my elbow, doubting whether I would be heard, but in a moment Philip had opened it.

'Jesu!' he said. 'Is he killed?'

'Hit over the head,' I managed to say, 'but breathing. Need to put him in the kitchen.'

'I'll take his shoulders.'

I shook my head. It would be easier for me to carry the man the few remaining yards than to change places now.

Once we were in the kitchen, Margaret assumed command, clearly forgetting her earlier annoyance with me.

'Put him on the cushioned chair by the fire,' she said. 'Rafe, bring that stool for his feet.'

She wrinkled her nose. 'Where did you find him? He is filthy.'

'That alley down the side of Hamo Belancer's shop,' I said. 'He has taken a vicious blow to the back of his head.'

Emma was already ladling warm water into a bowl, from the large pot Margaret kept beside the kitchen fire.

'Cloths, Margaret? Where do you keep your cloths?'

'In the still room. And there is a pot of wound salve on the bottom shelf, on the left.'

As Emma ran to the still room, Philip pulled off Winchingham's boots, which, like his robe, were filthy.

'Set them outside the garden door, Philip,' Margaret said. 'We must take off this robe, he cannot stay in that, wet and dirty as it is.'

She was right. The Saints only knew what diseases might be breeding in the refuse of that alley, dangerous for a man with an open wound in his head. Between us, Jordain and I managed to half lift Peter Winchingham and peel off his robe. That, too, Philip rolled up and deposited outside. With it, some of the stench departed. Without his robe, the merchant was clad in a cotte of fine wool over his shirt and hose, which the heavy robe had protected from being fouled. Now he slumped in the chair, his face grey, his breathing irregular and faint.

Emma held the bowl of warm water while Margaret gently wiped away the blood which had clotted in the merchant's hair and on the back of his neck. It had not begun to dry, so the injury was recent.

'How bad is it?' I asked. The man had shown no signs of life apart from that laboured breathing. Not even his eyelids had flickered.

'A hard blow,' Margaret said, 'the skin broken the

width of my palm, and plenty of bleeding, but I can see no fragments of bone. I think his skull is intact. Worse than the blow you took in the spring, Nicholas, but as long as the brain is not damaged, I think he will recover.'

'Should I fetch a physician?'

'Let us see what I can do for him first.'

Silently Emma passed her the pot of wound salve, and Margaret spread it gently and generously over the whole damaged portion, while the rest of us stood about, helpless.

'Alysoun,' Margaret said, 'run and fetch the feather bed from my chamber. He may have a fit of the chills after such a blow. The loss of blood will have unbalanced his humours.'

'Fetch mine instead,' I said, 'better if he bleeds on mine than on Aunt Margaret's.'

Alysoun galloped up the stairs, more excited than worried. She could have little idea how dangerous a blow to the head might be.

Once the feather bed was tucked around him, it seemed that Peter Winchingham breathed more regularly, and began to lose some of that grey pallor from his face, but there was no sign yet of him waking.

'Where was he, do you say?' Philip asked. 'Near Belancer's shop?'

'Aye,' I said. 'They told us at the Mitre that he was going there to buy a flask of wine to bring to supper. That was why Philip and I went there, else we would never have found him. He must have gone down the alley to the back door.'

'Sneak thieves, then. Pickpockets abroad at night.'

Silently I pointed to the fat purse attached to the merchant's belt. Philip leaned over him.

'I see. Not a thief then.'

'I wonder–' I paused and everyone looked at me.

'This matter of the stolen books from St Frideswide's Priory. They were offered to Master Winchingham. He brought them to me to value. I wrote to Canon Aubery this very day to warn him about thefts from the library. Might the canon have spoken of it within the hearing of someone . . . someone implicated in the theft? Master Winchingham would be able to identify the man who brought the Bible and the book of hours to him. Could this have been an attempt to silence him?'

'It could be,' Philip said slowly. 'But did it need such violent action? The man selling the books could easily have kept out of sight while the merchant was here in Oxford, for he will surely be gone back to Bruges once the fair is over. Yet if you had not found him when you did, the merchant could have died, and it would have been a case of murder, a far more serious crime than the selling of books, whether or not they were stolen.'

'Aye,' I said, 'but if they were *not* stolen, but removed by someone within the priory, that is another crime altogether. A man's future career within the church would be jeopardised.'

'Still, I cannot think–'

Our speculations were interrupted by a groan from the patient. I spun round and leaned over him. His eyelids fluttered, but did not open. I laid my hand on his.

'Master Winchingham? This is Nicholas Elyot. You are quite safe now, here in my house, where you were coming to supper. You have taken a blow to the head, but it is not too serious. Your head will pain you, but my sister is certain you will soon recover.'

His hand moved under mine, and he groaned again, but this time his eyes did open, and his glance wandered unfocused over the room. For some moments he continued to sit slumped in the chair, then his eyes sharpened and he struggled to sit more upright. I gripped his shoulder.

'Do not try to get up. Give yourself time.'

'Master Elyot? By Mary and all the Saints, I feel as though my head has been hit by one of the king's new siege guns. Is there aught to drink?'

Emma was already beside me with a cup of the small ale, weak enough for children to drink. He took it in a hand that trembled slightly, but drank it down thirstily.

'I thank you, mistress.' Looking around, he caught sight of Margaret. 'Mistress Elyot, is it? I believe I saw you when I came before.'

'Margaret Makepeace.' She dropped a curtsey. 'I am Nicholas's sister. How do you feel now, apart from your head? Are you dizzy? Queasy?'

He started to shake his head, then thought better of it. 'Nay, somewhat bruised, I think.' He turned his hands over, and we saw that the palms were grazed.

'You fell,' I said, 'in the alley beside Hamo Belancer's shop. Someone appears to have struck you from behind.'

'Everything is muddled in my head,' he said. 'I remember leaving the Mitre, on my way here. I think . . . aye, I was going to buy some wine. Hamo Belancer? Aye, that is it. I used to buy from him years ago. Thought I could . . . but I do not remember much after that.'

'Do not try,' Philip said. 'It will all become clear if you leave well alone. Usually the mind cures itself.'

'Forgive me,' I said, 'this is Master Philip Olney, Fellow and Librarius of Merton College. And this is Jordain Brinkylsworth, Regent Master of Hart Hall.'

Emma had drawn back a little, but I caught her hand and drew her forward. 'This is the Lady Emma Thorgold, granddaughter of Sir Anthony Thorgold. All three are, like you, lovers of books, come to meet you and sup with you.'

Alysoun was tugging at the hem of my cotte. I drew her forward. 'This is my daughter Alysoun, and the young man crouching by your stool is my son Rafe. And that is the whole company.'

Alysoun, following Emma's lead, curtseyed, but Rafe just grinned shyly around the thumb he was sucking.

Peter Winchingham struggled to his feet and gave a general bow. 'My apologies to you all. I have disrupted your evening. I am well recovered now.' He turned to Margaret. 'Mistress Makepeace, is that handsome leg of mutton our supper? Let me keep you no longer from table.'

Margaret protested that he should rest for a longer time, but he said he was quite able to sit down to supper and was sure that food would do him good, would even steady his shaken brain.

'Indeed,' she said, 'you may be right. If you find you can eat without queasiness, food may be just what you need.'

'I have a hard skull, mistress. I was once struck by a ship's timber when sailing to Danzig, a blow a good deal harder than this one, for a gale of wind was behind it, and I was none the worse afterwards.'

Even so, he accepted my arm for support as we walked through to the small parlour. The candles had burned low, but they cast a warm sheen over the polished wood and the dull gleam of the pewter dishes. Alysoun brought us a first course of oysters cooked in some rich savoury sauce, while Margaret insisted on replacing the candles before she would sit down.

Considering how little warning she had had, Margaret had excelled herself. After the oysters, there were individual pies of pheasant, garnished with pickled quails' eggs, then a terrine of minced ham, all before we reached the magnificent leg of mutton, which more than justified its cost. Margaret served with it a sauce of pickled nasturtium seeds in cream, and followed it with a salad of lamb's lettuce and nasturtium petals. She must have found the very last flowers in the garden. By the time we reached the apple and blackberry pie – which Alysoun announced proudly she had made herself – we were all nearly too full to partake of it, but could not disappoint her. With every course, Master Winchingham looked a little better.

I had brought out a flask from my small supply of wine, but Margaret warned it would not combine well with an injury to the head, so we all contented ourselves with ale instead.

Our talk during the meal had been general, but after the children had been sent to bed and we settled back to a final cup of ale, toying with the comfits Margaret had retrieved from Mary Coomber's dairy, it was inevitable, I suppose, that we should turn again to the attack in the alley.

Philip looked across the table at me. 'When you found Master Winchingham, Nicholas, how was he lying?'

'Face down in the filth, I am afraid. Struck from behind, he must have fallen forward, and lay as he fell.'

'That was not what I meant. Was it his head toward the street, or his feet?'

I glanced across at Jordain. We had been too concerned at the time with carrying Winchingham away from that stinking alley, but now I realised what Philip was asking.

'Your head was toward the street,' I said slowly, turning to the merchant, 'so you must have been coming *away* from the back door of Hamo Belancer's shop.'

Until that moment I had been assuming that Winchingham had been followed, perhaps all the way from the Mitre, by the man trying to sell the books. He would know the merchant was staying there. Following behind, he could have waited for a suitably dark corner to strike his victim down, and the alley offered a perfect opportunity. But in that case, Winchingham would have been lying with his head *away* from the street, further into the alley.

The merchant's mind had been tracing the same path as mine.

'So I was not struck by someone coming after me from the street, but by someone approaching from further down that alley. Where does it lead?'

'A cluster of mean buildings,' I said. 'There is a maze of alleys and dead ends, but eventually it emerges at Merton Street. Your assailant could have come from a number of different directions.'

'But if I was facing the street,' he said, rubbing his temples and looking confused again, 'it means–'

'Aye,' I said. 'It means you had already been to Hamo's shop.'

'But there was no flask of wine beside me, was there?'

Jordain shook his head. 'Nothing. And your purse has not been taken.'

'Ah, now, if I had bought wine–' He unbuckled the purse from his belt, opened it, and swiftly counted the coin inside. He shook his head, though it made him wince. 'It is all here. I have spent nothing on wine.'

Emma had said very little during the meal, but she was listening to this exchange intently, her chin resting on her steepled fingers.

'You walked from the Mitre to Hamo's shop,' she said, 'hurrying to buy the wine and reach here in good time. You saw that the shop was closed and remembered the ban on Oxford shops during the fair. However, you remembered Hamo's ways from the past and thought he might still be willing to sell you a flask of wine at the back door.'

'Aye, mistress,' the merchant said thoughtfully, 'you have it exactly. I have been trying to remember through the fog that has invaded my brain, but that was just how it was.'

'You went to the back door and knocked?'

He rubbed his temples again.

'Nay.' He thought for a moment. 'I went to the back door and it was slightly ajar. I heard voices. Two men talking. And I thought I should wait a moment before I made myself known.'

'And then?' Philip said.

The merchant closed his eyes. 'I am trying to remember. Two men speaking. One was Hamo Belancer. It's a distinctive voice, I remembered it. High pitched. He talks through his nose.'

'Like a Frenchman,' I said.

'Aye, that will be it. And – of course! – they were speaking French.'

He opened his eyes and we all stared at him.

'So,' I said, 'it was not the fellow who tried to sell you the books who struck you down. From what you told me of him, I would not think he could speak French.'

'Unlikely.'

'There are a number of Frenchmen here at the fair,' Margaret said. 'We have seen them.'

'As have I. Hamo told me he knew one,' I said, 'a vintner, who was to supply the wine for the prince's dinner.'

'Then it was nothing more than old acquaintances meeting together,' Jordain said.

Peter Winchingham sat up straight, pressing his fists down on the table. 'I remember now. They were not talking idly, as old acquaintances do. Hamo Belancer was telling the other man of a secret way he knew, to gain entrance to the Priory of St Frideswide. Can it be that they are somehow caught up in this business of the theft of the priory's books? It seems strange, for a pair of vintners.'

'Very strange,' Philip said. 'I do not much care for Hamo Belancer, but he is – or at least he was – a prosperous burgess of this town, until he lost his French vineyards. I can see no reason why he should stoop to stealing books. And why should this Frenchman have any interest in such thievery?'

'It makes no sense,' I agreed. 'The one obsession in Belancer's life is that lost patrimony in France. I can well imagine him discussing that with a Frenchman, especially a French vintner, but what business could they have with the priory?'

I paused, turning a marchpane comfit over and over until my fingers became sticky. I looked at Peter Winchingham. 'Nevertheless, could it have been one of those two men who struck you on the head? They were there, nearby.'

He looked at me bleakly and nodded slowly. 'I think you have the right of it, Master Elyot. It comes back to me more clearly now. I did not like the sound of their discussion, so I decided to come away. I turned. My feet may have made some noise, for there was rubbish at foot there in the alley. And, aye, I think there was a moment when there came more light. I had forgotten that. As though the door was opened wider.'

'The door opening,' Emma said quietly, 'and the men looking out into the alley.'

'Aye, that must have been it. And then I was struck.'

'They thought you had overheard them, heard more than you did. And it was something they needed to conceal.' I passed a hand over my face. 'Needed seriously enough to risk killing you.'

'Yet I hardly heard anything.'

'They would not know how long you had been listening,' Jordain said.

'I wish now that I had asked Hamo which of the Frenchmen he knew,' I said. 'It must surely have been the same man.'

'Perhaps it may be possible to learn the name of the man who supplied the wine for the priory dinner,' Margaret said.

'Aye, Canon Aubery may know. Though what may be afoot . . .' My voice trailed off. Suddenly I remembered my conversation with Alice Walsea, which had gone quite out of mind with all that had happened since.

Could this Frenchman be the one she was seeking? And if it was, what had he to do with Hamo Belancer or with the Priory of St Frideswide?

Chapter Six

When it was time for our guests to depart, we made a party of it, for I accompanied them along the High. I think we all felt nervous of possible danger in the street after the attack on Peter Winchingham. All of us carried lanterns and did not trouble to keep our voices down, for a large noisy group is in less danger than a solitary pedestrian on his own.

We had gone but a dozen or so yards, and were about opposite Hamo Belancer's shop, when the merchant suddenly stopped. Both the shop and the domestic quarters above were in darkness.

'I have just remembered something,' he said, rubbing his hand across his face. 'I did catch sight of the other man. The Frenchman who was with Belancer. Just for a moment, at the edge of my sight. He was not a big man, medium height, medium build. Very dark, though. I would say that his complexion marked him as a man from the south, from Italy or Provence, hardly a Frenchman.'

'Could this be the vintner Hamo spoke of?' I wondered. 'Are not the wines of France grown further north?'

'Not all of them. And a wealthy vintner might have lands in more than one region.'

'The vineyards Hamo used to own were in Guyenne. My knowledge of the geography of France is somewhat hazy,' I admitted.

He nodded. 'Guyenne is good wine-growing country.

This man might well have been his fellow vintner in the same part of the country. But what their interest in the priory could be, the Saints alone can know.'

'Too much is happening,' I said, 'which is somehow connected to the priory. First the books you showed me. Then the fire at the fair gatehouse. Now this conversation you overheard between Hamo and the Frenchman. And the whispers which have reached Alice Walsea. She thought they might mean nothing, but that seems less and less likely.'

I thought for a moment.

'Even earlier, Canon Aubery was concerned about valuables disappearing from the priory. Tomorrow I will try to discover from him which of the Frenchmen supplied the priory with wine for yesterday's entertainment of the prince. There can have been nothing amiss with the wine, or we should have heard of it by now. But a merchant providing expensive goods to the priory would have easy access to it. He would need no secret entrance, such as you heard them discussing. Perhaps this is not the same man, but another Frenchman seeking out Hamo Belancer on the recommendation of his friend.'

'Whoever he was,' Emma said, 'it is clear that they mean some mischief, like the scoundrels who set fire to the fair's gatehouse.'

'Aye,' Philip said thoughtfully. 'There is still plenty of ill-will abroad in the town about the profits the priory makes from the fair. Only this afternoon our porter was reminding me of what happened in '44.'

'What was that?' Winchingham asked. 'I was last here a year or two before that.'

'The mayor and bailiffs of the town captured the senior lay steward of the priory and seized all the tolls, rents, and profits of the fair, swearing that the monies were the town's by right, after the previous prior and canons had sworn to give up their claim.'

'That was forced from them, under threat of death,' Jordain said.

'Aye, so it was. It seems the amount in '44 was a thousand pounds or more.'

The merchant gave a soft whistle. 'That much? No wonder the matter remains in dispute. Did the priory get its money back?'

'I think so. The royal charter entitles them to it. But you have the right of it. There is a great deal of ill will because of the enormous sums of money. Not only does the town have no claim on the profits of the fair. There is also all the trade lost during the time it takes place.'

We all knew these disputes by heart, but it seemed that this year matters were growing more dangerous than usual.

'If some attack is planned on the priory itself, they must be warned,' I said. 'If I can manage to see Canon Aubery tomorrow, I will tell him.'

'But,' Emma said, putting her finger on the nub of the problem, 'why should any mischief planned by the town concern a Frenchman?'

None of us had any answer to that. We had reached the corner where St Mildred Street met the High, with All Saints Church on one side and the Mitre Inn on the other

'I will escort Lady Emma to her door,' I said, 'and you are here safely at your inn, Master Winchingham. I'd recommend a quiet day tomorrow, resting that head of yours.'

He grinned like a boy. 'It will do me good to be about my business at the fair. Far better than moping around the inn like a maid with the green sickness. I am always the better for staying busy. I give you good night, gentlemen and my lady Emma, and with all my heart I thank you for rescuing me, else I might now be stone cold in the filth of that alley. Not the way I would choose to end my days.'

He had put on his boots before we left, but Margaret insisted on keeping his robe to clean.

'My sister will return your robe,' I said. 'As soon as it is fit.'

'She is a wonder,' he said, 'your sister. That was a

meal fit for the king himself.'

We saw him safely inside the inn, then Jordain and Philip were determined upon accompanying me to Emma's door, although I would have preferred to have had that duty to myself. Her farewells were brief.

'It has been an unexpectedly interesting evening, Nicholas,' she said. 'I like your merchant, even if he *is* old enough to be my father. And it seems we are on the scent of an intriguing puzzle, involving murderous Frenchmen. God give you all good-night.'

With that she slipped through the door of Mistress Farringdon's house, quietly, so as not to wake those sleeping inside. Once we had heard her slide the bolts, we turned back to the High.

'Now,' said Philip, 'our numbers are diminished. We could spend the rest of the night seeing each other home, for fear of attackers, but I will walk with you as far as Magpie Lane, then take my life in my hands and walk the rest of the way to Merton alone.'

'Are you sure?' Jordain said anxiously. 'It is not far from where Master Winchingham was attacked.'

'I am certain the man – Frenchman, if he was – is long gone. I'll be in no danger from the whores of the lane. They will be long abed by now. Alone or in company.'

After Philip had left us, Jordain and I quickened our steps.

'Now we have a dilemma,' I said. 'Either you escort me home, then walk alone to Hart Hall, or I see you to Hart Hall and I walk home alone.'

'A pretty conundrum,' Jordain said, and we both began to laugh. Perhaps we had washed down our supper with a little too much ale.

'I have found a solution,' I said. 'Your students, like the whores of Magpie Lane, will be long abed and will not take kindly to being knocked up at this hour. Come and spend the night with us. You have slept in the truckle bed in my chamber before now. What do you say?'

'With the prospect of one of Margaret's breakfasts

tomorrow? Bread fresh from the oven, instead of the baker's stale leftovers? It would take a stronger man than I to say you nay.'

It was only after we were settled in our beds, and the candle blown out, that Jordain spoke into the darkness.

'However these broken pieces fit together, Nicholas, I fear they make an unpleasant whole. Whether or not the secret way into the priory is somehow to do with the thefts which have taken place, I do not like the sound of it.'

'The other possibility,' I said, stifling a yawn, 'despite the presence of this Frenchman, is that it is another attack by the town on the priory. The firing of the gatehouse may have been no more than a warning. If a fire should be started in the priory itself, there will be lives lost, and not only amongst the canons. It would quickly spread through the town.'

'Can any of the townsmen be so foolish as to risk that? Their own homes might be reduced to ashes.'

'When men reach a certain pitch of anger,' I said, 'they do not reason clearly.'

'That is very true.' He was silent for a few minutes. 'I cannot see how any of this is related to what Mistress Walsea has heard. No dangerous Frenchman would have come all the way to Oxford to set fire to a priory.'

'It seems unlikely.' I turned over in bed, setting the ropes creaking. 'Of course, the Frenchman may have an interest in valuable books, or church silver. It may be a case of robbery on a large scale. The priory does also possess some relics. There are those, both inside and outside the Church, who will not hesitate to sully their hands with crime in order to get those same hands on some coveted relic.'

'Indeed. In that case, is the Frenchman working with the fellow who showed Master Winchingham the books? That would make a third man involved in this, besides Hamo Belancer and this French fellow. It cannot be Hamo who took the books to the merchant, for he already knew him. It was a stranger.'

'You are making my head hurt,' I said. 'Go to sleep. Tomorrow it may all seem clearer. In any case, I must see Canon Aubery urgently.'

I set off early the following morning, immediately after breaking my fast. As usual, Margaret fed Jordain as though she were stuffing a goose for a Twelfth Night banquet. She considered that he would come near to starving at Hart Hall if she did not feed him whenever she could. We both knew that the scanty provisions Hart Hall's meagre budget could purchase went mainly to the students, while Jordain took little for himself. Such short commons would have driven away the students from any other hall, but Jordain was a fine teacher and looked after his students as carefully as their parents, so they stayed. It was known to be difficult to secure a place at Hart Hall. Whenever a student finished there, either to return home or to take up a position in one of the colleges, there was a rush of others eager to take his place.

Jordain and I left together and parted near St Mary's, Jordain to head up Catte Street, while I crossed the High. I decided I would call on Alice Walsea, if she had not yet left for the fairground. I had promised that I would let her know if I discovered anything which might relate to the Frenchman she was seeking. The man whom Peter Winchingham had glimpsed might not be the same man, but there was no harm in passing on the information.

I found Mistress Walsea in the parlour of Tackley's inn, still at her breakfast. She looked like any decent merchant's wife, come to St Frideswide's Fair either to buy or to sell. Pleasant, but unremarkable. You would not have taken her for the elegant and discreet lady's waiting woman that she had been just a few weeks before. She motioned me to a chair at her table, and called to the pot boy to bring another ale cup.

'This place has changed, since I was a student,' I said, as I took a seat. 'It has been freshly lime washed, and the pot boys and maid servants are looking very spruce. It used to be more down at heel.'

She smiled. 'It is very pleasant. Not as fine as the Mitre or the Cross, but a good, honest, comfortable inn, such as a moderately prosperous merchant would choose.' She looked about her. 'I do not see any students here.'

'I believe that nowadays their quarters are in the back premises, well away from the more well-to-do guests. The student lodgings provide a regular income during the whole of the university year, but the inn must make what profit it can from such opportunities as the fair.'

'Aye,' she said shrewdly. 'The inns and taverns must be the only businesses in Oxford which welcome the advent of the fair. Now, have you something for me?'

'I am not sure whether this is your man or not, but I saw no harm in telling you of an attack which took place last night, not many yards along the street from here.'

'An attack?'

'Aye, an English merchant over to the fair from Bruges. He thought to buy a flask of wine to bring to dinner with me, by the back door at the vintner's shop of Hamo Belancer, a man who had a French father and used to own vineyards in Guyenne, until they were lost to the French king in one of the skirmishes along the border. It was he told me of the French vintner who was to supply wine for the prince's dinner.'

'I see.' She ate the last of the bread and cheese on her plate, laid aside her knife, and wiped her lips on her napkin. 'And where – and indeed why – was this merchant attacked?'

'He had reached the door, then heard voices speaking French, and hesitated to knock.'

'He speaks French, naturally.'

'Fluently.'

'So he heard something dangerous?'

'Odd, rather than dangerous. They seemed to be discussing a secret way into the Priory of St Frideswide. He decided to come away, without buying any wine.'

'Wise, no doubt.' She smiled grimly. 'How did he

come to be attacked?'

'He thinks his feet may have made a noise amongst the litter of the alleyway. He was struck over the head from behind, and – had a friend and I not gone searching for him – he might have died.'

I realised I had not touched the ale she had ordered for me, so I took a sip.

'We are not sure . . . this may be nothing to do with the man you are seeking. There have been a number of disturbing matters connected to St Frideswide's Priory in the last week or so.'

She knew of the firing of the fair gatehouse, of course, but I reminded her of it, then I told her briefly about Canon Aubery's discovery of the missing church treasures, and about the books belonging to the priory which had been brought to Peter Winchingham, under the pretence of being books from a gentleman's library which was to be sold up.

'Now,' I said, 'we may have three distinct problems here.' I numbered them off on my fingers. 'First, antipathy toward and attacks on the priory from disgruntled townsmen. Second, thefts of books and church silver from the priory. And third, your whispers about a French criminal coming to Oxford. They may all be unrelated. Talk of a secret way into the priory might be concerned with further thefts, or with an attack on the priory itself – perhaps arson, which could prove dangerous to the town. Your man may be quite unconnected.'

'But they were speaking French.'

I nodded. 'They were speaking French.'

'This Oxford vintner who told you he knew the merchant who supplied the wine for the prince – he did not tell you his name, or point him out?'

'He did not, but I could certainly ask him.'

She rested her chin on her clasped hands. 'The vintner from France would need no secret way into the priory. He could come and go as he pleased, without any need for an excuse.'

'My thought also.'

'It is unfortunate that your merchant from Bruges was not able to see his attacker.'

I realised I had not told her this part of the story. 'Oh, but he did. Just before we parted last night, he remembered that he had a glimpse – no more than a glimpse. Medium height, medium build, swarthy complexion.'

She sat up suddenly, rattling her plate and knocking her knife to the floor. I bent to pick it up.

'Now that, Nicholas, is an important piece of the puzzle. The man I seek is said to be a Provençal, though he lives in France. That would account for a darker colouring. The people of Provence have little love for the French, but this man is for sale to anyone with a heavy enough purse. It could be. It could be.'

She looked remarkably pleased, but I was not so sure.

'Master Winchingham had no more than that momentary sight. It was dark in the alley, with nothing but a little light from the open door. He could be mistaken. Most Frenchmen look dark to our English eyes.'

She brushed this aside. 'This is no provincial Englishman you are talking about, but an international merchant, accustomed to trading in many countries, with men of many nations. He would not make that mistake. I must speak to him, ask if he remembers anything else. He has a stall at the fair?'

'One of the largest booths.' I could understand her sudden excitement, and I knew her to be discreet, but I feared for Peter Winchingham's safety.

'I think it would be best if you were not seen talking to him at the fair. If his assailant recognises him there, he could be in danger. And just as you are watching out for your Frenchman, it is possible he might be watching out for you.'

'It is unlikely that I would be known to him,' she said, 'but you have the right of it. We should proceed with caution.'

'I agree,' I said. 'Let us go about our normal affairs, you to your stall at the fair, I to the priory, where I was already bound. I am going to warn Canon Aubery about the possibility of an attack on the priory, or an attempt at further thieving. I will also ask him to describe to me the vintner who supplied the wine to the priory, if he had the opportunity to see him. He is not the cellarer. Once I have a description, we will be better informed.'

'Aye,' she said, 'sound thinking.'

'And I am sure I can arrange for you to meet Master Winchingham less publicly than at the fair, perhaps in my shop.'

'That would be best.'

'It is good that Prince Edward is no longer here,' I said. 'Oxford has already suffered in his eyes, with that fire at the gatehouse. It will do the town no good in the king's opinion if there is further trouble.'

'Oh, but Prince Edward is still here,' she said. 'He had some business with Osney Abbey and spent the day there yesterday, but he is back at St Frideswide's now.'

'Do you know how long he stays? When does he leave for Wallingford?'

'That I do not know.'

I was surprised she needed to admit to ignorance on the subject of the prince's movements. Was his visit to Oxford something decided suddenly, on a whim? Or had Mistress Walsea known of it beforehand? Her purpose in Oxford might be twofold, but I thought it wiser not to ask.

'I must be on my way,' she said, rising. She wiped her knife on her napkin and restored it to the sheath hanging from her belt. When I had picked it up, I had noticed that it was longer and sharper than those most people carry with them for eating.

'I must see to it that my girl is not neglecting our trade. She is a good girl, but with little talent for selling our goods. She is inclined to drift off into a dream.'

I could imagine that Alice Walsea, behind the counter of her stall, would prove as excellent a merchant as any whose livelihood it truly is.

'If you will permit,' I said, 'I shall make haste to be

away before you. Probably best if we are not seen together.'

She nodded. 'Aye. In any case, I needs must fetch my cloak from my bedchamber. These late October days may start fine, but they can turn cold before evening. You will let me know anything you discover?'

'Most certainly.' I bowed, and made my way quietly out into the street again. As far as I could see, no one else at Tackley's had paid us any mind. I had seen a few known Oxford faces, but from our brisk discussion they would probably assume that Mistress Walsea was purchasing a book from me, or else ordering to have one made to her requirements. Perhaps she would be interested in buying some of Emma's work?

Out once more in the High Street, which had become busier while I was in Tackley's, I turned left, then walked down past Oriel toward the main gate of the priory. I had no wish to approach from the fairground. I was no fair-goer, but a serious local visitor, come to see one of the canons who – in the past, at least – had regularly done business with me and with my father-in-law.

The porter at the priory, a lay servant who knew me well, simply nodded me through, and I wondered why anyone should find it necessary to use some secret entrance, since people were coming and going all day long between the priory and the town.

'Can you tell me where I may find Canon Aubery?' I asked.

It was well past Prime by now, a part of the day when the canons would not be praying in church, but occupied about any duties they might have in the priory. The talk in Oxford was that these duties were few and undemanding enough. Unlike the rural Benedictines and Cistercians, who laboured hard in their fields and orchards, or the various monastic houses in Oxford which were devoted to scholarship, the Augustinian canons of St Frideswide's Priory had long had a reputation for pleasing themselves, making themselves, indeed, at home in the town like secular folk, in the taverns and – some claimed – in the whorehouses. It was not true of them all, certainly not of Francis Aubery, but a few bad apples, as they say, may cause the rot of others, or at any rate tarnish them with their evil reputation.

'Why, Maister Elyot,' the porter said, 'most of the canons, they be mortal busy carrying things into the church, see, for safety. Canon Aubery and Sub-Prior Resham, they reckon as how some valuables has gone missing, and they're making certain sure that nothing else be taken. Stacking everything precious up behind the high altar, where surely no man durst touch them, not even some misbegotten thief.'

'Is Prior de Hungerford with them?' I asked.

The porter rolled his eyes. 'Not he.'

He looked as if he would like to spit, but the porter at a religious house must refrain from such vulgar gestures. 'Prior's gone into town, on one of them new horses of his.'

I made my way to the church of St Frideswide, and, crossing myself, paused on the threshold to admire again the sheer beauty of the place. When I had come to the service before the opening of the fair, it had been past dark, the shadowy interior only lit by the candles on the altar and in the choir. Now, in the early morning, it was flooded with light, the great east window beyond the high altar glowing as if with the colours of precious stones – ruby, sapphire, emerald, topaz. The whole soaring space was almost deserted, although I could hear the soft murmur of prayers from the Lady Chapel, where a few pilgrims had come to the tomb of St Frideswide, our own Oxford saint, to leave offerings and light candles.

As I made my way slowly up the nave toward the choir, I could hear other noises, subdued by the holy nature of the place, but nevertheless busy, even urgent. This part of the church was normally reserved for the canons, and I passed between the choir stalls with a sense of intruding, before hesitating at the steps leading up to the high altar. It was not for me to go any further, but fortunately Canon

Aubery emerged at that moment, together with another canon who was unfamiliar to me.

'Nicholas Elyot!' Aubery's exclamation was muffled by the atmosphere of sanctity with which we were surrounded. 'What do you here?'

'I have some information for you.' I spoke quietly. 'But I understand you are hard at work. May I help?'

'That would be most kind of you,' the other canon said. 'Most of us are far from young, and there is a good deal of heavy lifting yet to do. All of the lay servants are needed to keep order at the fair, lest more trouble break out.'

'I am happy to help you with the heavy lifting,' I said, 'but I fear it would be wrong of me to venture into the most holy of places within the church.'

'There is no need for you to be reluctant,' Canon Aubery said. 'By lending your aid to the protection of the priory's valuables, you will be doing God's work. We have already moved all of the church plate, but have only this moment started to bring in the books from the library.'

'I am very used to carrying books.' I smiled up at them. They were both dusty, and Canon Aubery's tonsure was crowned with a garland of cobwebs.

They led me to the library of the priory, a small separate building which I had visited before, when Canon Aubery was their *librarius*. It now had a neglected look. This was clearly the source of the dust and cobwebs. I looked around.

'Is there no *librarius* now?' I asked.

Canon Aubery shook his head. 'Our present prior feels there is no need for the position.' He glanced about despairingly. 'That is why there is such a look of neglect.' He laid his hand on the nearest books, stacked up ready to be moved, and sighed. 'My poor books. There is so much of my life stored up here, and memories of your father-in-law, and of you, dear Nicholas. I could recall for you every discussion we had over each of these volumes.'

I smiled sadly at him. It was a fine collection, of

several hundred books, which he had built up on earlier acquisitions with loving care. I could understand his grief at seeing them so neglected.

'Well, let us move them to a place of safety, and then, if you will provide me with a cloth and a pot of leather polish, I will rub up those most in need of care. If you have no polish, I can bring some tomorrow.'

'Let us be sure to move them first,' the other canon said, introduced to me as Canon Fitzrobert. 'I have the keys for the chained volumes here.'

While the two ecclesiastics set about unlocking the chains which secured the more valuable volumes, I carried the first heavy pile of books across to the church. I thought it unlikely that the chained books were in danger from thieves, unless they came provided with the means to cut through heavy chains. Which, if they were greedy and determined, they might.

Behind the altar I found Sub-Prior Resham and several more canons packing the church plate in soft cloths and storing it in three large coffers.

'Where shall I put these?' I asked.

'For now,' the sub-prior said, 'you may lay them on top of the furthest coffer. We have finished with that one. We have yet to bring in chests for the books.'

Sub-prior Resham was a small, elderly man, devout and scholarly, and it had been the general expectation that he would succeed as prior when the previous incumbent died. Instead Nicholas de Hungerford had come from without and been appointed in his stead. No one seemed to know how it had been brought about. Such appointments are not always made on merit, but may be a reward or a bribe. Someone, somewhere, must have owed de Hungerford a favour. For what, I suspected it was better not to ask.

I had had little to do with Prior de Hungerford, although I knew him by reputation. A big, coarse man, he would have looked more at ease wielding a cleaver in a butcher's shop than conducting God's worship in this beautiful place. The fact that he was frequently seen in secular dress seemed to bear out my impression that the habit of an Augustinian prior sat ill with him. Physically, Sub-Prior Resham was no match for him. Intellectually, he soared far above him. Since de Hungerford's appointment, the unwelcome prior had done much to undermine the priory's already fragile finances and – in the opinion of many – to line his own pockets. Resham was said to have made a stand against him. I wondered whether this present move to protect the priory's treasures would bring matters to a head between them. It would be difficult for de Hungerford to oppose it on any lawful grounds, but the man had not shown himself to be much troubled by what was lawful.

I spent about an hour moving books into the church, then another polishing the older volumes whose leather covers had begun to dry out with neglect. By the time our tasks were finished, and both church plate and books stowed away in heavy double-locked coffers, I was as festooned with dust and cobwebs as the others.

'Come,' Canon Aubery said. 'I will show you to the *lavatorium* so that we can wash off this grime, and then I hope you will accept a cup of good French wine in thanks for your hard work.'

'I should be glad of that,' I said, 'and then I can tell you of this odd news I have heard.'

Once we were settled in his chamber with a flask of excellent wine, I asked him first whether it was some of the wine supplied for the prince's dinner.

'It is indeed. There was a good deal left over, so our cellarer told us to help ourselves.' He gave an ironic smile. 'He did not wish to see it all consumed by the prior's rough companions from the town.'

I raised my eyebrows in query at this.

'Aye, it is true. De Hungerford prefers the company of his secular friends. They are here most evenings, drinking and dicing. He rarely attends Vespers or Compline. Nor does he rise for Matins and Lauds. Or rather, he has not been abed by then. We often see lights at midnight from the prior's lodgings.'

This was even worse behaviour than I expected, but I supposed the other canons were not sorry to have the man absent from their religious services.

'This wine the French vintner supplied,' I said, 'did you ever see the man himself, the Frenchman?'

Aubery shook his head. 'I did not. His business was entirely with the cellarer.'

I was disappointed, but not surprised. It would not have been Canon Aubery's affair to deal with the wine supply. I was reluctant to speak to Hamo Belancer, particularly if he was mired in some criminal affair with the Frenchman, but he would be able to tell me the vintner's name, and perhaps even point him out.

'Well,' I said, 'you have fallen heir to a very fine vintage, Francis. But tell me, did your cellarer not want to reserve the wine for the prince's use? I have heard that Prince Edward is still here. How long does he remain?'

'He has not said for sure. There was word from Wallingford that some repairs to the castle were not quite complete. He will wait here until he hears that all is ready for him. I suppose he is more comfortable here, even with the noise and crowds of the fair, than surrounded by masons and plasterers.'

He drank deeply of the wine, and sighed with pleasure. 'One forgets the simple delights of youth, like a good vintage, foresworn when taking the habit.' He gave a wry smile. 'Although we would probably allow ourselves such wine were the priory's monies not in such a perilous state.'

Of course. I recalled my father-in-law telling me that Canon Aubery was a younger son of the nobility, sprung from some ancient landed family in Worcestershire or Gloucestershire.

'Now, Nicholas, what was this news you were bringing to me.'

As briefly as I could, I gave him an account of the

previous evening's events – what Peter Winchingham had overheard, and how he had been attacked.

'And this is the man who came to you about the books?' the canon said. 'I should say that when I went through our library this morning, before we began to move anything, I found that the little book of hours, and a fine bible given to us by a benefactor about fifty years ago, are both missing. I have not had the time yet to check everything, but, in addition, I could not find a copy of St Augustine's *De Doctrina Chritiana*, nor Bede' *History*. There may be other books missing. So you think this talk of a secret way into the priory may be something to do with further thefts?'

'Truly, I do not know. It might be so. Or could it be that the townsmen who set fire to the gatehouse are planning to slip into the priory and cause further damage, perhaps by fire? Yet why should that involve the Frenchman? It would be clearer if we knew that this is the same Frenchman who supplied your wine. He is known to the vintner Hamo Belancer. But I cannot see why either harm to the priory or the theft of your books should be of interest to a Frenchman.'

'The books are valuable. They would fetch good prices.'

'But would a French vintner know how to find buyers in England? Surely he would not risk trying to take them back to France. We may have a temporary peace with France, but I am sure that any Frenchman passing through an English port will have every scrap of his luggage and goods examined down to the last inch by the royal officials at the port.'

'Aye, you are probably right,' he said, raising the wine flask and looking at me.

I shook my head. 'Nay, I thank you, but I have much to do today, and I do not want to find myself falling into the arms of Morpheus.'

'However,' he said, 'the Frenchman seems more likely to have an interest in books than in the local youths' fire-raising, do you not think?'

'I agree,' I said. 'And in any case, if this man is the vintner, he has every right to come openly into the priory on business. No need for some clandestine way.'

We pondered the subject a little longer, but could make no more sense of it.

'One thing I have not asked you,' I said, as I rose to leave. 'Do you know what this secret entrance might be, that Belancer and the Frenchman were discussing?'

He shook his head.

'I never heard of such a thing. We have that small postern gate through the town wall, which opens on to the meadow – or on to the fairground at the moment – but it is hardly secret.' He made a face. 'The town fathers are threatening to take control of it, and make it a public right of access to the town. They say we have no jurisdiction over gates through the wall. If they can win their case, it will mean our priory will become as public as Fish Street, with any man, woman, or child cutting through here to use the gate.'

I tried to reassure him that the South Gate was much more convenient for most people, leading as it did to Grandpont and the main road heading south from Oxford, while the priory's postern merely opened on to the meadows lying south of the town. It was convenient for the priory, since the priory grange lay some distance away, at the far side of the meadow land. Without this gate the only way to reach the grange would be to go into the town, down the High Street to the East Gate, then walk nearly to the East Bridge and come at the grange from the far side, almost twice the distance. I thought the town's threat of seizing control of the postern was made merely from spite, and not from any real need to possess the gate.

On leaving Canon Aubery, I made for this postern gate myself, for although of little general use during most of the year, it was very convenient for reaching the fair. I had told Alice Walsea I would bring her any information I had gained at the priory. There was little enough of interest to her, although Aubery had confirmed that the two books I had seen were indeed missing from the priory's library. I was glad to see the church plate and the books safely stowed away behind the high altar in the church. Sub-Prior Resham had told me that he was organising a watch to be kept there by the canons and, when they could be spared from duties at the fair, also by the senior lay servants of the priory, including the steward. Unless a veritable army of thieves broke in, everything should be safe.

None of this, however, seemed to have any connection with Mistress Walsea's mission and the suspected French criminal.

I stopped at Peter Winchingham's booth and found him displaying a bolt of the finest woollen cloth in a rich forest green to a stout matron with a commanding voice and the look in her eye of a woman who would be prepared to stand there an hour haggling over the price. The merchant spared a moment to smile at me, and he seemed well enough recovered from his injury, although he wore a capuchon wound over his head in a fashion which hid it from view. Satisfied that he seemed none the worse for the attack, I gave him a quick nod, then made my way briskly down to the lower end of the fair, where a row of modest stalls was set out near Trill Mill Stream, close to the temporary jetty. It was here that Peter Winchingham had berthed his boat, I recalled. There were half a dozen or so moored there now, from wide, substantial barges, with plenty of room for cargo, down to one small craft which was probably poled up here by a single man, from somewhere not far away.

Alice Walsea's stall was neat but not ostentatious, between one selling embroidered gloves and girdles and another from which an enticing scent of gingerbread arose. One of the maidservants I recognised from the Mitre was just concluding the purchase of a bunch of bright ribbons, laughing with Alice over some exchange, while a girl laid out a fresh wheel of ribbons in different colours to fill the empty place where they had lain on the counter.

The maidservant turned away and, catching sight of me, dropped a curtsey.

'Good morrow to you, Master Elyot.'

'Good morrow, Millie.'

She could be no older than Juliana Farringdon, I thought, but I knew that she had been working at the inn for at least two years.

'I am going to buy some gingerbread, Millie,' I said. 'Would you like some?'

Her face lit up. I do not suppose she was often given such small treats. I bought four gingerbread babies and she went away, nibbling hers, as I carried the others to Alice's stall.

'Can you eat these without harm to your stock?' I asked, handing one each to Alice and her girl.

'Indeed, if we are careful. Joan, take yours down by the stream, well away from the ribbons. And Nicholas, you may sit on Joan's stool.'

Eating the gingerbread was excellent cover for a private discussion, but I had little to tell her.

'I have warned Canon Aubery of what Peter Winchingham overheard, so he will be on the alert, but they have stored all the priory's valuables behind the high altar. Unfortunately, he never saw the French vintner, so I must try to persuade Hamo Belancer to tell me who he is. Moreover, Francis Aubery knows of no secret entrance to the priory, so I wonder whether Hamo was deceiving the Frenchman in speaking of one, for some reason we do not know.'

I shook my head, and brushed the crumbs from my fingers.

'I am never sure whether Hamo loves or hates the French. He is half French himself, of course, and likes to boast of it, as though that makes him superior to mere native Englishmen. Yet he is implacable in his hatred of the French army and the French king, who have seized his Guyenne vineyards. Master Winchingham thought he seemed to be conspiring with the Frenchman, but perhaps there *is* no secret way into the priory and it is all a scheme to make a fool of the man. Who can say?'

Alice frowned. 'Is he a man given to such foolery?'

'I barely know him. He is a man on poor terms with his neighbours, and even with his fellow members of the Guild of Vintners, always aware of any perceived slights or insults. But would he devise a plan to humiliate a Frenchman he claims to know from the days when he owned his French vineyards?' I shrugged. 'It seems unlikely. What could be his reason? Although I do believe he might be spiteful, if he thought the man had done him an injury.'

'It seems we are hardly any further ahead,' she said. 'This afternoon I might stroll past the vintners' booths and see whether I can overhear aught, or pick out the fellow with the southern complexion.'

'And I shall visit Hamo Belancer. I will make some excuse about wanting to buy French wine, and would like his recommendation of one of the vintners.'

I was just rising from my stool when a growing noise from the riverside caused us both to exchange worried glances. We had already heard some shouting. Now it was beginning to sound like a fight.

Chapter Seven

The noise was getting louder and more menacing. 'Stay here,' I said to Alice, 'and mind your goods. It only needs a disturbance like this for the petty thieves to take their chance. I will find your girl and send her back to you.'

I ran along to the end of the row of stalls, where a crowd of buyers and stall-holders had already gathered, looking down toward the jetty with more curiosity than fear. About half a dozen men were brawling on the narrow wooden platform of the jetty, and one man was in the water, struggling with an awkward kind of dog paddle to reach the bank. I pushed my way to the front.

'What's amiss?' I asked my neighbour, a tin smith I knew by sight, though not by name. He would have a stall in this lower part of the fair, selling cooking pots, candlesticks, and cheap plates.

'Don't rightly know, maister. Them Frenchies was shouting insults at our lads, and our lads give the same back. Then somebody threw a punch, and they was all at it.'

It would be difficult to tell who had started it. The prosperous merchants who owned the larger boats would leave a man here to keep an eye on their goods, despite the few lay servants of the priory who were paid to provide a guard. It was a tedious job, kicking your heels while everyone else was enjoying the fair. No wonder tempers flared.

'So much for the truce between our countries,' I said. 'It looks as though war has broken out again here in Oxford.'

'Aye, well, 'tain't natural to be friends with a Frenchman, treacherous, thieving bastards. Never trust 'em, myself.'

I caught sight of the girl Joan, who was standing on the bank, far too close to the jetty, watching the fight with her mouth open. I half ran, half slid down the bank to her. With all the to and fro of merchants unloading their goods, the grass was worn down to mud, and this part of the meadow was always damp and slippery. I came near to losing my footing and following the first casualty into the water.

I grabbed Joan by the arm. 'Come away,' I said. 'This could quite easily spill over on to the bank here and you would not be safe. Come back to your mistress.'

She looked at me in some surprise, as if she thought the fight was nothing more than entertainment laid on for her amusement, then she turned obediently and followed as we made our awkward way back up to where the watching crowd was standing.

'There's been blood drawn now,' the tin smith said, giving me a nod. He sounded almost satisfied.

'Knives?' I said.

'Nay, nobbut bloody noses.'

'Go back to Mistress Walsea,' I said to the girl.

Once I was sure she was on her way to the stall, I turned back to the fight. The man from the river was climbing into one of the French boats, bowing out of the combat and presumably in search of dry clothes, but the rest of the men were pounding each other even more furiously. One of the Frenchmen – distinguishable by their different style of dress – hooked an Englishman's legs from under him and tipped him into the river.

'Where are the priory's lay servants?' I said. 'And some of the town constables should be here.'

'They'll be away by the rich booths,' the tin smith

said. 'They don't bother with the likes of us. But a lad run off to fetch 'em.'

Now I looked, I could see a purposeful group of men heading down towards us. I hoped they were enough to put an end to the fight, for it was looking increasingly nasty. A few more had joined in. I saw the flash of a knife – no, a dagger. These men would not carry swords, but even a knife can kill as easily as a sword. Set to guard their masters' goods, all of these men would be armed.

Before the priory's lay servants could reach us, there was a cry of pain, and one of the English servants fell to his knees, clutching his left side. Even from where we stood, we could see the blood welling between his fingers. Instinctively I stepped forward, but the tin smith laid his hand on my arm.

'Best not, maister. You'll likely be struck yourself. Let them as are here for it take care of the trouble.'

I felt like a coward, yielding to his advice, and there was a raised outcry amongst the younger men in the crowd.

'That's one of ours down! Come on, lads!'

Fortunately, before the skirmish could turn into a full scale battle, the senior steward of the priory arrived, attended by half a dozen of his men, and including two of the town constables. They herded the would-be volunteer soldiers back amongst the rest of us, and began separating the combatants, wielding their clubs indiscriminately amongst both native and foreign heads.

As they began to march the men away, now relieved of their weapons, I said to the priory steward, 'That man is badly injured,' pointing to the man who was bleeding freely.

'Never fear, Master Elyot,' he said. 'We'll take him to the infirmary before we lock him up. It won't be the first fight we've had at the fair, though one of the worst. No surprise, with the French here.'

'The owners of these boats will not be pleased,' I said to the tin smith, as we watched the procession making its way back to the priory. 'Their goods must stay unguarded, or they must lose the work of one of their other servants to guard them.'

He smiled sourly, and spat. 'I'd not mind having the problems of a rich merchant.' With that he turned on his heel and returned to his stall.

I noticed that the unintentional French swimmer was peeping from his master's boat with what looked like a smile of relief. He might have had a soaking, but he had avoided imprisonment. As I was about to step back and give a brief account of the affair to Alice Walsea, a dripping figure emerge from behind the row of stalls. The Englishman who had been dumped into the river.

He winked at me. 'Let myself drift downstream when I saw the knives coming out. Kept out of the way of them constables.'

He went off whistling to his own boat, no doubt – like the discreet Frenchman – in search of dry clothes. Honours were about even.

I told Alice what I had seen, but she had already heard most of it from the other stallholders. Indeed, while so many were absent, she had been able to stop some pilfering from the glover's stall.

'So knives were used,' she said, 'not just fists. That is a bad omen.'

'There might have been deaths,' I said, 'if the steward and constables had not arrived when they did, but all is quiet for the moment.'

As Margaret was today serving at the fair, along with Beatrice, I took my dinner again at the Cross's stall close by the postern gate to the priory. As I ate my rabbit pie and bread (neither as good as my sister's), I turned over in my mind the puzzle of this secret entrance to the priory. On all sides St Frideswide's Priory was protected by a stone wall, here on the south side making use of a portion of the town's own wall, a formidable fortification. The rest of the walls were not so impressive, but ample enough. The main gatehouse was on the north side of the enclave, opening directly into the town. Short of some easy route to climb over the wall, I could not see what was meant by this secret way. And in any case, climbing over a wall was far from secret. One would be observed from the surrounding houses, and even from Oriel college.

I wondered whether I could persuade Hamo Belancer to let me into the secret, but I dismissed the idea, for it would merely serve to warn him that Peter Winchingham had indeed overheard at least part of his conversation with the Frenchman. Better to restrict myself to discovering which of the French vintners was known to him, and then try to see whether his appearance matched that of the man Winchingham had seen briefly last night.

Before going to visit Belancer, I went home and checked on the work Walter and Roger were doing while the shop was closed. On my desk, I found Lady Amilia's book of hours, which Roger had collected from the bookbinder. Henry Stalbroke had achieved a superb purple for the leather, which I knew would delight my demanding customer. With some regret, I turned over the pages. Some had been carried with Emma in her flight from Godstow, some had been completed on the small table at the house in St Mildred Street. There seemed too much of our lives, mine and Emma's, caught up in the book, to be handed over to that heedless woman, but there was no help for it.

'Walter,' I said, 'I need you to deliver this to the Lady Amilia and collect the payment. Do not let her put you off with delays. You know the tricks she plays.'

He grinned. 'Aye. I'll be the thick headed servant – "Maister said as how I must wait for payment". And just bide there until she hands me the chinks.'

'Well, do not over play it. She is aware that you are my journeyman. Their town house is almost opposite the Guildhall.'

'I know it. My own window overlooks it.'

'So it does. You may as well go now.'

I found Mistress Farringdon and Juliana in the garden with the children. They had brought Maysant with them and were looking after all three children – and the dog – while Margaret was occupied at the fair. During this period of busy activity, I had come to realise just how much of Margaret's time was taken up with my children. Normally, of course, I was at work in the shop, so that Margaret could go to market or attend to other errands without worry about Alysoun and Rafe, but when I took myself off, it was Margaret who must make arrangements to care for them. More than once I had suggested hiring a girl to help her, but she had scorned the idea. I suppose that if all such girls were as empty headed as Alice Walsea's Joan appeared to be, Margaret might find a maidservant simply one more burden.

'You have all that you need, Maud?' I asked.

'Indeed,' she said. 'We have found a few more apples that were missed the other day, and I told Margaret that I would make a start on separating the honey from the combs she has already brought in from the skeps.'

'There is no need for you to do that.'

'Oh, I like to keep busy. And Margaret has promised me a pot of the honey.'

I laughed. 'More than one pot, I hope. Well, I shall leave you to your labours. I am going to call on Master Hamo Belancer.'

'Emma told us what happened last night. I hope he will not be violent.'

'It was the other man, we believe, who felled Master Winchingham. I know Belancer of old. I think he is unlikely to strike me. Where is Emma?' I added casually.

'She has gone to Beatrice's cottage to see Stephen. She had promised to hear him read, and he wants her to help him learn to draw.'

I nodded, sorry that Emma was not here, but glad that she was befriending the boy. I suspected that he was often lonely. I had a sense, sometimes, that there was a whole separate world of women and children which was conducted out of the sight of men.

When I reached the vintner's shop, I was surprised to

see that it looked as shut as it had when we had passed it last night. All the shutters were closed, although it was a bright, clear autumn day. The whole building – the shop below and the house above – had a curiously abandoned look. Yet it was not quite abandoned, I realised as I crossed the street, for I could hear a dog barking. Hamo Belancer owned a big rangy beast, heavier built than a lymer, but without the great square head and vicious jaws of an alaunt. It was a dog which he claimed he had used for hunting when he was on his estates in France. How extensive those estates had ever been, no one knew. They seemed to grow in the telling with the passing years, the longer they were lost to him.

The dog was elderly by now, but he still had a hearty pair of lungs. His ceaseless barking was interspersed with long, mournful howls, which put me in mind of the howling wolves which found their way into some of Walter's more sinister stories, banned by Margaret before the children's bedtime.

I stood hesitating in front of the house, wondering whether to venture down the unsavoury alleyway. It did not appear quite so dangerous by day, but it was still filthy and odorous.

'Tell him to silence that dog, or I will come round myself and shoot it.'

A man had emerged from the house on the opposite corner of the alley, glowering at me, as if the dog's noise were my fault.

'Good day to you, Goodman Brinley,' I said, for I knew the man, a cobbler who, like every other shopkeeper in Oxford, had idle time on his hands for the duration of the fair. 'What is afoot with the dog? Is he sick?'

'Sick? How can I know?' He planted his feet far apart and folded his thick arms, which would have been a credit to a blacksmith. 'All I know is that dog has been howling without taking breath since the middle of last night, and none of us had a morsel of sleep. I've knocked on Hamo's door three times already today – three times! – but can he stir himself to answer? Not he! Thinks himself a cut above ordinary folk, does Hamo Belancer, yet his mother was nothing but a poor serving wench at the Swindlestock tavern before she married that French wine merchant.'

He gave a derogatory snort. This was all new to me.

'I was just on my way to fetch the constable,' he said. 'To tell him to make Hamo do summat about that bastard of a dog. Still, maybe as he'll open for you, *Maister* Elyot.'

I did not think Brinley had any reason to blame me for the dog's howls, but a man who has had no sleep may be forgiven much.

'Let us go together,' I said mildly. 'Perhaps two voices calling to him may have better effect than one.'

He gave an assenting grunt, relaxed somewhat, and walked over to me.

'Was it the street door you tried?' I asked.

'Aye.'

'Perhaps he did not hear you, with the shop closed and the dog barking. Best we try the back door in the alley.'

Brinley pulled a disgusted face. ''Tis his responsibility, not mine, to keep this portion of the alley clean, that runs past his house and shop. And I must endure the state he leaves it in. My wife will not use our side door, for the filth.'

'Well, if we are to make ourselves heard, I think we should try the other door.'

We picked our way down the alley to the door, and I was glad I had not been able to see the state of it more clearly in the dark the previous night.

'I cannot blame your wife,' I said, with a shudder.

It was strange that a man who dealt in wines, and who took some pride in their quality, should allow this festering alley so near to his shop. Although it was true that Hamo had become idle and discouraged, as well as obsessed, of late, ever since the loss of his lands in Guyenne. I did not particularly like the man, but it must have been a severe blow to one in his position, with his trade.

As we neared the door, the dog's barking sounded louder. It was clear that he was here, at the back of the building.

I looked round at the cobbler dubiously. 'Perhaps Hamo has gone out and left the dog shut in. That may be why you could not rouse him. He may be down at the fair.'

'Ever since the middle of last night?' The man raised his eyebrows incredulously and gave a disbelieving snort. 'He has not taken a stall there, I know, for he told me so. Said it was not worth the rent, for the little profit he would make. Not with merchants coming from France with their fine wines. Like the rest of us, he has to put up with the loss of trade.'

'Well, let us see,' I said.

I raised my fist and banged on the door.

The only response was even more frantic barking from the dog.

I banged again.

It did seem very strange. Hamo had definitely been here last night, after Vespers, for Peter Winchingham had heard him. He knew the vintner's voice. And as the cobbler said, it was extremely unlikely that he would have gone out in the middle of the night, leaving the dog shut in the house all this while. Hamo was a surly and unsociable man, but he was not cruel, and he was fond of that old dog.

No answer.

The cobbler took me by the elbows and moved me to one side, then leaned close to the door.

'Belancer!' he bellowed, 'we know you are in there. Here's Master Nicholas Elyot come to see you, and I want you to silence that dog, lest it drive us all mad.'

Then he raised both meaty fists and hammered on the door as though he were beating a tattoo on a drum.

Apart from ever more desperate cries from the dog, there was no response. We looked at each other, and I knew the same thought was suddenly passing through both our minds. During the time of the Pestilence, you might bid a healthy friend goodnight, then in the morning find that you could not rouse him, for he and all his household lay dead behind the door.

'Perhaps,' I said quietly, 'he is ill.'

The cobbler, looking suddenly smaller and older, nodded. 'Aye, perhaps he is.'

He seized hold of the latch and rattled it, as though the more noise he made, the more the spectres of the past could be chased away.

''Tis not locked,' he whispered.

Now, for a purveyor of wines, even if they were no longer of the highest quality, not to lock his door during the hurly-burly of St Frideswide's fair, with so many strangers about, was a matter for concern. The cobbler turned to me, raising his eyebrows in query.

I hesitated. I was reluctant to enter another man's house unbidden, but the dog was in distress, while Hamo Belancer might be seriously ill and in need of help.

'Aye,' I said. 'Best open it. If there is nothing amiss, we will apologise and leave.'

By now I was losing any desire to question Hamo about his acquaintance amongst the French merchants. The barking of the dog was beginning to make my head throb, and I felt considerable sympathy for the cobbler and his family. I also felt a growing unease about Hamo.

Cautiously, Brinley began to push the door open. The room beyond, which I took to be the kitchen, was gloomy, with all the shutters closed and little light coming from the door leading from the dark alley.

'It is stuck,' Brinley said, when the door was not yet halfway open.

He heaved at it, but it did not move. Together, we both put our shoulders to it and leaned as hard as we could. The door groaned and yielded a few more inches, just enough for us to squeeze through.

It took a few moments for my eyes to accustom themselves to the gloom. I could smell spilt wine, but I supposed that was not unusual in a vintner's home. Perhaps he and the Frenchman had downed several flasks of wine after Peter Winchingham was laid low, and now Hamo was sleeping off the after effects, still too drunk to be woken by the dog's noise, despite the fact that the afternoon was already well advanced. There was another smell, metallic.

Brinley had gone in search of the dog.

'Found him shut in a storeroom at the back,' he said, returning with the old dog fawning and quivering with gratitude. 'Poor fellow. He must have been there for hours.'

Now that the dog had stopped barking, instead leaping about in excitement, and licking his hand with enthusiasm, Brinley seemed inclined to forgive the beast.

I turned back to the door, peering behind it. 'There is something blocking it,' I said. 'No wonder we had trouble getting it open.'

I took a step forward, but the dog was ahead of me. He circled warily, whining.

He was reluctant to allow me to come any nearer, but yielded at last and I knelt down on the floor.

'Can you find a candle?' I said over my shoulder. 'I think I have found Belancer.'

As Brinley fumbled about behind me, I ran my hands over the object which had blocked the door. It was certainly a man. Almost certainly Hamo Belancer. When the cobbler finally approached with a lit candle, I took it from him and leaned forward, holding the candle high. But I did not need the candle to tell me what I already knew, for I had felt the man's flesh.

No one could be that cold, and live.

I sat back on my heels.

'It is Belancer,' I said, 'and he is dead.'

I heard the hiss of the cobbler's in-drawn breath.

''Tis not–' he dared not speak the word.

I shook my head. 'It is not the Death.'

It was not disease that had taken the vintner's life. The whole front of his cotte was soaked with blood, and more blood had pooled on the floor. That was the metallic smell I had noticed. But the blood was blackening and dry. Belancer had been dead for hours. I leaned forward again, for I had noticed something else.

'Look at this,' I said.

The cobbler came uneasily to stand beside me. For such a big, confident man he looked exceptionally queasy at the sight of blood.

'What is it?' He glanced down, then looked away again.

I spread wide the collar of Belancer's cotte, and pointed at his neck, which was marked with a wide line of purple bruising.

'Strangled *and* stabbed,' I said. 'Someone wanted to make very sure of him.'

Brinley gulped. 'I know he was not a popular man, but why should anyone want to kill him, unless . . .' he glanced round the room, which was indeed a kitchen.

'. . . unless they meant to rob him in the night, and he tried to stop them.'

I did not respond to this. Belancer was not in his night shift, so he had not been disturbed in his sleep. And would the dog have been shut away in the small storeroom during the night? More likely he would have been left to roam loose, to deter any such burglars. As far as I could see, the room did not appear much disturbed, only as untidy as any kitchen is, belonging to a man who lives alone.

'If I stay with him, will you look into the shop? See whether there is anything amiss there.'

He nodded and hurried away, clearly glad to escape from the horror on the floor. He was back almost at once.

'Too dark.' He lit another candle, and returned to the shop, leaving the doors between open.

'Nothing disturbed here,' he shouted. 'Everything as it has always been. He kept a tidy shop.'

He returned and sank down on one of the stools beside the table. I got up and joined him. I saw that there were two cups of fine pottery, on long stems and with broad circular bases. The glaze was a costly, glowing blue. Hamo had brought out his best drinking vessels to entertain his guest last night. There was a large flask standing next to them, all at the far end of the table. I did not draw Brinley's attention to the flask, in case he took it into his head to pour a drink to steady himself after our discovery. I thought everything should be left for the sheriff to see.

'What are we to do?' he asked bluntly.

'I think one of us should stay here,' I said. 'It will be best if no one else comes interfering with aught until Sheriff Walden has seen it. I will stay, if you wish. Then, if you will fetch the sheriff as quickly as you may?'

'Aye.' He sprang to his feet, clearly glad to escape. 'What of the dog?'

We both looked at the dog, who was sitting by the body, perhaps hoping his master would get up from the floor.

'Can you take him to your house?' I said. 'If your wife will not mind? He'd best have some water, and some scraps to eat, if you can find something. He has had a hard time. Afterwards, we will decide what is to be done with him.'

'He's not a bad hound,' Brinley conceded. 'It was just the endless barking we could not stomach. I'll tell my wife to feed him, and I'll fetch Sheriff Walden as quickly as I may. I hope he is at the castle.'

'Indeed,' I said, but he was already through the door, the dog obediently following his whistle.

Once he was gone, I went round opening the shutters, both in the kitchen and in the shop, although not the shop front. With a little more light, I was able to examine both the body and the room more easily, but there was little more to see.

Belancer had been stabbed neatly, once, in the chest, by someone who knew exactly where to strike. It was difficult to tell whether he had been strangled first and stabbed afterwards, or t'other way about. I had been unfortunate enough to see the result of a strangling only weeks before, but this was different. Belancer's neck bore the clear imprint of fingers, and of two thumbs pressed into his windpipe. The other strangling I had seen had been done with a thin *garrotte*, from behind. This murderer had been facing his victim. I wondered whether Belancer had fought back. He was neither small nor weak, but this murder bore the signs – or so it seemed to me – of a skilled killer. Alice's Frenchman, able for any crime if he were paid enough? I was almost certain of it.

Peter Winchingham had heard them talking together sometime shortly after Vespers, when he was on his way to sup with us. It was probably about an hour later that Jordain and I had found him in the alley. As far as I could remember, closing my eyes and trying to visualise it again, he had been lying about halfway between the back door Brinley and I had come through now and the far end of the alley, where it emerged into the High Street.

Try as I might, I could not remember whether there had been any sign of life about Belancer's house when we found the merchant. We had been too much occupied with carrying him where he could have his injury treated and be kept safe and warm. Though I thought I recalled a light being extinguished. By the time Winchingham's head had been physicked, and we had eaten a leisurely meal, at least another two hours must have passed, perhaps even three.

And by the time we were walking the merchant back to the Mitre, Belancer's shop and house were certainly in total darkness.

But the dog had not begun to bark then. We would have heard it, even from across the street, in the darkness of the late night.

Was the murderer still here when we passed? Probably not. The dog could have lain quiet for a time, before he became anxious. He was an old dog, probably usually content to lie and sleep. It was likely, therefore, that the murder had been committed between, let us say, half an hour after Vespers and perhaps two hours after that.

I hoped the murderer had no intention of coming back. I wished now that I had kept the dog with me.

I was eying the open door uneasily when I heard footsteps approaching along the alley. I rose quietly, looking about for some kind of weapon, for I had nothing but the knife I used for eating. Even the slender blade I used for cutting parchment or paper would have been better than that, but coming here I had merely crossed the street to ask Hamo about the French vintner, meaning to return home in a few minutes.

The footsteps paused at the door, and the cobbler's wife leaned her head warily in.

'Master Elyot?'

'Aye, Goodwife Brinley.' I went to the door, making sure that I blocked the view of the body on the floor.

'My man, he asked me to tell you as we've got the dog, and he's off to the castle to fetch the sheriff.'

'I thank you,' I said. 'Could you oblige me? I do not want to leave the . . . That is, I think I should stay here. Could you step over to my shop and tell my journeyman why I am delayed? And ask him to explain to my sister, when she comes back from the fair?'

'I'd be glad to oblige, Master Elyot.' She dropped me a curtsey. Then she smiled. 'Your sister and those others, they're making a fine showing at the fair. And their goods are the best quality. I don't often buy others' cooking, but I had some of their bullace cheese myself. 'Tis a bother to make, what with the gathering of the fruit, and then all them stones. Always seems there's more stones than fruit. I do believe some of those damsons and bullaces has two stones.'

I nodded distractedly, not being in the mood for a culinary discussion. I watched from the door as she picked her way, with distaste, down the alley, then set off to cross the High Street. I sat down again on the stool. It would be at least an hour by the time the cobbler had walked all the way to the castle and then returned with Sheriff Walden. I decided to examine the room again, to see whether it had anything else to tell me.

My second examination of the kitchen revealed no more than the first – Belancer's body, the usual cooking pots and ladles, and the presence of the two wine cups with the flask – although as I pulled out the stool to sit down again I saw a rough scrap of parchment on the floor. I picked it up and tilted it toward the meagre light from the window. It bore no writing, just a sketch of a few lines, which meant nothing to me. I shrugged and slipped it into my scrip. It did not seem to be of any importance.

As I had feared, it was a long wait before Brinley returned with Sheriff Walden and two of his officers. One of these, I noticed, was the fellow who had behaved with such arrogant rudeness to me, when I had sought entrance to the castle a few months ago. I hoped it was not he who had delayed the cobbler when he arrived seeking the sheriff. I did not ask whether Brinley had needed to search long for the sheriff, but by the time they arrived the afternoon light was fading into evening and I had lit more candles.

'Well, Nicholas,' Walden said, 'Brinley here tells me you have found a body. Hamo Belancer, he says.'

'Aye,' I said, 'we found him together. The dog had been barking for hours, and no one answered the door. The door itself was not locked, so we entered and found him, just where he lies now.' I wanted to be sure that Walden understood there had been two witnesses to the discovery of the body.

'Aye, Goodman Brinley has told me, while we were on our way here.'

'Do you need me any further, sir?' The cobbler had begun to edge toward the door.

'Nay. You live next door, do you not? You will be there, should I need to speak to you again?'

'Where else should I go?' He spoke with a touch of his previous grumpiness. 'There will be no trade for another three days, and I'll not go to the fair, to put my money in that prior's pockets.' He went off, though we heard him mutter, 'Not that a man can stop his womenfolk wasting their coin.'

Walden and I grinned at each other.

'He had no sleep last night,' I said, 'for the dog's

barking.'

'So he has been telling me. Now let us look at your man.'

I wished he would not call him that.

Walden knelt down to examine the body and I said nothing until he had finished. He stood up and brushed off his knees.

'Stabbed and strangled,' he said, just as I had.

I nodded. 'He wanted to make quite sure. I think he must have attempted strangulation first. With that stab wound, he must have known that he had made an end to his victim.'

'I think you are probably right. Perhaps Belancer struggled and fought back, so the murderer's hands slipped from the throat. Then he drew his knife to finish the job.'

'Knife or dagger, do you think?' I asked.

'A long knife or a slender dagger. Difficult to say. Either would be effective, going in there, at that angle.'

'That was what I thought. It's a narrow wound, under all that blood, but he knew just where to drive it in.'

'Are you become an expert on killing, Nicholas?'

I shuddered. 'I hope not. It is no more than common sense. And I studied a little of Galen as a student. Medicine never appealed to me.'

'Well,' Walden said, 'like you, I think the murderer knew what he was doing. He has killed before, I would say. I wonder which of our Oxford villains had listened to Master Belancer's complaints about Guyenne once too often.'

'I do not think it was one of our Oxford villains,' I said quietly.

I glanced aside to where the two officers were waiting, somewhat impatiently, I thought.

'Could your men remove the body to the castle? It need not remain here, surely, to upset the neighbours.'

He took the hint. The men brought in a simple litter which they had left propped up against the wall outside. Since it was not quite dark, and the identity of the body would be visible to everyone in the streets, I found a blanket from the bedchamber and laid it over Hamo once they had lifted him on to the litter.

'No talking to anyone on the way,' Walden warned. 'I want no rumours flying round the town. Keep your tongues behind your teeth. Not even his name. An unfortunate death. At the moment we can say nothing about who it is. Or how. Or why.'

They both nodded as they picked up their burden. I saw that the insolent fellow had less to say for himself when the sheriff was by. I did not think he remembered our previous encounter.

'Now,' Walden said, taking a seat when they were gone, 'what is it you know, that you did not wish to speak of, except to me.'

'First,' I said, pointing, 'these wine cups. Hamo Belancher's finest. The wine in the flagon is finished, but the scent of it lingers. I would say that is from the last precious store imported from his French vineyards. He did not sell it. He would not serve it to me. Perhaps to you. But perhaps not.'

'So Belancer had an important guest,' Walden said, humouring me. 'Are you saying that this important guest was also his murderer?'

'Almost certainly. There is no sign that either the shop or the house was broken into. Nothing has been disturbed or stolen, as far as I can see. Also, the dog was shut away in a storeroom.'

'That is significant?'

'It's an old, familiar dog. Quiet. He knows all Belancer's acquaintances.' I paused, thoughtfully. 'He had not many friends, but all the neighbours, all the shopkeepers in the High, all his customers, knew him and knew his dog. He would not bother to shut the dog away if one of them came visiting. Nor, I think, would he bring out his finest wine and his best wine cups. His father brought those cups from France. He boasted of them.'

'So.' Walden tapped his teeth with his fingernail.

'You are saying that Belancer had a guest who was a stranger – he did not know the dog – and he was important enough for him to bring out this wine and these cups.'

I nodded.

'And this man was also his murderer? I suppose you are now going to tell me who he is.'

I smiled. 'Not quite. But I think I know what manner of man he is.'

I rested my folded arms on the table and told Walden about Alice Walsea's warning of a dangerous criminal from France, a man for hire, who would certainly have the skills to kill quickly, efficiently, and silently. Then I recounted all the events of the previous night, what Peter Winchingham had seen and heard, and how he had been attacked. I also explained how I had arrived at a rough idea of the time when Hamo Belancer was probably killed. He listened without interrupting me, only nodding from time to time.

'That is all very convincing, Nicholas,' he said, 'and I agree you are probably right, but until we know which of the French vintners Belancer knew, and whether it was the same man who visited him last night, we are still floundering. I believe there are about eight of them.'

'I realise this,' I said. 'I came here this afternoon to try and discover the name of the vintner he knew.' I gave a shrug. 'I came several hours too late.'

Walden drummed his fingers on the table and I sighed. I had been here for hours now. I was tired and hungry, and I could not quite rid my mind of that sight of Hamo Belancer lying cold on the floor, in his own blood.

'Have you ever heard anything of a secret way into St Frideswide's Priory?' I asked. 'As I said, that was what Master Winchingham heard them discussing.'

He shook his head. 'I have not. I cannot see how there could be such a thing. And why would that be of any interest to the French vintner, who has every reason to come and go there as he pleases?'

'And why,' I said, 'the most unfathomable question – *why* would the Frenchman want to kill Belancer? They were friends, or at least acquaintances.'

'That,' Walden said, 'I cannot even begin to answer.'

I got up and began to pace restlessly about the room.

'A sudden quarrel? Were they planning some crime together, some trick to pass off cheap wine as the best vintage, and then fell out about it? It's possible, you know. Belancer could claim he had bought some fine French wine from the other man, and then pass off his poorer stuff for a high price.'

'Surely his customers would notice?'

'There are some men will pretend they have a great knowledge of wine, but is it not often no more than talk? How many true experts in the quality of wine do we have here in Oxford? Very few, I should guess. Hamo could buy one barrel of the best quality from the Frenchman, and offer that as samples, then substitute the inferior wine to his customers.'

Walden grinned. 'I see you have the makings of a fine criminal mind. Such a scheme might well be tried, but I cannot see how a falling out over a devious plot to cheat customers could lead to murder. Everyone knows that it goes on all the time. That is why we have assessors for the quality of bread and ale, the accuracy of a merchant's scales, and the length of his cloth yard.'

'You are right.' I flung myself down on the stool again. 'And in any case, what could such a cheating scheme have to do, in the first place, with Alice Walsea's information about the man she is looking for, and, in the second place, with a secret way into St Frideswide's Priory? Nay, it will not do.'

'I think we can do no more here.' Walden got up and began closing and barring the shutters.

I extinguished all but two of the candles.

'I will have discreet enquiries made,' he said, 'into the group of French vintners who have come to the fair. As you know, the management of the fair is not really my business, it is handled by the priory through their steward and their lay servants, and they may call upon the parish constables if they need help.'

'Did you hear about the fighting this morning? One man was stabbed.'

'Aye, but it was nothing to worry us. The combatants have been locked up till tomorrow to cool their tempers and learn restraint. It was never serious enough for me to intervene.'

'And I will continue to try to discover the identity of the man Master Winchingham glimpsed last night,' I said. 'A man of Provençal appearance, it seems. There surely cannot be more than one such amongst the French merchants. I shall keep my eyes open, and I shall also ask the cellarer at the priory to describe the man who supplied the wine for the prince's dinner.'

Walden dropped the bar across the last shutter, leaving us in the gloom lit only by the two remaining candles. 'The prince is still here, so unless he dines with the mayor, Prior de Hungerford will be obliged to provide more dinners, and therefore to buy more wine.'

'Very true.' I realised I had not told the sheriff about the thefts from the priory and the steps taken by Sub-Prior Resham and the canons to move all the treasures and books to the safety of the high altar, but it seemed I had burdened him enough already.

I blew out the candles, and we groped our way to the door, which still stood open. A chill wind was getting up, with the bite of autumn in it. Once we were outside, Walden felt in his scrip and drew out a bulky lock, which he clamped around the latch of the door.

'The shop door is barred on the inside, as well as locked, and this should deter any sneak thief, once word gets about that the place is empty.'

We walked up the alley together.

'This place is worse than a pig run,' Walden said, 'and your poor friend, the merchant from Flanders, was lying in this?'

'Aye, face down and half smothered.'

We had reached the High Street and I noticed that

Walden's horse was hitched to a ring in the wall. Across the way, I saw that light was shining from my own house. My stomach was hinting that it was long past the hour for supper.

Walden mounted and nodded toward the cobbler's house, from which we could hear the shouts of his children.

'At least they should have peace tonight.'

How wrong he was proved to be.

Chapter Eight

When at last I reached home, I found the children abed, and Margaret half asleep in her chair by the fire. I crept into the kitchen as softly as I might, but the hinges of the door creaked and she started awake.

'I am sorry to disturb you,' I said.

I crouched by the fire, holding out my hands to the blaze. I had suddenly realised how cold I had grown in that bleak fireless room across the road. 'I have been all this time at Hamo Belancer's house, and Sheriff Walden has but this moment left.'

Margaret got up and lifted a pot which had been staying warm by the fire.

'I have kept you some of the leek and barley pottage,' she said. 'There is bread under the cloth on the table.'

With some reluctance, I left the fire, but I was very hungry. It was hours since I had eaten that meagre rabbit pie at the fair. When I was settled with a steaming bowl of pottage and had cut several slices of bread, Margaret sat down opposite me and poured us both a cup of ale.

'This venture of Mary Coomber's was a fine idea, no doubt, and we shall all have earned some chinks to lay aside, perhaps for a new winter cloak, or shoes for the children, but by St Frideswide herself, I shall be glad when this fair is over. My feet and my back have never ached so much.'

I smiled at her over my spoon. 'I am sure you work every bit as hard about the house.'

'Perhaps, but it is different, standing in a stall all day long, keeping a polite smile on your face while customers taste first one thing and then another. And then, like as not, walk off without buying anything! I have some sympathy, now, for you shopkeepers.'

I laughed. 'Most of my customers behave better than that, although sometimes it is difficult to remain polite, with such as Lady Amilia. Comfort yourselves that there are only three more days of the fair. And you are not there tomorrow, are you?'

'Nay, 'tis Emma and Mary tomorrow, with Juliana coming in the afternoon, so that Mary may be away in time for her milking.' She cut herself a slice of bread and nibbled at it. 'I give you due warning that Alysoun is fretting to go to the fair.'

'Perhaps I may take them tomorrow. I have an errand in the morning, but after that I will take them both, and you may have a quiet day.'

She smiled. 'That would be good. Now, what is this matter that Johane Brinley brought word of? I was not here when she came, but heard it from Walter. Hamo Belancer has met with an accident?'

'A severe accident,' I said grimly. 'He is dead. He was murdered.'

Margaret pressed her fingers against her lips, then stretched out her hand to me.

'Nicholas, you are not being caught up again in dangerous affairs, surely? If Hamo Belancer has been murdered, it is no concern of yours.'

I reached across and patted her shoulder. 'No need for you to worry, Meg. I am concerned only because Cobbler Brinley and I discovered his body, I sent at once for Sheriff Walden. It was some time before he could come, and then we put our heads together over what may lie behind it. I told him about what Peter Winchingham had heard, and how he was struck down. He needed to know everything I could tell him. And there was also Alice Walsea's information about the Frenchman, since it was certainly a

Frenchman Master Winchingham overheard.'

'So now you are free of it?' She took a sip of her ale, and eyed me narrowly over the rim of her cup.

I returned to my meal and kept my eyes on my bowl.

'I have said only that I will try to learn from the cellarer at St Frideswide's which of the French vintners has supplied the priory with wine. That is my errand, first thing tomorrow morning. Walden is a good man, but the fellows under him are little help, I would guess, in seeking out the truth of a crime. The killing of Belancer seems senseless. Yet it must have been the Frenchman, since there was no sign of a break-in at the shop, and the Frenchman was certainly with him last night. Unless–'

I paused, tapping my spoon against the bowl.

'Unless what?'

'Unless someone else visited Hamo *after* the Frenchman left. It must have been someone he knew. Someone for whom he would open the door readily at night. But he had not let the dog out of the storeroom, so it needs must have happened immediately after the other man left.' I shook my head. 'Nay, I think not.'

'The dog? What dog?'

'That old dog of Hamo's.'

I explained how the dog had been shut away, and so had alerted Brinley and me that something was amiss.

'However much we may wish to complicate the matter,' I said, 'the finger points clearly at the Frenchman, but why should he have any reason to kill Belancer? They were planning something together. Something involving this secret way into the priory.'

'Nicholas, you are making my head ache, as well as my back and my feet. You are starting to repeat yourself. Finish your meal, then let us get to bed before we fall asleep over the table.'

She was, of course, as always, perfectly right. I scooped up the last of the pottage, which had banished my slight feeling of dizziness, and wiped up the final drops with the heel of my bread. We took our candles and went quietly up the stairs, although I paused for a moment at the children's room. Rowan was sprawled over most of Alysoun's bed, leaving her hardly any room, while Rafe, as so often, was hanging over the side of the truckle bed, in danger of rolling on to the floor. I set down my candle and tucked Rafe more firmly in place. The dog, who was not supposed to sleep on Alysoun's bed, I shoved over to the far side. She woke and licked my hand in a forgiving manner. Alysoun muttered something in her sleep, but did not wake, as I took possession of a larger portion of the bed for her from the dog. Probably before morning Rowan would have spread herself across it again.

Once in my own bed chamber I was too tired even to change into my night shift, simply kicking off my shoes, dropping my cotte on the floor, and rolling myself in the feather bed. Yet despite the fatigues of the day, I could not sleep at first. The image of Hamo Belancer, sprawled on the floor, his neck bruised and the front of his cotte soaked in his life's blood, kept pressing on my mind. I thought I could hear the old dog's puzzled whine. And my brain would not abandon its attempt to sort out the confusion of ideas – a French vintner supplying wine to the priory, town youths firing the gatehouse, the king's intelligencer masquerading as a merchant, books and silver stolen from the priory, Winchingham struck down, the fight on the jetty, a secret way into the priory, and Hamo dead in his own kitchen.

There seemed to be no connection between them, apart from the priory, and I wished I could silence the chatter in my head. In irritation I flung myself on to my side, then on to my back. Having earlier in the day wanted to avoid the lures of Morpheus, now I longed for him to throw the comforting blanket of sleep over me.

In the end, I must have slept.

Until a clamour penetrated even through my sleep-dulled ears.

In Oxford we are a city of bells. Some say that there is a church on every corner, but that is an exaggeration. Yet it is true that there are many churches within the small circle of the town walls, and many of the colleges have built their own chapels. At all the canonical hours, the bells ring out their discreet summons to prayer, although here in the centre of the secular town we are mostly out of earshot of the bells that rouse the ecclesiastical orders from their beds at midnight, to celebrate the coming of the new day with Matins and Lauds. They may whisper at the edge of our hearing, but we have learned to shut our ears to them.

This was different.

A single bell, tolling over and over again, as if it rang for the funeral of some centenarian. Nay, it was not so measured, so sober. This was a shout, a clamour, an alarm.

I threw off the covers and sat up. When there is a fire in the town, or if the flooding in the outskirts begins to creep too near for safety, the church bells ring out a warning. But this was one bell, one church, and even in the dark I guessed that it came from St Frideswide's. Had the fire-raisers returned there? Was this why a secret entrance was needed?

I fumbled until I had lit my candle, pulled my cotte over my head and pushed my feet into my shoes. It seemed like a repetition of the other night, only there had been no bell then. This time the danger must have reached the priory itself.

Margaret was already at the top of the stairs as I emerged carrying my candle, and Alysoun stood in the doorway of the children's bed chamber, white-faced and frightened.

I leaned down and hugged her. 'Nothing to worry about, my pet. It is something at the far side of the town.'

'Is it another fire?' she whispered. She was shivering, and her bare feet were turning blue with cold.

'Never you worry,' Margaret said briskly. 'I've looked from my window and there is no sign of a fire. No doubt some mischievous novice playing a prank. Get you back into your bed before you wake Rafe.'

I did not think there were any novices at the priory,

but I did not contradict her.

'Aye, Alysoun, back to your bed. I am sure Aunt Margaret will stay with you until you go to sleep again.'

Margaret raised her eyebrows at that but I nodded, and murmured, 'You stay with the children and I will see what is afoot. At least they have not set a fire this time.'

'I cannot go to sleep with that bell clanging,' Alysoun objected.

'They will grow tired of it soon,' I said, with more conviction than I felt.

Before there could be any more arguments, I clattered down the stairs so fast I nearly extinguished my candle in the draught, then, lighting a lantern from it, I went out into the street. This time there were not such crowds as there had been before, since there was no sign of a fire which might endanger the town. There was no mistaking that the sounding of the bell was some sort of alarm or cry for help, but unless the town itself was threatened, I suspected that many of my fellow townsmen would shrug and return to their beds. If the priory was in trouble, then let the priory take measures to contain it.

Even so, there were a few of us, running down in the direction of the priory, and this time it had needed no messenger to fetch the sheriff and his men, who caught up with me as I passed Oriel College, where a number of lighted windows showed that the Fellows there would get little sleep until a stop was put to the clamour. Indeed, as close to the priory as this, the noise was deafening and I realised that Oriel must needs endure the bell for Matins every night.

'Wait,' I said, seizing the sheriff's stirrup leather. 'Is this what we were discussing earlier?'

He leaned down from the saddle. 'It may be so. As you are in this to your chin, you had best come with me.'

The narrowness of the street here had slowed his horse to a trot, so I was able to keep my hold of the leather and run alongside.

The main gate of the priory stood wide open, and the

porter lay sprawled beside it.

'No coming in by a secret entrance here,' I said, as Walden slid from his horse. 'Have they killed the man?'

Walden threw his reins to one of his officers and we bent over the porter. As well as my lantern, the night flares beside the gate were lit, and in the combined light we could see that the man's eyes were open. He groaned and tried to sit up.

'Stay,' Walden said, pressing him down again. 'I can see you've taken a blow. My men will look after you. Was it the Frenchmen who broke in?'

'Nay,' the man croaked. 'No Frenchmen.' Then, strangely, he began to laugh, a weak, hysterical laugh. 'No Frenchmen. It was–' He began to retch, then vomited, barely missing Walden's feet.

I realised that the bell had stopped ringing.

'The church,' I said, scrambling to my feet. 'All the treasures are there.'

'Look after this fellow,' Walden called over his shoulder, and we both broke into a run, heading for the church.

Before reaching it, we stopped dead. The door of the church was wrenched half off its hinges and hung askew, flung back against the wall. Light flowed out from within, showing a struggling mass of men just within the doorway.

Walden turned and shouted for his men. 'Here, to me.'

It was a scene which seemed barely to make sense. A large number of townsmen, rough, dangerous looking fellows, were attacking the canons with fists and clubs. From all the signs – the candles lit along the choir stalls and on the altar, service books scattered on the floor – the canons must have been in the church celebrating Matins. Some were lying on the ground, senseless and bleeding. I saw Canon Fitzrobert, Sub-Prior Resham, and the cellarer, the man I had hoped to see in a few hour's time. Few of the canons were young, yet they were struggling valiantly against their attackers. So at first glance it seemed to be what I had expected, another attack by the town on the priory, except that this time, instead of mischievous youths who started a fire and ran away, it was hardened men of violence, who looked ready to kill.

Then I realised that what was strange was their leader. Clad in secular dress and wielding a sword in one hand and a heavy club in the other, was Prior de Hungerford, and he was bent on injuring or killing Canon Aubery. With a yell, I leapt forward and seized his sword arm as he raised his blade against Aubery. I must have taken him by surprise, but nevertheless he swung the club, aiming for my head.

I ducked just in time, and felt the edge of it brush my hair. Then two of Walden's men grabbed him from behind. I released his sword arm as the sword fell to the ground, while one of the soldiers twisted his other arm until he dropped the club. More of the intruders appeared from the direction of the dortoir, dragging two very elderly canons, who must be allowed to remain in their beds during the midnight services. One was bleeding from a gash in his temple, and both stumbled and staggered in confusion. At the sight of the soldiers, these new attackers dropped their hold of the old men, and tried to run for the gate, but they were caught and held before they could reach it.

Some time later, all the canons, together with Walden and me, and two of his senior men, were gathered in the infirmary of the priory, where the present infirmarian and his predecessor were treating the wounded. The three worst of the injured we had found lying at the church door were still unconscious, and the porter kept vomiting, but the remaining wounds were mostly minor, although the two old men from the dortoir were badly shaken. Someone had found some red wine and doled it out to both the victims and the rescuers.

Francis Aubery came to sit beside me on a bench against the wall, and sank down with a sigh. He put his head in his hands.

'I thank you, Nicholas, for saving me from a beating, or worse. It was brave of you to rush in like that, unarmed, but foolish. You could have been killed.'

'So might you. I do not understand what has happened here.'

Walden pulled up a stool and joined us.

'Your medical men think that all will recover, although the three worst may take some time.'

Aubery raised his head and gave a weak smile. 'Our present infirmarian has little medical knowledge. He holds the position only because de Hungerford has made it his practice to move us from pillar to post, so that no man may become too secure in his position and his knowledge of what it requires of him. Fortunately, our previous infirmarian, Canon Younger, is indeed a skilled physician, so we may rely on his opinion.'

'As I heard Nicholas saying,' Walden said, 'we do not understand what has been afoot here. These men came in through the gate, then? Let in by the prior?'

'Nay,' Aubery said, 'from what I can gather from poor Donster – our porter – de Hungerford came *with* the men from the town, demanded entrance, as was his right. But when the other rogues tried to enter, Donster did his best to stop them, and it was the . . . the prior himself who clubbed him down.'

He could hardly bring himself to speak de Hungerford's title.

'You were at Matins?' I said.

'Aye, we were just beginning the service. Because of the earlier trouble at the fair, and our worries about the thefts, we have been keeping the church door locked, even during services.'

'And de Hungerford was not presiding at the service?' Walden asked, in a puzzled voice.

Aubery gave a grim smile. 'He rarely attended service, sheriff. He has been living a life quite separate from the rest of us, almost since the day he arrived. It was Sub-Prior Resham who was leading the service. The first we knew of what was happening was when we heard the attack on the door, the splintering of the wood and the tearing of the hinges.' He paused. 'They sought principally to attack the sub-prior and me, of course, since we had been responsible for removing everything of value to the church. They were bent on stealing it.'

'So they were not deterred by the holiness of the place of sanctuary,' I said.

'They were not.'

Aubery turned to me. 'How do you come to be here, Nicholas? I can understand Sheriff Walden and his men, but you?'

'The ringing of your bell woke me, even as far away as the High Street, though I think I was not deep asleep. It was well thought on, to ring the bell.'

'I do not even know who rang it,' Aubery said. 'There was the splintering of the door, and then they were upon us. I believe we were fighting for our lives.'

'So I believe also,' Walden said, 'and I can tell you who thought to ring the bell. It was your steward. He was woken in his quarters by the breaking of the door, and ran straight for the bell rope, like a man of good sense. It would have been impossible for you to fight off this party of rogues if we had not been warned by its tolling.'

'Then we owe our lives to him,' Aubery said soberly, 'as well as to you.'

'And they committed this act of sacrilege,' I said, 'as well as attempted murder, purely to steal the priory's treasures? And under the leadership of Prior de Hungerford? It seems almost past belief. Is the man deranged?'

'Sometimes I think he must be. He was shouting during the fight, something about how we had no right to confiscate *his* church silver and *his* library of books.'

Canon Aubery twisted his hands together in distress. 'Yet we were only trying to keep them safe.'

'Of course you were,' I said, 'and so you have done. The rogues never reached them, did they?'

He shook his head and I turned to the sheriff. 'Where are the villains now, and where is the prior?'

'The villains from the town I have sent off to be confined up in the castle,' he said. 'De Hungerford is locked in a chamber in the prior's house here at St Frideswide's, with two of my men guarding him.'

He ran his hands through his hair. 'It is a difficult matter. Since it took place on Church property, but most of the attackers are from the town, which one is the competent authority? As for Prior de Hungerford, I suppose an ecclesiastic's attack on his own church and canons must be a matter for the Church. However, Bishop Glyndwelle is away at the heart of his see in Lincoln, or at least I suppose he is. In the morning I will send a messenger to him, with details of what has happened here, but we cannot expect to hear from him for some days. In the meantime I propose to keep de Hungerford locked up here, but under my guard, if there is no objection from the priory?'

Aubery shook his head. 'I cannot think there will be.'

He glanced across the room to the four beds where the porter and the three most injured canons were lying.

'Normally, it would be Sub-Prior Resham who would take charge in the absence of the prior, but until he is able . . . I think we will meet in Chapter tomorrow and decide how best to carry on. We must not forget that there are still three more days of the fair to run, with dozens of merchants here to do business, and hundreds of folk come to buy, some of them gentlefolk, who have travelled a distance to be here.'

As he spoke, a sudden thought struck me with such force that I half started from my seat.

'The prince!' I cried. 'Edward of Woodstock! Is he not still staying in the priory? He is not harmed?'

Walden patted my arm. 'No need to fear for him, Nicholas, though if my men had not stopped him, he would have been there, in the thick of the fighting.' He laughed. 'What a man! What a prince! He was hardly more than a child when he won his spurs at Crécy. The French cower before him. His men would follow him into the jaws of Hell if he said, "Onward". And when a band of Oxford ruffians sets upon a group of defenceless canons, the Prince of Wales buckles on his sword over his night shift and comes roaring in. Barefoot.'

'In his night shift?' I said.

'In his night shift.'

I grinned. 'Indeed, what a man! What a prince!'

It was a cheering thought on which to end the night. Though to tell truth, it was nearly dawn. It was cause for relief, too, that the attempt to steal the priory's treasures, quite likely at the cost of several lives, had been frustrated, and the perpetrators now all held under lock and key. What would the Church do about de Hungerford? The usual practice was to draw a veil of secrecy over any misdemeanours committed within the purview of the Church, to keep out prying secular eyes, but in this case an attack had been made upon other churchmen and upon Church property. Moreover, laymen had been involved, and the secular hand of justice had saved lives and property. It was a bewildering tangle. I hoped Bishop Glyndwelle was a man of exceptional ability and shrewdness.

By the time Walden and I left the infirmary, the porter was looking better, sitting up and sipping red wine under the stern supervision of one of the infirmarians. The three more serious cases seemed more at ease, as though they had slipped from the unconsciousness due to injury to a more natural, healing sleep. Walden and I crossed the outer court together, both of us now given to fits of yawning. The main gate was closed and barred, but it was guarded by two of the men from the castle, who opened the wicket for us, and we stepped through.

'Ah, he's still here, the poor fellow,' Walden said, slapping his horse's shoulder affectionately. Someone had hitched him to a post beside the gate, and he blew a moist greeting into his master's ear.

I held Walden's stirrup for him as he mounted.

'What puzzles me,' I said, looking up at him in the

flickering light cast by the gateway torches, 'is that this seems to have nothing to do with Frenchmen, secret entrances, or the murder of Hamo Belancer. Can there be two plots afoot to steal the priory's treasures?'

'That, my dear Nicholas, we have yet to discover. There was nothing either secret or French about this attack. It was good open English villainy.'

He turned his horse. 'God give you good night, what is left of it.'

'And to you, Cedric.'

I shivered. I had no cloak. Somewhere in the confusion I had lost my lantern. I would need to walk briskly on the way home.

The following morning Alysoun woke me in her favourite way, by jumping on my stomach. I groaned and threw my arm over my eyes. It seemed that the women in my family were unwilling to let me sleep once they were astir themselves.

'What is afoot?' I croaked. Truly, I hardly seemed to have seen my bed.

'Aunt Margaret says you will take us to the fair today.'

I struggled to sit up, and Rowan placed her front paws on my chest to hold me down flat on my back. When had the small puppy grown so much?

'I have an errand at St Frideswide's Priory first,' I said. 'Then we will go.'

Pushing the dog down from my chest, I managed to sit up.

'Why do you want to go to the fair, my pet? To purchase some lengths of French brocade to make a new gown? Some embroidered gloves, perhaps, for your next visit to the king's court?'

She giggled. 'Of course not. I want to see the tumblers. And Jonathan told Rafe there is a dancing bear. Can a bear truly dance?'

'Well, a few clever bears can shuffle about a little,

while their master plays a pipe. Not what I would call true dancing, such as you might see at a wedding, or on Twelfth Night or May Day. Still, I suppose it is remarkable that a poor dumb beast can do even that. Rowan could not.'

'Rowan is not a poor dumb beast!' she said indignantly. 'She is the cleverest dog in Oxford! Do you not remember how she found her way home, when she was just a tiny puppy?'

'Then if she is so clever, perhaps you can train her not to pin me down with my bedclothes. *And* you can train her not to sleep on your bed. I found her there again last night. She should sleep down in the kitchen.'

'Oh, but she would be so lonely all by herself there at night. And besides,' she added cunningly, 'she keeps me warm, and it will soon be winter.'

Rafe wandered in, half dressed and dragging his cotte behind him by one sleeve. 'Are we really going to see the dancing bear?'

'We shall never go to the fair if I am not permitted to dress,' I said. 'Alysoun, help Rafe put on his cotte, then both of you go to your breakfast. I needs must go out first. After that, we shall see about the fair, if Aunt Margaret tells me you have been good and have helped her while I am out. She has been working very hard, and we want her to have a rest today.'

Once they were gone, I crawled reluctantly from under the bedclothes. Had I had even as much as two hours' sleep? My head ached and my eyes felt as though they had been doused in sand.

Down in the kitchen, I thought Margaret looked as tired as I felt, though she had had more sleep than I, for when I returned from the battle at the priory she had gone back to bed, leaving a candle lantern lit for me in the shop. Though, to be sure, we had earlier in the evening both been late abed after I came back from Belancer's house.

'I will take as little time as I may,' I said, hurriedly eating a slice of bread and cheese, without pausing to sit down. Tired as she was, Margaret had already baked the morning's loaves. 'I need only speak briefly to the cellarer at the priory, no more than a few minutes.'

I drank my ale quickly, and wiped my mouth.

'Will you not tell me what was afoot last night, with all the clanging of the bell?' Margaret said. 'You were a long time returning.'

I glanced at Alysoun, who was listening eagerly, and I remembered she had been woken by the bell. Rafe was busy slipping bits of bread to Rowan under the table.

'Later,' I said. 'All was settled, but it took some while. Cedric Walden arrived at the same time as I did.'

Before Alysoun became too inquisitive, I hurried out, catching up my cloak from its peg on the wall. Now we were so near the end of October, I would need it. The stallholders at the fair would be cold today, standing still for hours, with little protection from the wind. I was glad Mary Coomber had insisted on a booth for her little enterprise.

As I left, I saw Walter and Roger both approaching and stopped to speak to them.

'I must call at the priory, then I am taking the children to the fair. There is not a great deal to do in the shop today, and with no customers to serve, you may go to the fair yourselves, if you wish.'

Roger brightened. 'Aye, I should like that. They say 'tis bigger this year than ever, at least since I was a boy.'

'Mayhap I'll go.' Walter was less enthusiastic. 'Mayhap not.'

'Come you with me,' Roger said, slapping him on the shoulder. 'We need not spend our chinks. We can watch other folks spending theirs. And there will be plenty to look at, not just your seller of spectacles. All I have seen when I go to mind the booth at night, is a row of closed doors and folded stalls. I have never even been to the end of the row. We can have our dinner there. Both the Mitre and the Cross have stalls.'

I left them to it, Roger persuading and Walter – I could see – gradually yielding. There seemed to be more people than on previous days making their way through the streets toward the fair, their curiosity roused, perhaps, by last night's disturbance.

At the priory's gate, one of the other lay servants was on duty, with a soldier from the castle in attendance.

'How is Donster?' I asked.

'Nursing a sore head, maister' the man said, 'but otherwise none the worse. He's pleased to have a day free of work. 'Tis not often us gets one, not even on saints' days, for them's often the busiest, here at the gate.'

This was good news about the porter. I had thought the vomiting the night before was a bad sign, after a blow on the head, but it seemed the man was recovering.

'And the canons?' I said.

'Nursing their own wounds. There's four still in the infirmary. The three worst hurt this night past, and one of the old men, who took a fainting turn this morning. The rest are in Chapter, though they'm likely done by this.'

Giving him a nod of thanks, I made my way to the Chapter House, where the canons were just leaving. I caught up with Canon Aubery.

'How are you this morning?' I asked. 'I saw you take some shrewd blows.'

'Stiff,' he said, 'and some fine purple bruises under my habit, but a few days will cure all, which is more than can be said for this poor house of ours.'

He sighed. 'They have asked me in Chapter to take charge until Sub-Prior Resham is fit again, so I must see to the managing of the fair for the last days, a task I fear I am not fit for. And there is the church door to repair. I needs must send for a carpenter this morning.'

'How are the sub-prior and the other two faring.?' I asked.

'Mending slowly, but still very weak. I cannot think they will be fit to rise from their beds for several days.'

'I had hoped I might speak to your cellarer,' I said. 'You know that I am trying to discover which of the French vintners has been supplying wine to the priory.'

Aubery shook his head. 'I am afraid you are out of luck this morning, Nicholas. All three have been given a dose of poppy syrup to help them sleep, for sleep is their best cure for now.'

I supposed it was no more than I expected, but it meant I had wasted a journey.

'I had word from Sheriff Walden this morning,' Aubery said. 'He is sending a letter telling of last night's attack to Bishop Glyndwelle in Lincoln and asked if we wished to add a letter of our own, but we have left all to him. I am sure he will report it fairly.'

'Aye,' I said. 'I think you may trust to that. If the bishop or one of his household comes to investigate, then you may apprise him of anything more he needs to know. You will be more familiar with de Hungerford's conduct than the sheriff can possibly be. And you can also tell him about the thefts of priory treasures.'

He sighed. 'I am not a man always to be looking over my shoulder at the past, Nicholas, but I could wish that our last prior were still alive. He was a kind man, pious and gentle. Not a good manager of money, but honest. Everything about the priory has suffered since de Hungerford came.'

'And do you still have your royal guest?'

'Aye, he is to remain another three or four days. The repairs to Wallingford Castle should be finished by then.'

'I must leave you to all your duties,' I said, 'but it is good to know that the priory is in your capable care.'

By the time I reached home again, the kitchen was spotless, Alysoun and Rafe were waiting in their best Sunday clothes, and Margaret was seated in her chair, pretending to be asleep.

I put my finger to my lips and whispered, 'Do not disturb Aunt Margaret. We will slip away quietly.'

'We have been *very* good.' Alysoun's whisper was loud enough to be heard in the street. 'We cleared the breakfast, and swept the floor, and fetched in logs for the fire.'

'Can we bring Rowan?' Rafe asked.

I shook my head. 'She would not like it, and she might frighten the bear.'

The ghost of a smile played around Margaret's lips, and she opened one eye a slit. I smiled back.

'Fetch your cloaks,' I said.

Walking through the streets with the rest of the fair-going townsfolk, I kept a firm hold on the children's hands, for they were apt to skip ahead in their excitement. I hoped the fair would not prove a disappointment.

As it was, the jugglers and acrobats were some of the best I had ever seen. From their dark hair and olive skins, I thought they must be Spanish or Italian, and from their strong likeness, one to another, they must all belong to one family, though a large one. Four of the men juggled balls and rings and cups, each man by himself, then passed things back and forth between them so fast you could hardly tell what was flying through the air. Then one of the women flipped over and over in somersaults, before balancing on her hands on the tips of two swords, which the men raised high in the air, parading about as though they were carrying a banner instead of a mortal woman at risk of falling and breaking her back.

There were two children, no older than Alysoun – boys or girls I could not tell – who performed amazing contortions, turning themselves into hoops and rolling about the dusty ground, then three women joined them, and they formed patterns, rolling then turning cartwheels, then throwing the children in the air until they landed on the shoulders of two of the men. Alysoun and Rafe watched with their mouths a-gape.

To finish, all of them, men, women and children, formed themselves into a human pyramid, men at the bottom, women leaping on to their shoulders, and the men tossing the children up to stand on the women's shoulders, as carelessly as if they were sacks of grain. The whole crowd gasped as the children sailed through the air, but they landed neatly, with impish grins, then they stretched a banner between them which read, in rather shaky letters: 'Long live our good Prince Edward".

That brought a great cheer from the crowd.

'Will the prince be watching?' Alysoun asked.

I hoped he might be, but feared he might not.

'He would only be able to see from one of the high windows of the priory,' I said, 'but if he has not seen it, then I am sure someone will tell him.'

And perhaps he will send a purse to the acrobats, I thought.

They leapt down from their pyramid, bowing to the applause, and one of the women began to go round with an upturned hat, collecting coins. I gave the children each a whole silver penny to drop in the hat. She smiled at me and sketched a curtsey.

'Gracias,' she said.

From a distance the women had looked graceful and delicate, but up close I saw that she was as hard and sinewy as a mercenary soldier or a country labourer. A cruel life, I thought, and a body trained from early childhood to those terrible contortions. I wondered how she had managed to balance on the sword points without piercing her hands, but it must be a secret of her profession. Perhaps she wore thick pads to protect her palms, but let her keep the illusion.

Rafe tugged at my sleeve. 'And now may we see the dancing bear, Papa?'

'I asked at the gate,' I said. 'The bear keeper will be having his dinner soon, and so shall we. Afterwards, the bear will dance further along from here, where there is an open space beyond the stalls. But first, let us see what is to be seen in the rest of the fair.'

We spent half an hour or so happily strolling about the stalls, and visiting those of the stallholders we knew. Mary Coomber gave the children marchpane sweetmeats, then we called on Master Winchingham.

'I have the very thing for you, my maid,' he said. 'I am left with the end of a bolt of sky blue linsey-woolsey which is just enough to make you a gown.'

He drew it out from under the counter and spread it out for Alysoun to see. Her eyes glowed.

'Oh, it is beautiful.' She reached out a finger to touch it but, mindful of the sticky marchpane, I wiped her hands first. 'May I have it, Papa?'

I laughed. Alysoun was by nature a little ruffian, playing most happily with Jonathan Baker, even scrumping apples from the orchard at Holywell Mill, under the nose of the fearsome Miller Wooton, but of late her admiration of Juliana and Emma had given her a taste for more ladylike clothes.

'Very well, my pet, but you must help Aunt Margaret in the making of the gown.'

I reached for my purse, but Peter Winchingham shook his head.

'Nay, Nicholas, I owe you much more than a length of cloth for saving my life the other night. Now, what might I have for the little lad?'

He disappeared into the room at the back of the booth, and emerged with something hidden behind his back.

'Now,' he said, handing a carved wooden toy to Rafe. 'See whether you can make the monkey climb the stick.'

He smiled at me. 'I planned to bring these round to your shop, but you have saved me the journey.'

It was a clever thing. I had once had one myself, though it had been broken long since. By manipulating a weight on the end of a string, the wooden monkey could be made to climb the stick. This was a better one than mine had been, purchased by my mother from a pedlar when I had been quite ill with the measles. I could remember long days when I was too tired to do anything but play with the monkey, for hours on end, it seemed. This one was finely carved, the handle of the stick and a hat upon the monkey's head painted red and blue.

At first Rafe did not manage the trick, and Alysoun could not keep her hands from reaching out.

'I can see how it is done!' she said. 'Let me!'

I put my hand on her shoulder and shook my head. 'Let Rafe find out for himself,' I said.

Peter Winchingham winked at me.

It did not take long before Rafe had mastered it, and in delight he made the monkey climb the stick again and again.

'There is an excellent toy stall,' Winchingham said, 'in the next row over from here. Bavarians. I used to buy toys for my children when they were young, whenever I had business in Bavaria.'

'They have come a long way to our Oxford fair,' I said, 'and those acrobats as well.'

'Spaniards. Have you seen the players yet? They perform a play late each evening, just before the fair closes.'

I shook my head. 'I hope they at least are English! To say truly, I have been caught up in such wild events as would make a play, which have left me little time for visiting the fair.'

I gave him a brief account of events at Belancer's house and the priory, while Rafe, watching jealously, allowed Alysoun a turn with his toy.

Winchingham grew grave as he listened. 'There have been whispers about what has happened at the priory, but I did not realise how serious matters had become. So Belancer is dead, and you suspect the Frenchman who struck me down. Very probable, I would say, though like you I can see no reason for it. And this attack on the priory by their own prior – that is shocking news! Yet you do not think the one is connected to the other?'

'I cannot see how, and I still have not been able to discover which vintner supplied the priory. I do not suppose you have recognised your attacker amongst the Frenchmen?'

'I have not. They keep very much to themselves. Nor have I seen the man who offered me the books, although I expected him to return to the inn last night. Perhaps he will come tonight, unless something has caused him to take fright.'

'If he comes,' I said, thinking fast, 'perhaps you should say that you will, after all, buy the two books, but it must be the day after the fair, when you have had time to pack up your remaining goods and make up your accounts. Bid him come to the Mitre – at midday, shall we say? – and I will bring Sheriff Walden. He can catch him in the very act of selling stolen property.'

'An excellent plan. I will do so, if the man shows his face again, which surely he must do, for I still have the books in my possession.'

'I wonder whether he was amongst those with de Hungerford last night,' I said, and described the men as well as I could remember, from the confusion and the erratic light of flares and lanterns.

'Nay,' he said. 'I think not. This was no big bully of a man, but a weak, weedy little fellow, with the look of a lower servant about him, or perhaps an under-fed clerk, such as might be employed in the imaginary gentleman's household.'

We were no further forward, but Winchingham promised to send me word if the man should come to the Mitre at any time.

Rafe had regained possession of his monkey, and he tugged again my sleeve. 'The bear? You promised.'

'May I leave the length of cloth with you?' I asked Winchingham. 'I fear it might suffer in the crowds around the dancing bear.'

'I will have it made up into a parcel for you, and send one of my lads round this evening with it. I would come myself, but if I am to await the fellow selling the books–'

'Aye. It would be best it you kept to the inn.'

We needed to find somewhere to eat, or the children would be fretting, even with the excitement of seeing a dancing bear. The crowds had grown so much today that we found all the tables set out by the Mitre and the Cross were already full, but I remembered that there had been a stall not far from Mistress Walsea's which sold hot pies, so we made our way there. For the moment I had forgotten the hostile men of two nations guarding the boats and barges moored at the jetty, but remembered them as we drew near. Many of them were clustered about the pie stall. The trouble-makers must still be under lock and key, and the present company eyed each other warily, but for the moment no blows were being exchanged.

The pie stall did not provide tables and chairs, so we carried our pies to the jetty and sat there, swinging our legs over the river. For cheap pies they were surprisingly good, if somewhat messy. When I had rinsed my handkerchief in the river and wiped faces, we went in search of gingerbread and Alice Walsea.

She remembered the children from her brief encounter with them at my cousin's farm, and insisted on buying them an extra gingerbread babe each.

'So, you are going to see the dancing bear,' she said. 'Keep well clear of him, for if anyone provokes him, he may turn nasty. Bears are wild beasts, and you should never forget it.'

'Aye,' I said, 'Mistress Walsea speaks truly. Do not try to stand too close.'

For once it was Rafe who did not seem to be frightened by this warning, though Alysoun looked thoughtful.

Alice Walsea and I both admitted our failure to trace the swarthy Frenchman, who might be the man she sought, or might not, although he was certainly the man who had attacked Peter Winchingham, and probably the murderer of Belancer.

'And I hear that you were caught up in the trouble at the priory this midnight past,' she said.

I did not ask how she knew. To discover what others do not know was her profession, but I told her what had happened.

'And now,' I said, 'we must be off to seek this bear.'

'Aye,' she said. 'He usually performs a little way

from the fair, to be away from the stalls and draw his own audience. Follow the path in the lee of the town wall, toward the priory grange, but not nearly as far.'

Rafe set off at once, and Alysoun and I had to hurry to keep up with him. A crowd of people was already moving from the main part of the fair along the path below the wall, and Rafe tugged anxiously at my arm.

'Hurry, Papa! We might miss him.'

We reached an area which had been marked out with rope strung round a large circle of wooden pegs driven into the turf. The rope could not have kept the bear in, had he taken it into his head to lunge at the crowd, for it was no more than a foot off the ground. I assumed it was meant merely to hold back the audience and give the animal room to perform. A lanky youth in shabby finery was standing just inside the circle, calling out as people made their way nearer.

'Come and see the remarkable bruno, Radofitch, all the way from the frozen wastes of legendary Muscovy. A bear who will dance for you as dainty as any gentlewoman.'

His speech was also a little threadbare with use, for he spoken the words as though they had lost their meaning for him. I saw that he had a small drum slung on a baldric.

I made our way to the front of the crowd, but far enough from the rope that I hoped a swipe of the bear's paw could not reach us, and put the children in front of me, so that no one blocked their view. However, I kept a tight grip on their shoulders, so that I could whip them behind me if it seemed there might be danger.

From a tent erected next to the wall, the bear keeper appeared. Like the youth, he wore bright but worn garments of a curious cut, designed to suggest that he came, like the bear, from some exotic land, although I doubted whether he (and the bear) had come further than from one of the German states. He led the bear on a chain, which was attached to a wide metal collar, trimmed with vicious looking spikes. They both stepped easily over the rope.

The bear ambled along on all fours, ignoring the crowd. He was a little grey around the muzzle, but otherwise looked healthy enough. Sometimes these performing bears are so old they can barely stagger.

Once inside the ring, the bear keeper held up his hand to hush the crowd.

'Good people,' he said, 'you must keep quite silent while the magnificent Radofitch performs. Noise disturbs him, and I will not answer for the consequences.'

Alysoun moved a little closer to me, but Rafe was watching with shining eyes.

The bear keeper unclipped the chain from the bear's collar, and drew a double pipe from a cloth sheath at his belt. The youth lifted a pair of drumsticks and began to tap out a rhythm, while the man raised the pipe to his lips and started to play a lively dance tune. For a moment the bear simply stood where he had halted, then he rose up on to his hind legs.

There was a gasp from the crowd, and Rafe pressed back against my knees, seizing a fistful of my cotte for safety. Standing upright, the bear was nearly eight feet tall, towering over both the man and the boy. Somehow he seemed to grow when he stood thus, almost like a man, and I would have been glad to back away myself, but I did not want to alarm the children.

Slowly the bear began to shuffle around the circle, more or less keeping time with the music. When he slowed, the man and the boy slowed their music, so that the bear seemed somewhat cleverer than he was. Nevertheless, it must take some hard work to train such a fierce, such a large and dangerous creature to do your bidding. I have seen bears who were half-starved and ill-used, but this animal looked well enough.

The performance did not last long. The music came to an end, the bear sank down on to his four paws, then sat, almost like a domestic dog, scratching and parting his fur, searching for fleas. There was a collective sigh of pleasure from the audience, and clapping, and the boy began to come round, as the woman acrobat had done, with his hat for coins.

Alysoun looked relieved, but Rafe was distressed.

'Papa,' he said, 'aren't they going to give the bear anything? We always give Rowan something when she learns a new trick.'

'Perhaps when they are back in their tent,' I said.

When the youth reached us, Rafe went up to him boldly, holding out the gingerbread which Alice had given him. It was somewhat squashed from being clutched tight during the performance, but still whole.

'Please,' Rafe said to the youth, 'will you give this to the bear, from me?'

The youth looked surprised, then he grinned, not unkindly.

'Aye, give it here. Now watch!'

He flung the gingerbread high in the air, so that it dropped down in front of the bear, who caught it neatly and began to eat it with every sign of pleasure.

'Did you see!' Rafe cried. 'He likes my gingerbread!'

That raised some smiles from the people standing near, and Alysoun leaned toward Rafe. 'You can have half of mine,' she whispered.

The bear was led away to the showman's tent and the crowd began to disperse.

'Time we went home,' I said, and we headed back toward the main fairground.

By the time we had passed through the South Gate and started up Fish Street, Rafe was stumbling with tiredness, so I took him up onto my back.

'That was kind of you,' I said the Alysoun, 'to give Rafe half your gingerbread.'

She smiled. 'I liked to see the bear eating the gingerbread, but it was only fair that Rafe should have a share too.'

Rafe's head drooped on to my shoulder and he whispered in my ear.

'When I grow up, Papa, I am going to have a bear.'

Chapter Nine

The following morning one of the lay servants from the priory brought me a note from Canon Aubery, saying that Canon Basing, the cellarer, was much recovered and sitting up in bed, if I still wished to speak to him about the French vintners. I could not go at once, for Lady Amilia had sent one of her waiting women with an order for another book. Although I could not open the shop to sell any goods, I supposed I might discuss the matter without breaking the terms of the St Frideswide's Fair charter.

'My lady wishes to have a book of troubadour songs,' the woman said. 'Words and music both, but not one of your plain music books, such as common folk use. It must be illuminated and gilded, like the book of hours you made for her. Bound in matching leather. And you must use the same scrivener. Here are her instructions.'

She laid a sheet of parchment in front of me, on which Lady Amilia had set out her demands in some detail. I did not greatly care to be ordered about like one of her lesser servants, but we humble shopkeepers must maintain a polite demeanour to our rich customers, however much our hearts rebel.

I nodded and smiled and agreed that all should be made as requested. Emma, I thought, would enjoy the task, for setting out the words and music together requires some skill. To find enough troubadour songs to make up an entire book would need some time and effort on my part. I hoped, also, that Henry Stalbroke would remember how he had made up that unique purple dye for the cover of the book of hours. I knew that he rarely wrote such things down, but experimented with his colours until he found what satisfied him. And the final result could also be affected by the underlying leather. Still, we would all do our best.

The waiting woman was inclined to linger, especially when Margaret brought her spiced ale and a plate of comfits. I daresay she was glad of an excuse to absent herself from Lady Amilia's demands for a while. She was gone at last.

'Who is minding your booth today?' I asked Margaret, when she came to clear away the ale cup and the plate, on which not so much as a crumb remained.

'Maud and Beatrice today. Emma and I tomorrow, although the others will come at the end of the fair, to clear all away. Roger has said he will bring Mary's handcart and pull it home for us.'

'Good,' I said, 'I am glad Roger is proving a help to you.'

'Aye, he was a somewhat surly lad when he first came to work for you, but he has grown up of late.'

'He has.' I thought for a moment. 'So Emma is not working today. Do you think she would enjoy seeing the play? Have you heard anything of them, the players, in the gossip going about the fair?'

'These wandering players,' she said, 'they are often a dirty, scurrilous lot, but 'tis said this group are decent folk, as decent as such vagabonds could ever be. They are under the protection of some lord's household. And their plays are said to be moral pieces, not some low stuff, meant for drunken louts reeling out from a tavern.'

I smiled. That was probably the highest praise that could be extracted from Margaret for a group of people she naturally regarded with suspicion – rootless wanderers, with no settled home, no parish church, no neighbours able to recount the life histories of their grandparents.

'Well, I have not seen a play since last year, when that group came to the Mitre. Their tale was taken from the

Bible, and performed respectfully. 'Tis a pity we have no guild plays here in Oxford, as they do in Coventry. Surely what Coventry can do, Oxford could do! I should like to see some of our respectable burgesses portraying Adam and Eve in the Garden, or contriving an Ark for Noah.'

I rubbed my chin. 'The boat builders over by the castle could contrive something, I am sure.'

Margaret laughed. 'Tease how you will, Nicholas. Did you not tell me the students sometimes put together a play? Though perhaps not Adam and Eve.'

'If they did, they would prefer a fairer Eve than one of their fellow students in a wig of frayed rope, and a gown of felt fig leaves. A student play would never match what true players can perform. I shall find out which piece they are to give us this day and ask Emma if she would care to see it. After a year in the nunnery, she is starved of the sort of entertainment youth craves. And you have all worked hard these last days.'

'So as a kindly uncle, you will take the girl to the play?'

'Indeed,' I said with dignity.

With a knowing smile, she returned to her cooking.

At the priory, I sought out Canon Aubery first. He was sitting in the parlour of the prior's house with another canon, whom I had last seen acting as infirmarian, and who was introduced to me as Canon Pultney.

'I have no skills in physic,' he said with a rueful smile, 'and have happily handed over my duties to my predecessor. However, I used to assist our former prior with his accounts. Poor man! He was often in a fine muddle. Canon Aubery and I have put our heads together and are attempting to make some sense of de Hungerford's account books, but I fear we are not making much progress.'

Aubery sighed. 'It seems they have been deliberately set out to confuse, but with all the monies of the fair to account for, after it ends tomorrow, we feel we must make a start somewhere.'

'I will not interrupt you,' I said. 'I have no love for columns of figures myself. I came only to ask whether Canon Basing is still well enough to see me.'

'Indeed he is,' Canon Pultney said. 'He is chafing to quit his bed, but we feel he had best stay there another day. Everything is in hand for the prince's entertainment, so he need not fret. And the few other noble guests who were staying here for the duration of the fair have taken themselves off to the Mitre after the disturbance of the other night.'

'And small blame to them,' Canon Aubery said.

'But the prince stays? I said.

They both laughed.

'More determined than ever,' Canon Aubery said. 'It seems his only regret is that he was unable to join the battle.'

At the door, I turned back.

'And where is de Hungerford now?'

'Still locked in his bedchamber,' Canon Aubery said, 'with two of the sheriff's men to guard him. And two more outside. Last night he tried to climb out through the window, so they are taking no chances.'

I shook my head. It seemed to me that de Hungerford would have been better suited to life as a mercenary soldier than as a senior man of the Church, though perhaps the ease and comfort of the ecclesiastical world was more to his taste than the rough soldier's life.

Leaving them to their labours, I made my way to the infirmary. Canon Basing was indeed sitting up, looking curiously like a layman in his night shift, but a layman who had taken on the fashions of some of the crusaders returning from the East, for his head was swathed in a turban of bandages like a very Saracen. I pulled a stool up to his bed.

'How do you find yourself this morning?' I asked.

'I've still a mighty headache, but otherwise none the worse,' he said. 'I need to be up and doing. This priory will not run itself without care for food and drink and all the ordinary daily needs of us all.'

I thought he looked agitated, which would be no benefit to healing his wounds, so I sought to distract him.

'I am trying to learn what I can about the French vintner who supplied wine to the priory for the entertainment of Prince Edward, around the time when the fair began. Can you tell me what he looked like? And perhaps his name?'

'As for his name, that is easy enough. He is called Claude Mateaux. As for his looks? I hardly paid them any mind. I was more interested in sampling the wine he brought, for he was charging a great price for it, French wine or not.'

He frowned.

'I was reluctant to pay so much, although the quality was excellent. After a considerable argument, I was able to persuade him to lower the price a little.'

I now had a name, but without a description I only had Hamo Belancer's offhand remark that he knew the vintner who was supplying the wine. I did not know whether it was the same man Peter Winchingham had glimpsed in the doorway of Belancer's house.

'Can you remember anything of his appearance?' I asked, without much hope.

'He looked like a Frenchman,' the cellarer said impatiently.

I noticed that he seemed a little feverish, and thought I should not try him too far. I stood up.

'French because of the way he dressed?'

'Aye, that, of course. But he was dark. You would never take him for an Englishman. Black, bushy eyebrows. I remember that. And his skin was darker than an Englishman's. Closer to the colour of new polished oak,' he added, with an unexpectedly poetic touch.

'Like a Barbary pirate?' I was startled.

'Nay! New oak, before it darkens with age.'

He was clearly annoyed with my dim wits.

'Perhaps like a labourer,' I suggested, 'who has worked much in the summer sun?'

'Aye,' he conceded. 'Somewhat of that hue.' He lay back and closed his eyes.

'And he spoke English?'

'He did, like a Frenchman, but not like a nobleman.'

I was not quite certain what he meant by this. All English gentlemen speak French, and I have been told by those with greater familiarity than I with such things that this English-French is somewhat antiquated. Those Oxford scholars who have visited the university in Paris avow that the French spoken there is much altered from the language spoken here at the king's court. Perhaps all that Canon Basing meant was this difference. Yet I was sure that the language spoken by a man from Provence would differ even more, for the Provençal language is partly akin to Italian. However, I did not want to press the cellarer further, for I could see that he was tired and in pain, so I thanked him, and bade him farewell.

As I was leaving the infirmary, he called after me.

'Master Elyot, there was another delivery of wine this morning, although I do not know whether it was the same vintner. You must ask our lay steward, Master Shrewsbury. He will have seen it bestowed.'

I found the steward in his office, which was attached to the Chapter House. It was fortunate, I thought, that the priory employed such a resourceful and competent man, for he would be needed over these coming weeks.

'Today's delivery of wine?' he said. 'Aye, it arrived early this morning and was stowed in the buttery next to the canons' refectory. We do not pitch it down into the ale cellar. These costly wines must be handled with care.'

'I have been speaking to Canon Basing,' I said, 'about the French vintner who supplied the original wine for the prince, one Claude Mateaux. Was the new supply provided by him? And did he see it delivered himself?'

Master Shrewsbury eyed me thoughtfully. 'You are asking some strange questions, Master Elyot.'

'I am doing so at the bidding of Sheriff Walden,' I said. 'We are trying to discover whether this man Mateaux might have been caught up in some trouble in the town.'

He tapped his fingers on his desk. 'Might it concern the killing of the Oxford vintner, Hamo Belancer?'

He was no fool, the steward.

'It might,' I said cautiously. 'Belancer had mentioned to me that he knew the French vintner who was supplying your wine.' I thought it unnecessary to say anything of what Peter Winchingham had overheard, and how he had been attacked.

'Well, whether he knew Belancer or not, it was Mateaux who brought the wine today, and oversaw the delivery himself, making sure that his servants, and ours, handled the wine casks with due care.'

He eyed me thoughtfully. 'And you are not the only one asking questions today. This Monsieur Mateaux was very curious about the priory, wanting to know which buildings were which, and how the priory was managed, and how matters stood after the attack.'

'Indeed? That is very interesting, Master Shrewsbury.'

'Is it? And is there any other way in which I can help you and Sheriff Walden?'

'Can you describe Mateaux to me?'

'A man about thirty, strong but not heavy. Of medium build. He looks more like an Italian than a Frenchman to me. Very dark hair.'

An observant man, the steward. He had confirmed what I was already almost sure of. 'That is most helpful,' I said. 'And you are to be congratulated on your quick thinking during the attack the other night. Had you not rung the bell when you did, the sheriff and his men might not have arrived in time.'

'It was the only thing to do. I knew our old men could not withstand those villains from the town, though they fought more valiantly than I could have expected.'

'They did indeed.' I smiled at the memory. 'Who

would have thought a group of elderly clerics, interrupted in the midst of their midnight service, could have withstood de Hungerford and his ruffians as they did?'

'It was a bad business,' he said, frowning. 'What is the world come to, Master Elyot, when an ordained prior turns on his own church and his own fellow canons?'

'Let us hope,' I said, 'that Bishop Glyndwelle will soon take the matter in hand.'

So now I had a name and a description of the vintner known to Hamo Belancer, who had supplied wine to the priory, and who seemed to fit Peter Winchingham's description, as far as he could give one. I borrowed a piece of parchment from the steward and wrote a short note to Sheriff Walden, also requesting that he should meet me at the Mitre at noon on the day following the fair, in the hope that we might catch the man trying to sell stolen books to Winchingham. The steward sent one of the lay servants to the castle with my message, and I took the information about the Frenchman to Alice Walsea, who was selling almost the last of her ribbons and laces to goodwives from the town.

She left the girl Joan in charge of the stall and we strolled down to the main branch of the Thames, as though we had nothing more in mind than a pleasant walk in the meadow. Once we were beyond the hearing of those buying and selling in this part of the fair, I told her all that I had managed to learn about Claude Mateaux.

'I think you have the right of it, Nicholas,' she said. 'His true name is probably not Mateaux, but this could be the man – by his appearance a Provençal, though passing for a Frenchman. He is most certainly not merely a vintner by profession, although it would provide excellent opportunities for his other activities – an excuse to travel without question, to enter the homes of noblemen and great men of the Church, even the Pope himself! What he can be doing in Oxford, I cannot conceive.'

'I have wondered whether he intended to meet de

Hungerford,' I suggested. 'It is not clear to me what the prior intended by his attack on the priory church. Was it merely to steal the treasures which had been put out of his reach, and which he had already begun to plunder? And if that was the case, did he intend to steal them simply for his own enrichment? Or had he some other purpose in mind? Could he and Mateaux be in some devilish scheme together?'

I realised I had not told her of the questions Mateaux had been asking about the priory, so I repeated what the steward had told me.

'He might have asked such questions because he needed to know where de Hungerford was held,' I said, 'so that he could release him.'

She nodded. 'That is certainly possible. Although I have heard nothing to connect de Hungerford with our man, or even with France. However, our information was very limited.'

She stood still and stared out over the river, which was flowing swiftly past our feet.

'How long does it take to reach London by boat?'

I was startled. 'I am not sure. Quicker than by road, I suppose. It would depend on whether the boat was rowed, or sailed, and the wind direction, the speed of the river . . . I am not the person to ask.'

'Not even London,' she said thoughtfully. 'Westminster, which is nearer. The king's court will be at Westminster.'

'Someone who could tell you is the merchant, Peter Winchingham,' I said. 'He brought his goods upriver from London, and his barge is moored at the jetty by Trill Mill.'

'He is trustworthy, you believe? And he is somewhat mired in this business already?'

'I believe him an honest man,' I said. 'He has shown himself so in all my dealings with him. And he was an old friend of my father-in-law, who was a shrewd judge of men.'

'Then let us consult him.' She turned sharply about

and began striding briskly up the meadow toward the wealthier part of the fair.

Although surprised at first, Peter Winchingham repeated my own qualifications as to how long the journey would take, given various conditions.

'However, downriver, with a sail and the wind in your favour, with oars when the twists of the river rob you of the wind, it may be done in a full day. Coming upriver, against current and wind, it can take a good deal longer.'

'Do you know where I might hire a boat?' Alice said.

Winchingham studied her thoughtfully, then looked at me, although he did not express what must be going through his mind – why a respectable middle aged woman, here selling ribbons at the fair, should have a sudden desire to make a hasty trip to Westminster.

I glanced at Alice, who gave me a brief nod.

I drew Winchingham and Alice out of hearing of his journeyman.

'As I have told you before, Mistress Walsea is employed by the king's court,' I said, 'and is concerned in this matter of the Frenchman. I now have his name and a description of his appearance, which seems to match yours. She is anxious that she should take word of it as soon as possible to those at court who will know how to proceed.'

He nodded briskly. 'Then there is no need to seek further, mistress,' he said. 'I am happy to place my own barge at your disposal, with two of my men to handle it. Free of its load, it will move fast, and it carries a large sail. At the moment the wind is from the west, which will serve you well. When would you start?'

'As soon as I have left word with the girl who helps on my stall. We have few goods left. She can close all up now and stay at Tackley's Inn until I return. Allow me half an hour.'

If Winchingham was surprised by such haste, he did not show it.

'It is near midday now,' he said. 'You cannot reach Westminster before dark, and it is not safe to continue through the night, too many hazards in the river. It will be necessary to tie up for the night and continue after dawn, but you should reach Westminster sometime tomorrow morning.'

'Very well. I thank you, Master Winchingham. I will send your men back as soon as they have delivered me. I am certain we will return by road. Now, if you will forgive me, I will see to my girl. In half an hour, at the Trill Mill jetty?'

Then she was gone. Winchingham and I looked at each other in some bemusement.

'She has been described as a formidable woman,' I said.

He laughed. 'Indeed. If I have but half an hour, I must hurry. I will see to provisioning the boat, for they will need food and drink. There are blankets on board, and there is a cabin, where the lady may be private. I will alert two of my best men.'

He was turning on his heel, when he paused. 'The fellow selling the priory's books came last evening. I have told him to return at noon, on the day following the fair, and I will have the coin ready for the books. We may seize him then.'

And he was away, almost running in his haste.

All of this had left me somewhat breathless, for I had not expected my information about Mateaux to stir Alice Walsea to such prompt action. However, it probably meant that she would bring back with her a party of men from amongst the king's closest advisors, who would have the authority to arrest the Frenchman on some pretext or other, before he could carry out whatever crime he was planning. If we were right in conjecturing that he might try to release de Hungerford, I was sure that Sheriff Walden's men could easily prevent any such attempt.

Curiously, I felt disappointed, as though, having fulfilled my small part by discovering the identity of the Frenchman, I was no longer of any use. I wished I might be setting off on a desperate voyage down river to

Westminster, to bring news to the king. Instead, here I was, standing stranded in St Frideswide's Fair, where some of the stallholders were shouting the bargains they were offering, now the fair was nearing its end, and the bear keeper's boy was calling out the time of the dancing bear's next performance.

Then I shook myself. I was being absurd. Let the king's intelligencer take the matter in hand. When I reached home, I would send another message to the sheriff, apprising him of what was afoot. In the meantime, however, I had other errands to undertake.

On my way out of the fairground, I asked the gatekeeper if he knew which play was to be performed that afternoon by the travelling players.

'Why, maister, I do believe 'tis to be the story of our St Frideswide herself, though how they mean to make a play of that, I do not know.'

I went on, satisfied. This would certainly not be the kind of lewd piece that Margaret feared. The players would surely not dare to insult the saint at her own fair, beside her own priory, and close by her own tomb. I hoped Emma would consent to come with me, to see what they made of the story.

I set off up Fish Street to the narrow alleyway near the Guildhall that led to John Shippan's carpentry workshop. He had urged me to come and see how the desk I had ordered was progressing, but I had not found time before this. And now that I had so much idle time on my hands, I thought I would call in.

His journeyman directed me again up the rickety steps to the workshop where Shippan did his final finishing of the better pieces, and I found him there, squatting down and rubbing wax into the legs of a beautiful desk.

'Is that mine?' I said, suddenly rescued from my gloomy mood.

'Aye, Master Elyot, 'tis that,' he said, straightening himself and standing up with a small groan. 'Eh, I'm not so limber as I once was.' He stroked the softly glowing wood as if it were a child's head. 'I haven't affixed the movable shelf yet. I've still to wax that, for 'tis easier done before 'tis in place.'

'Aye, I can see,' I said, 'for it would swing about.'

I walked round the desk, admiring it from all sides. Shippan watched me anxiously. ''Tis as you wanted?' he asked.

'Better, far better, than I could have imagined.'

I ran my fingers over the silken finish of the writing surface. The stand raised above and behind this, to hold the text to be copied, was set at just the right angle, with two cords of gold silk ending in brass weights to hold the book open at the required page. There were five holes on each side of this stand, stepped one above the other, to hold pots of coloured paints, while along the back edge of the writing surface there was a trough for quills, a wooden cup to hold more quills, and a hole at either end for the pots of scribing inks – one for black and one for red.

'This is the movable shelf,' he said, taking it up from his workbench.

Although it was not yet waxed, it was otherwise complete, and he had made two neat little lidded boxes, one to hold the thin sheets of gold foil, one to hold the pellets of gesso, which fitted into their own square slots on this shelf.

'You are a marvel amongst master craftsmen,' I said. 'I have never seen such a beautiful desk. I shall be jealous of my scrivener now, and want its fellow for myself.'

Shippan looked embarrassed at this praise, so I became businesslike.

'When will it be ready for me to collect?' I said.

'Two-three days. I can deliver it for you.'

I wanted that pleasure for myself. 'Will it be too heavy for me to carry?'

'Aye, likely. I can lend you a hand cart.'

I suspected that I was not his first customer who could not wait to lay hands on a beautiful purchase.

'I'll call round for it then. It is beautiful, John. I am grateful to you.'

He blustered out something in protest, but truly I was in awe at his skill. The carvings alone, of trailing vines and flowers, were as fine in their way as the border of a manuscript. They would not disgrace a cathedral.

On my way out, I paused. 'How does that parrot fare, with the perch you made for him?'

Shippan grimaced. 'The bird was delighted. He liked it so much, he has been nibbling away at it ever since, till he has created some fine new decoration of his own. The lady has requested a new perch, but I declined regretfully. I have no wish to spend my life making that foul creature a whetstone for his beak. I told her to fetch him a dead branch from the woods. He will enjoy the rough bark all the more.'

Laughing, I left the workshop and went cheerfully on my way, hoping I could contain my eagerness to burst out with a description of the desk before time, though it would be a sore trial of my patience.

In St Mildred Street, I found Emma and Juliana elbow deep in washtubs. Emma wiped her hot face with the back of a soapy wrist and apologised.

'I fear you find us in some disarray, Nicholas. We have been all at sixes and sevens with the fair. This washing should have been done yesterday, for we are near out of clean linen, and now we are more than halfway through the day, with it still not finished. Will you take a sup with us?'

I could see that they were far too busy to entertain an idle visitor and she asked merely from politeness, so I shook my head. 'I came only to ask if you would like to come to the play with me this afternoon? At four o'the clock. 'Tis the story of St Frideswide. Or perhaps you are too busy with your washing?'

'Nay, 'twill all be spread out to dry by then.'

I realised that I must not ignore Juliana. 'Would you like to come?' I said, turning to her.

'Nay, I must mind Maysant,' she said. 'Let Emma go with you. She has worked far harder than I these last days.'

I could not help but notice a certain knowing smile she gave Emma.

Firmly ignoring it, I said, 'I will come for you half an hour before, if that will suit?'

'I will be ready,' she said.

As I made my way home, my mood was quite lifted. By now Alice Walsea would be on her way down the Thames in Peter Winchingham's barge, helped along by a brisk autumn breeze. I knew by repute that the river did not lay a straight course to Westminster and London, but below Oxford it abandoned its whimsical wanderings which fretted the town in its web of waterways. And with the flow of the Cherwell joined to it at the edge of the meadows where the fair stood, there was a goodly body of water to carry the barge along. They would tie up for the night somewhere on the way, then reach Westminster tomorrow, where Alice could entrust the matter of Claude Mateaux and his doings to an authority higher even than Sheriff Walden.

De Hungerford was in the hands of the sheriff, and I hoped that, between us, Walden, Winchingham, and I could arrest the rogue selling the stolen books the day after the fair. All of this was cause for satisfaction. As for the murder of Hamo Belancer, that too would be the responsibility of those Alice would be bringing from Westminster. I could shake off all responsibility in these unpleasant affairs. Once the fair was over, life would take up its normal course, I could reopen the shop, and the university term would begin in earnest.

I must give some thought to this book of troubadour songs, ordered by Lady Amilia. I knew few, and there must be someone in Oxford who would know more. You could always find someone in Oxford who was deeply learned in a subject, however unlikely and obscure.

It was long past the dinner hour when I reached home. Margaret was in the garden, lifting the last of the carrots, with some uncertain help from the children, so I found a leftover cold pasty and took it into the shop, where

Walter and Roger were sorting the *peciae*, ready for our reopening in two days' time.

I told them about the order for a song book. 'I shall be expecting your help,' I said. 'Any troubadour songs you know, I shall want words and music.'

They both looked dubious.

'I am not one for songs,' Walter said.

Roger grinned. 'I could sing you many a good English song, the sort you can hear any evening in the taverns, but French songs? Nay, I think not. And I doubt Lady Amilia would approve of our good rousing English songs.'

'I have a very clear idea of your good rousing English songs, Roger,' I said. 'I hardly think Mistress Makepeace would approve of them, either. You have the right of it. They will not do. The troubadour songs are mostly not even French, they are in the *langue d'Oc*, the language spoken in the far south, Provence. Very different from French. I fear this will be a task almost beyond me.'

'What you need,' Walter said, 'is a troubadour.'

'Not easily come by in Oxford,' I said. 'Now, you may both be off early today. We shall be busy enough when we reopen, the day after tomorrow. Roger, before you go home, I want you to take a letter to Sheriff Walden at the castle.'

Sitting at my desk, I quickly set out Alice Walsea's plans and the loan of Peter Winchingham's barge to reach Westminster by river. However well she fared, I did not believe she would be able to reach Oxford by road, with reinforcements from the king's court, the following day, not even by nightfall, and nightfall came ever earlier now that we were near the end of October. It would be the day after that when she would return, at the earliest. The day after the fair.

I folded and sealed my letter, stamping the soft wax with my seal, and gave it to Roger to deliver.

'And now,' I told them, 'I am going to make my last visit to the fair, to see the play with Mistress Thorgold.'

I ignored their leers and winks as I let myself out of the shop.

Emma was ready and waiting when I reached St Mildred Street, a little before the time I had appointed, and we set off down the slight slope of Fish Street to the fairground.

'It is strange to think that all this will vanish away again in a few days' time,' she said, as we passed freely through the gateway. Canon Aubery had ruled that no entrance fee was to be charged for the remaining time of the fair.

'It is like those visions the crusaders spoke of seeing in the eastern deserts,' she went on, 'when they were sure that trees and water were to be found just over the next rise in ground, but when they topped the higher ground, all had vanished and there was nothing but the dry and lifeless land stretching ahead of them.'

'It is called a mirage,' I said. 'Some believe they are conjured up by devils to drive men mad, who are already exhausted and dying of thirst.'

She nodded seriously. 'I could believe that. Or perhaps they are a kindly vision sent by God, to encourage travellers not to abandon themselves to despair, for in the end, there *will* be water, and shade, and safety.'

I smiled at her. 'Let us incline to that belief, then. I am feeling more optimistic today, after a week of alarms and ill deeds.'

'I have hardly seen you,' she said, slipping her arm through mine. 'We have both been so busy about our separate affairs. Mine have been very dull, although our earnings have been excellent. Tell me about yours.'

It was difficult, but I tried not to show how the warmth of her arm against mine affected me, and the brushing of her skirts against my hose. As we made our way past the stalls and along below the town wall, I told her all that had been happening, from Peter Winchingham's first visit to the shop, to Alice Walsea's departure down the river to Westminster. By the time I had finished, we had walked past the bear's dancing ring to the stage erected by the players, backing on to the town wall, some yards further on. Just behind this portion of the wall lay the grounds of Merton College. The bear had given his last performance for the day, and all the crowds here had come for the play.

'She must be a very brave woman, this Alice Walsea,' Emma said thoughtfully.

'Aye, I believe she is. I know very little about her work as an intelligencer. Selling ribbons at our fair was not dangerous, but living in the Mordon household, where she might have been discovered by the murderer of her cousin, was very perilous indeed.'

She pressed my arm. 'However it all turns out, I am glad you are out of danger, Nicholas.'

In some ways this gratified me, but I also had a niggling sense that I cut a somewhat pathetic figure, leaving the murder of Hamo Belancer and the attack on the priory, and whatever additional crimes might be brewing, in the hands of others, and one of them a woman.

However, there was no time to brood on it, for a player had stepped forward on to the stage, emerging from between curtains hung at the back. They had a space there, between the curtains and the wall, which must serve them as a changing place, and allowed them their entrances and their exits.

The player raised a trumpet to his lips and played a short fanfare. The crowd, which had been milling about and chattering, fell silent and drew close to the stage. We had managed to secure a spot near the front, which would give us a good view of everything.

'*Know, good people of Oxford,*' the player said, pitching his voice clearly, so that it could be heard by those at the very back, '*that we come to present to you the story of Oxford's own dear saint, St Frideswide, a Saxon princess, daughter of Dida of Eynsham. Now this Dida was a king, but a king over a small kingdom, and he answered to his overlord, King Algar, ruler of all the great lands of Mercia, as the central part of England was known in those far off days.'*

Someone behind us whispered loudly, 'I did not come for a lesson in history.'

Several people hushed him.

'*Now*,' said the player, ignoring the interruption, '*the princess Frideswide, or Frithuswith as some called her, was an exceptionally beautiful child, but she also loved God above all else, and we begin her story one day when she came to her father, while still a young girl.*'

The player drew one of the curtains aside, and King Dida stepped on to the stage. He wore a long robe of rich crimson, trimmed with fur and with what looked very convincingly like thread of gold embroidery. He wore a crown, but a discreet, modest crown (probably brass) studded with 'rubies' and 'emeralds'.

King Dida was followed on to the stage by the princess. This was the crucial moment. The women's parts were always played by boys or men, sometimes with unfortunate and ludicrous results. I hardly dared to look up.

The players had found the perfect boy for the part. He was perhaps thirteen or fourteen, with a voice not yet broken, and a face as sweet as one of the carved angels in St Frideswide's church. He was clad entirely, and simply, in white, with a thin circlet of gold atop a head of thick chestnut curls. I glanced down at Emma. She was smiling.

The princess told her father that she had sworn herself to God and to celibacy, and begged that he would enable her to build a monastery.

'*In Oxford*,' she said, '*close by the sweet waters of the Thames, where both men and women may live a holy life, devoting themselves to God's worship.*'

King Dida promised that he would help her, if she was quite certain that she wished to give up the world. '*For you are yet young, and know nothing of men.*'

'*I know that men can be as devout as women*,' the girl said, innocently.

The king shook his head, and smiled, but he agreed that he had a plot of land which he would give her. Here he made a grand gesture in the direction of the present day St Frideswide's Priory.

Plans for founding the monastery went ahead, and the two retired behind the curtain to consult.

Their place was taken by a big, swarthy man, bearded, and dressed all in black, but magnificent black, real velvet, I thought, with much richer fur trimmings to his robe than those of King Dida. Likewise his crown was a splendid affair, its height making him even more imposing and intimidating.

'*King Algar am I,*' he announced, in scornful tones, '*though some call me Æthelbald. All of Mercia I hold in my hands, and all my subjects must obey my will, or die. They tell me that the daughter of my subject king Dida is the fairest maid in all the world, yet she would hide herself away in a nunnery. It shall not be so, for I WILL have her, though she flee from me.*'

He swaggered across the stage and departed, through another gap in the curtains, accompanied by a chorus of hissing and booing from the crowd.

The first player, the one I thought of as the storyteller, returned to the stage. Behind him, some others from the company brought out a wickerwork frame, on to which green branches had been tied and woven. They set it up to the left of the stage, and slipped away.

'*Alas,*' the storyteller announced, '*the Princess Frideswide must flee before her monastery is complete, for the evil Algar has come to Oxford, intent on carrying her off against her will. She must escape him.*'

The princess appeared on the stage, gasping breathlessly and pressing her hands to her chest, then she fell on her knees, and raised her clasped hands to the sky. '*Heavenly Father, I beseech you, save me from the clutches of the wicked King of Mercia.*'

She scrambled to her feet. '*I must hide me. I shall flee to the Wychwood. There, he surely will not find me.*'

She hid behind the branches, and only just in time, for Algar strode on, swearing in a most unroyal manner, stamping about the stage and looking everywhere except behind the bushes.

He turned to the audience. '*Where is she, you misbegotten churls? I'll hang you, every last man of you, if you keep her hidden.*'

These threats were met by jeers from the audience, and he stormed out in a rage. Almost at once, from the other side of the stage, there entered a decent looking couple who, from their plain homespun attire, were country folk.

'*She is hereabouts, I am sure,*' the man said. He had a strong resemblance to King Dida, but surely it could not be, for he had sprouted a fine, full golden beard.

'*Come forth, my maid,*' the woman said, '*us'll care for ye. Be not afraid.*'

At this the princess emerged from her hiding place and the three went off together. The storyteller, who had remained quietly at the side of the stage, stepped forward again.

'*The princess remained some while with the farmer and his wife, tending the sheep and pigs, cooking and sweeping and mending the fire. As a princess, she had never done such things, but she was humble, and learned willingly. Then word came that she was sorely needed back at the monastery in Oxford, so with many tears she bade the kindly couple farewell and set off on the road back to Oxford. But alas!*'

Here he gave a great shout. '*Algar heard that she was on her way, and pursued her, even to the edge of Oxford itself!*'

At this point, a rumpus broke out at the back of the audience, and everyone strained to see what was happening. Suddenly we glimpsed a slender, copper-headed figure desperately thrusting through the crowd toward the stage. Somehow the princess had slipped around from the stage without our noticing it, and now was here amongst us. Close behind her came Algar. He had almost reached her.

'*People of Oxford,*' the storyteller on the stage cried

out, '*will you let this evil man catch the maid?*'

We all knew the story. '*Never!*' we shouted.

Hands reached out to grab Algar. Someone tried to trip him up, but somehow he fought his way through and climbed awkwardly on to the stage close behind the princess who turned to face him, her hands clasped in prayer.

Algar gave a great cry and fell to his knees. '*I am blind! I cannot see! Lord God, forgive me, I swear I will not touch the maid.*'

A great cheer went up from the audience, as the blinded and humbled Algar groped his way off the stage. Once he had gone, the princess departed, behind a different curtain. The narrator resumed.

'*Princess Frideswide completed the building of her monastery, and her fame grew, not only amongst her beloved people of Oxford, but far and wide throughout Mercia. Then one day, there came to her a nun from Binsey.*'

The princess returned to the stage, now with an abbess's habit over her white gown, a crozier in her hand. A nun, accompanying her, turned to her, pleading.

'*Reverend Mother,*' she said, in a voice not unlike the farmer's wife's, '*we are greatly troubled in our nunnery by lack of water. We have no well, and every drop we use must be carried a long, long way. Many hours which should be spent in prayer are wasted in the endless fetching of water.*'

'*We need only ask of Our Father,*' the princess – now an abbess – reassured her. '*Behold!*'

She tapped three times hard on the stage with her crozier and suddenly a spout of water shot into the air from behind the bushy branches. There was a gasp of amazement from the crowd, as the nun raised her hands in joyful wonder. The abbess blessed her, and they retired from the stage.

'*And so,*' the storyteller said, '*St Frideswide ended her days in the monastery she had built, where today stands the Priory of St Frideswide, and where, from her tomb, she still watches over all her beloved people of Oxford.'*

He withdrew, to rapturous cheers from the audience, who were delighted to have our own saintliness – in saving the young saint from the lecherous king – so publicly acknowledged. Perhaps the high tone of the piece was a little marred when two of the players came round collecting our approval in silver coins.

'How do you suppose they contrived the fountain?' Emma said, as she took my arm and we began to walk back toward the fair.

'Best not to ask, you will spoil the illusion.'

She laughed. 'Well, the play was not the work of a great poet, but they told a noble story with respect and piety.'

'They did. And they made us all feel that we were there, protecting innocence and purity against evil and cruelty.' I sighed. 'I wish it were that easy.'

She was quiet until we had passed out through the gatehouse.

'I suppose for some women, the monastic life is the fulfilment of a dream. It lifts them on to some higher plane, brings them closer to God. Do you suppose it is something lacking in me, Nicholas, that I could not feel that?'

'We are all different,' I said. 'We must all find our way through this life in our own way. I do not see why we should not be close to God, even living a secular life.'

'You are probably right.' She smiled at me. 'Last day of the fair tomorrow, and I must work hard.'

'I shall see you home afterwards,' I said. 'Oxford is apt to turn rough at the end of the fair, when the youths of the town suddenly realise that the holiday they have grumbled about has come to an end. They will be taking their last chance to get cup-shotten and roar about the streets. 'Twill be no place for a woman.'

'There is no need for you to see me home.'

I shook my head. 'I shall come for you.'

Chapter Ten

The final day of St Frideswide's Fair had arrived. As is so often the case, the end of any long festival is a mixture of relief and sadness. All those buyers who had hesitated over purchases had second thoughts and hurried back to the remembered stall, either to find a bargain or be faced with disappointment. The stall was gone! Nothing left but a gap in the street of stalls, some abandoned litter, some trampled grass. Up and down the fairground, the stallholders, their feet aching, their voices hoarse, were trying to sell the last of their goods at unreasonably low prices, to avoid carrying them back again to London or York or Wales or Brabant. Tonight they would celebrate at the town's taverns and inns, which would now be free to entertain all comers again, and many would spend perhaps too much of their earnings.

Sadness could be felt in the air, too, at the end of one of the town's greatest entertainments. To be sure, we had our own feasts and festivals, but only at this one time of the year could we gape at the foreign merchants and their exotic goods, marvel at the Babel of foreign tongues, and wonder wistfully about the strange places they would return to, which we would never see. And there was something melancholy in watching the bright fairground city gradually being dismantled and vanishing away, for many of the merchants would not linger even to the end of the final day. If trade had been good, and they had a long journey before them, some would pack up their remaining stock early, to make a start on the way to their homes or to the next great fair, leaving the streets of stalls looking like an old man's gap-toothed grin.

First thing in the morning, before she set off for her last turn of duty at the fair, I asked Margaret what I could do to help.

'Shall you need more hands to pack up your goods this evening?' I said.

She shook her head. 'There will be enough of us, and little left of our stock. We have decided to stay until the trumpet is blown to close the fair. Our small pots of preserves and our sweetmeats are the sort of thing folk will buy at the last minute, not like some costly saddlery or several bolts of silk damask. Those are the serious purchases, all made by now. But even the great merchants, as they prepare to close down, may buy a bag of comfits for a wife or sweetheart.'

I laughed. 'You have become a shrewd merchant yourself, this last week.'

'I think I shall not do it again next year,' she said seriously, 'though when we come to share out what we have earned, it will be good to have the extra chinks.'

I nodded. In the ordinary way of things, Margaret had only what I could give her from the takings of the shop, after my scriveners had been paid and my necessary materials purchased. I could understand that she might be glad to have in her hand money of her own.

'And Roger will bring Mary's handcart, to fetch away everything?'

'He will. And then we must pay him for sleeping in our booth every night, on guard. It cannot have been comfortable, and after the fire at the gatehouse it cannot have been restful.'

'Nay, I have said that I would pay Roger. It was my suggestion that he should be your night watchman, and I shall pay him.'

She argued a little at this, but I was firm.

'Alysoun is a little envious of Rafe's monkey,' she

said. 'Master Winchingham's blue linsey-woolsey is beautiful, but she cannot play with it.'

'I thought, if you do not need me, that I would take them for a final visit to the fair. Peter Winchingham told me about the stall where he bought the monkey. We could see whether there is a small toy I might buy for each of them.'

She nodded. 'Aye, but do not let them persuade you to spend too much. And I shall see you at supper time.'

'Before that. I have said I will come to fetch Emma and escort her home. You know how it can be in town after the fair. The rest of you are familiar with Oxford, and with how to avoid the trouble spots, but she is a stranger here.'

'She would be quite safe with us, I think. There will be Mary, Beatrice, Maud and I, as well as Roger with the cart. But, if you have promised–'

'I have. So I will see you then.'

The children were delighted at the prospect of another visit to the fair, although I warned them that I had heard the dancing bear had already left. Rowan was handed over to Walter to mind, and before we left I sent Alysoun to fetch Jonathan Baker to come with us. I did not think the boy had had any chance to visit the fair, and his father would not need his help until he prepared the dough in the evening, ready for tomorrow, the first fresh baking in a week.

With my troupe of children, I made my way to the fairground for almost the last time, and stopped first to buy a comfit each for them from Emma.

'I shall be here shortly after the fair closes,' I said. 'I know you must help to pack up, but it will be dark soon afterwards.'

'There is no need, Nicholas. I shall be quite safe with the others.'

'You will be even safer with me.'

She raised her eyebrows. 'You will be carrying a sword, then?'

'No need,' I said. 'My very presence will be enough

to affright any Oxford rogues.'

At which she laughed and shrugged, but did not attempt to dissuade me further.

Next, the children and I called on Peter Winchingham, who was supervising the wrapping of his fine cloths in canvas covers, keeping just a few on display to show to any late buyers.

'Where shall you store your goods until your barge is returned?' I asked. 'They can hardly bring it upriver until late tomorrow.'

'Nay, not that soon. The day after that, at least,' he said, 'with the current against them and the wind in their faces. I have made an arrangement with the Mitre. They have a storeroom we can use – the place is like a coney warren! My men will start moving some of my stock this morning, and we will have all stowed away before the fair closes. For the last hour I shall just be selling my ends of bolts, small lengths for children's clothes, mostly.'

'I will tell my sister.'

'And you will be with me at the Mitre, midday tomorrow?'

'Aye, and the sheriff too,' I said. 'Let us hope your fellow with the books suspects nothing.'

'Not as yet, I think. And I may leave much of my stock at the Mitre for now. If I am to move my business to England, there is little point in shipping it all over to Bruges again. I shall go back to arrange matters finally with my son, and stay for his wedding, but then I plan to move to England, with my daughter and my younger son, before winter sets in. The crossing is unpleasant in the bad weather.'

'It will be good to have you nearby.' I grinned. 'Perhaps I can help you to build up your library.'

He laughed. 'Perhaps you can.'

I sent Alysoun running back to tell Margaret about the bargains in short lengths of cloth, while I asked for directions to the Bavarian toy stall.

Like all the best merchants, the Bavarians, a husband

and wife, had sold most of their stock, but, confronted by three eager children, they cheerfully laid out what was left. Jonathan was immediately drawn to a slingshot, and I thought nervously of his neighbours' reaction, were he to be let loose armed with such a weapon. Seeing my alarm, the woman brought out from below the counter a carved box.

'See. Can you open?' she asked, in a thick accent.

'Of course!' Jonathan said scornfully. He began to wrestle with it and the woman winked at me.

While he was struggling, Alysoun was fingering everything laid out on the counter. Like Jonathan, she wanted a slingshot, but I shook my head firmly. There was another monkey like Rafe's, which she picked up and set climbing up its stick, but clearly she wanted to be different from her little brother.

Jonathan was turning the box over and over, running his fingernail over the carving, searching for an opening.

'Can I have that top?' Rafe asked.

'Do you know how to make it spin?' I asked.

'Maysant has one, and I can spin that.'

At least we had one decision. Alysoun finally picked up, to my surprise, a wooden doll with a painted face, which viewed the world with surprise. It was jointed simply at shoulders and hips, and dressed rather crudely in clothes similar to the woman's – exotic, foreign, and, I supposed, Bavarian. Alysoun had never before shown an interest in dolls, but I tried to hide my surprise.

'Juliana has a doll like this,' she said, 'only not as pretty. She says her brother William gave it to her when she was little, so she will keep it always. If I have this, I will keep it always, and remember the fair and the dancing bear.'

'You make clothes, Ja?' the woman said.

Alysoun nodded. 'My aunt has a whole basket of scraps.'

'It is gut.'

'I can't do it,' Jonathan said, in a dispirited voice, and

handed the box back to the woman.

The man took it from her. 'You see? Like so.' With a few quick twists that we could barely follow, he had opened the box to show three separate compartments. 'Now you.'

Jonathan tried again, and succeeded in opening one.

'I show you.'

They put their heads together and the man patiently took Jonathan through the movements.

'You keep secrets here, Ja? No one sees.'

'Aye!' Jonathan's eyes were shining.

I turned to the woman. 'The box, the doll, and the top,' I said, 'and I need one more.'

I picked up a beautifully carved dog. Its legs and tail were jointed, and its head could be set at a whimsical angle, but its real appeal lay in its lifelike appearance and especially its face, which was friendly and eager.

'This dog as well,' I said. 'For Stephen.'

I saw that Alysoun was now wishing she had noticed the dog.

'You know that Stephen would like to have a real dog, Alysoun,' I said, 'but he could not manage. It would probably knock him over, and he could not walk with it. You have Rowan. We will give Stephen this dog. It can sit beside his books when he is studying, and it will never need feeding.'

She smiled, and slipped her hand in mine. 'That is well thought on, Papa.'

'We shall take it to him this very afternoon.'

The rest of the day seemed to pass very slowly. As soon as we reached home, Jonathan ran off to show his box to his father, and no doubt puzzle him with its trick openings. I did not know what treasures he meant to keep in it, but children should be allowed to keep their secrets.

We ate the cold dinner Margaret had left for us, then walked down to the East Gate, and Beatrice's cottage. The sight of Stephen's face when I gave him the carved toy would have been worth a hundred wooden dogs. I saw tears in Beatrice's eyes as she turned away, but then she became very brisk, urging the children into the garden to feed the hens.

'Not that they need feeding, Nicholas,' she said, 'but I think Stephen is quite numb with gratitude, and 'tis best he has something to do. He has names for all the hens, you know, so I shall never be able to kill one for the pot, even if they stop laying.'

'He is looking much stronger, since our time in the country,' I said.

'Aye, he is. I believe he has even grown a little taller. And he continues to use just one crutch.'

'Do you think the leg is any stronger?'

'It must be, or he would still need both crutches. Sometimes he even rests a little weight on the toe.'

'Perhaps,' I said, 'one day he will walk without a crutch.'

She smiled, but shook her head. 'I pray so, every day, but I cannot believe it, for the leg is wasted, and twisted awry. I have thought of making a pilgrimage to Canterbury, but it would be difficult.'

'You could always appeal to our own St Frideswide.'

I gave her an account of the play Emma and I had seen the day before, until I had her laughing.

'And how do you suppose they made the fountain spring up?' she said.

'That I cannot imagine. It was spectacular, but, I suspect, not miraculous. They say the spring at Binsey still exists, and its waters have curative powers.'

The children came in then, Alysoun bearing a large brown egg cupped in her hands, which Beatrice said she must take for her supper. She found another for Rafe, and I placed them carefully in my scrip to carry home. Clearly Beatrice's eggs must be better than our own.

At last evening began to steal in, and it was time to fetch Emma away from the fair. Walter had agreed to stay with the children until Margaret returned, promising to tell them one of his mother's stories to keep them occupied.

'Nothing alarming,' I warned, 'that might keep them awake, or Margaret will skin us both.'

'Never fear,' he said, 'I have a-plenty that are not fearful.'

I considered changing into a better cotte and hose, then laughed at myself for a fool. Emma would either notice, and mock me, or fail to notice (for it would be dark) and my efforts would be wasted. As I slung my cloak round my shoulders, I told myself I was not some coltish boy, but a grown man with a business and a family to support. I was escorting Emma home merely because the streets of Oxford were always dangerous after the fair.

Indeed, there was already something of an air of menace in the streets before I even came to the fairground. The trumpet to close the fair sounded as I reached the gate, timed to ring out as the priory bells chimed for Vespers. The half charred gatehouse was almost dismantled, and there was chaos within, as stalls were being folded and stacked, merchants loaded their goods on to carts, and both merchants and late buyers jostled their way out to the street.

I found Margaret and the others well organised, their few unsold goods loaded into the handcart, together with some of Peter Winchingham's short lengths of cloth. Margaret, Beatrice, and Maud had all taken advantage of his late bargains. Mary was checking that everything had been cleared away inside, while one of the priory's lay servants stood waiting to collect the key to the booth. These more substantial structures would be dismantled during the next few days, after everyone had gone, and stored away in one of the priory's barns over at the grange, until next year's fair.

I noticed that Roger had brought two friends with him.

'Aye,' he said, when I mentioned this. 'I thought it seemed best. With three of us, we can fend off any light fingered churls who think to steal the mistress's goods.'

'Very sensible,' I said.

'Do you need Emma any longer?' I asked Margaret. I knew if I asked Emma herself, she would insist that she still had work to do.

'We are quite finished,' Margaret said. 'There is nothing more except to settle matters with the priory servant.'

I walked over to where Emma was talking to Roger's friends.

'Come,' I said. 'There is such a crowd, it will takes us some time to make our way through. Margaret says you are finished, and it is growing quite dark.'

I spoke no more than the truth, for clouds had crept over the sky almost without my noticing it, so that now the rising moon and the stars were quite blotted out and there was a thunderous feeling in the air. The good weather, which had held for the fair, might break at any moment. If there was to be a thunder storm, I hoped that Walter would be able to reassure Rafe.

'Have you a cloak?' I asked, as Emma turned to me.

'I never thought to bring one this morning,' she said. 'It was fine then, and the sun was quite warm.'

'Well, if the rain starts before we reach St Mildred Street, you may borrow mine.'

She took my arm as we tried to force our way back to the gate, but the crowd had grown thicker even in the short time I had been in the fairground. Everyone had suddenly realised the threat of those looming clouds and was pushing through the gateway, so that the crowd was like a river forced through the narrows. Unlike a river, however, it moved more slowly, not faster. As well as those who simply wanted to avoid a soaking, there were stallholders whose goods would suffer in the rain.

The priory servants had lit the pitch torches on either side of the gate, but the wind was getting up, so that the flames streamed out almost horizontally, scattering sparks which caused the crowd to bunch together even more. Their flickering light made the growing dark seem even darker. We were through the gate at last, and then through the South Gate of the town, and into Fish Street, but, if anything, here it was even worse. More of the larger, horse-drawn carts were ahead of us, as well as dozens of handcarts and the close pressed mass of people. There was hardly any forward movement at all.

'We shall never be home before the storm breaks,' Emma said, shrinking a little closer to me as she was shoved aside by a burly packman leading a laden mule.

'You have the right of it,' I said, 'if we stay on Fish Street. But there is a better way. Do you see St Aldate's Church there, just ahead, on the left? Across the street from it, on the right, there is a narrow lane which leads past the front of St Frideswide's Priory. If we go that way, we can turn up past Oriel College, and reach the High Street much more easily. It will bring us out not far from St Mildred Street. The way is too narrow for any of these carts, and most of the crowd are like sheep, anyway, all flocking along Fish Street. We shall slip around them.'

She nodded, and held my arm a little tighter as a cluster of rowdy youths pushed past us.

My plan was a good one, but for a time I was not sure I should be able to carry it out, for several of the carts had become entangled ahead of us, just before the church, and from the shouting and swearing, battle seemed likely to commence at any moment. I drew Emma over to the very edge of the street on the right, and we began to worm our way past the bulk of the crowd, which was now stationary, and not liking it. Some of them objected to what seemed to be our attempt to get to the front of the pack, but at last we reached the opening into the lane. I pulled Emma firmly into the dark tunnel, and we both paused for breath.

'I can hardly see,' she said.

Indeed, after Fish Street, where there were plenty of lanterns and torches lit beside the doorways of the big shops and houses, with even more further ahead, where the Guildhall stood, the lane seemed very dark.

'Our eyes will soon grow accustomed,' I said. 'And look, not far along, you can see the gleam of the torches beside the priory gatehouse.'

She nodded. I think she had been truly alarmed by the roughness and ill temper of the crowd.

'Let us carry on,' she said. 'I am glad to be out of that–'

It seemed she could not find the right word. I reminded myself that for over a year she had lived in the quiet and seclusion of Godstow Abbey. Before that, she had only known her grandfather's manor and then that of her stepfather. Although she had now spent a few months in Oxford, she had no experience of a town crowd in a bad mood.

'We'll soon be safe at St Mildred Street,' I said cheerfully, 'having circumnavigated them all. Let us hope Juliana will have some supper ready for you. I fear it will be a long time before your aunt reaches home.'

'I hope they will be safe.'

'I am certain of it. They will have the sense to wait until all this hurly-burly disperses. Had I shown some sense, we could have slipped through the priory's postern gate, and gone that way. I am known there, they would not have minded.'

We began to feel our way along the lane, which was very roughly cobbled, so that we were in danger of tripping in the dark, if we did not watch our feet – which we could barely see. As we drew nearer to the priory, we could hear the chanting of the service for Vespers, although the sound came fitfully, for the wind suddenly gathered speed and flung the first of the rain in our faces, not in a fine scattering of drops, but a hard fistful, mixed with sleet.

I stopped. 'Here. Put on my cloak.'

I wrapped it around her shoulders, but she objected.

'You will be soaked to the very skin, Nicholas. It is wide enough to shelter us both.'

She insisted on drawing me in under the shelter of the cloak, and although that meant that neither of us was entirely dry, neither of us was entirely wet. With the darkness and the driving rain and the broken cobbles, we made very poor, stumbling progress along the lane. There were a few small houses here, which I think belonged to the priory and may have been used to house their servants, but all were in darkness now. Probably the lay servants were occupied in closing up the fair, those who were not on duty in the priory itself, in the kitchen, for the canons would take their supper after Vespers.

We were, I suppose, about ten yards from the priory gatehouse, or a little more, with its welcoming pool of light cast by the gate torches, when I thought I saw a furtive movement. A man, silhouetted against the light. I did not like the look of him, or the way he moved. I stopped, holding Emma back. She was quick to sense that something was wrong.

'What is it, Nicholas?' she whispered. 'Why have you stopped?'

I put my lips close to her ear.

'There is something suspicious about that fellow. There. About halfway between us and the gate.'

Like the torches by the fairground, the priory torches were also twisted and wrenched by the wind. When the nearer one flared suddenly up, with a burst of sparks, I caught a brief glimpse of the man's face. Even in the poor light I could see that he was swarthy of complexion, with thick black eyebrows which nearly met over his nose. Unconsciously I gripped Emma's arm tighter.

'What's amiss?' she whispered, so low that I could hardly hear her.

'I think it is the man I have been seeking,' I said. 'The Frenchman Alice Walsea was warned about. The vintner who was known to Hamo Belancer, and almost certainly the man who struck down Peter Winchingham and murdered Belancer.'

'How can you know?'

'I cannot be certain, but he matches the descriptions given by Winchingham, and the priory cellarer, and the steward. Surely there cannot be two such. And why is he lurking here? If he was about some honest business, he would walk up to the gatehouse and declare it.'

I slipped out from under the cloak and wrapped it round her.

'Stay here. I am going a little closer, to try and see what's afoot.'

She laid her hand on my arm. 'Be careful, Nicholas!'

'I will. Stay in the shadows.'

I made my way cautiously forward. Fortunately by now I had gained my night vision, and the warm, if erratic, light from the torches meant that I was less likely to stumble.

Ahead of me, the man was groping his way slowly in the direction of the gatehouse, but with one hand braced against the priory wall. Then he stopped.

I froze. Had he heard me?

The figure stooped and seemed to be feeling for something on the ground. Then I heard a scraping sound, as of metal on stone. What could he be doing?

And then he disappeared.

One moment he was there, a figure clearly outlined against the light, bent over, and the next moment he was gone. The erratic light from the torches flowed toward me unimpeded by any intervening shape.

'What is happening?'

Emma had come up behind me so silently that I felt my heart jerk in momentary panic.

'He has disappeared. I am going closer.'

She clutched my sleeve for a moment, then let it go.

One cautious step at a time, I moved forward, until I thought I was near the place where the man had been standing, and I stopped.

Perhaps it was the blessed St Frideswide herself who laid her hand on me and made me halt, for had I gone two more steps, I would probably have been killed. No more than a yard in front of me, there was a patch of greater darkness in the dark of the cobbles. I squatted down and felt out with my hand. A hole. A great hole. But this was not some accidental pit in the street. It was squared off. I could feel chiselled and shaped masonry blocks around the edges. And just beyond the hole, lying on the ground, a square of metal, glinting faintly. That must be what the man had moved. The cover of the hole. A draught of cold air rose up into my face from the hole, and I sensed, rather than saw, that it was deep.

At first I thought it must be a well, or some sort of crude sewer. I suppose it was the dark and the rain and the alarming appearance and then disappearance of the man which had muddled my wits, for I did not realise at once what I had found.

And then I understood. This was something quite ordinary. It was the chute down which the barrels of ale could be rolled into the cellar of the priory, without the need to trundle them through the enclave itself, disturbing the canons at their prayers or their studies.

Nothing remarkable about this.

But I knew at once that I had found the secret way into the priory.

Something brushed against me, but this time I knew who it was.

'What have you found?' Emma's voice was no more than a disturbance of the air beside my cheek.

'I think it is the chute into the ale cellar, and the Frenchman has climbed down into it.'

'But why?'

'Because, for some nefarious purpose that I cannot guess, he wants to enter the priory in secret, despite the fact that he may enter at any time he wishes, on lawful business. Now why should that be? It is possible that he is caught up in some conspiracy with de Hungerford, and wants to release him from confinement. It seems he has been asking a great many questions about all the buildings in the enclave, perhaps trying to discover where de Hungerford is held.'

'Do you believe that?' I could hear the doubt in her

tone. 'From what I have heard, de Hungerford is a brutish, violent man, with no subtlety. While your Frenchman proceeds by stealth. If he worked with anyone, it was Belancer, yet he killed him.'

'From the start, I have wondered why he would want to kill Belancer, but now I think I understand,' I said. 'He needed Belancer to tell him how he might enter the priory secretly. Once Belancer had divulged that information, he was of no further use to the Frenchman Mateaux. Indeed, he was a danger, for whatever crime Mateaux committed, Belancer could have pointed the finger. So it was necessary to kill him.'

I felt her shiver as she leaned against me.

'He is a dangerous man, Nicholas. Alice Walsea told you so, and his killing of Belancer bears it out.'

'Aye, but he is now inside the priory, and must be stopped.'

'Not by you. We must fetch Sheriff Walden.'

'There may not be time.'

I sat back on my heels, thinking furiously. Mateaux would be feeling his way about the cellar now, trying to find the steps which I thought must lead up – not to the kitchens. From what I remembered of where they stood, we were too close to the gatehouse here. More likely to the row of pantries and storerooms on this side of the main court. With the canons at Vespers, most of the lay servants dismantling the fairground, and the remaining servants in the kitchens, the main court would be empty. Mateaux could not have come to steal the priory's treasures, for ever since the attack led by de Hungerford, it was common knowledge that they were secured in the church, which would be locked now, and again once Vespers was over.

Not de Hungerford, I thought. Not the church treasures. The Chapter House would be empty. The steward's office would contain important documents, but unless Mateaux was hoping to lay hands on the deeds to some property, they could have no interest for him. Besides, they would certainly be kept in a locked coffer, behind a locked door. Master Shrewsbury had struck me as a careful man.

The prior's house was guarded by Walden's soldiers. The infirmary contained nothing but a few sick and injured men. The library had been stripped bare of its books. There would be nothing of value in the dortoir.

Then remembrance hit me so suddenly that my stomach clenched and I felt sick.

Why had I not thought of it before?

'What is the matter?' Emma was so close to me, she must have felt me start.

'I am a fool!' I whispered fiercely. 'Ten times a fool! 'Tis the prince! He means to kill the prince.'

'You cannot be sure,' she protested.

But I *was* sure. Alice's French criminal, who would kill without a qualm, if the money was sufficient. Prince Edward, who was feared and hated by the French even more than his father the king. Now that the king was growing older, his concerns were more and more with the sound government of England, while more and more it was the prince who commanded the English army in the war against France. What more likely than to send an assassin to England, during this period of the truce, under cover of a fair? Had Mateaux some previous knowledge that the prince would be in Oxford? Or had his luck simply served him, so that he need not seek the prince at Woodstock or Wallingford, where he would have been more secure?

Emma's thoughts must have following almost the same path as mine, but she objected. 'Why should Belancer have aided a Frenchman to kill our prince? He was an Englishman.'

'Half an Englishman,' I said. 'But half a Frenchman. Perhaps he thought that the French king would reward him, even restore his French property to him.'

I got to my feet.

'I have wasted too much time. I must go after him.'

I put my hands on her shoulders.

'I will stop him if I can. If I cannot find him, I will try

to warn the prince. I know that he stays in the small guesthouse kept for noble visitors. Can you go to the castle? Fetch Sheriff Walden? The lane across from the priory gatehouse will take you past Oriel to the High Street. Nay, you need not go all the way to the castle yourself. Go to the Mitre. They can send someone on horseback. That will be best, and you can avoid the crowds that will be roaming the main streets, drinking themselves witless. Then go home and stay safely there.'

'Do not go, Nicholas!' she said desperately. 'You are unarmed. He is a killer.'

I took her face between my hands. I could just see, in the faint wash of light, that there were tears in her eyes.

'I will be careful.'

Without warning, she kissed me on the lips, light as the brush of a leaf, then she drew back, and began to walk away slowly toward the gatehouse of the priory.

I sat on the ground with my legs hanging down into the hole and felt around the top of the chute. It was unlikely that the barrels of ale would simply be dropped into the hole, for they would burst. To my relief, I found that I was right. There was a kind of sloping ramp, leading from the opening in the street into the cellar, down which the barrels could be rolled. I took a deep breath, leaned forward, and launched myself into the darkness.

It was probably the most foolish thing I had ever done.

My progress down the ramp was not, as I had hoped, silent. My shoes scraped against the wood, even my clothes swished as I slithered uncontrollably down what seemed a much greater distance than I had expected. I think, also, I may have gasped, without meaning to. It was hardly the stealthy approach I had hoped for. When I met the stone floor of the cellar suddenly, I fell sideways, hitting my head on something hard, the breath knocked out of me like a punch in the lungs.

Over the sounds my descent had made, I had just

caught some stealthy movement somewhere in the dark ahead of me. But now there was total silence. If Mateaux was there, he was holding his breath, frozen into stillness.

Bruised and shaken, I grabbed the side of the ramp and got to my feet, though my knees felt weak. Apart from the merest trace of grey light coming through the open hatch into the street, the darkness in the cellar was far worse than in the lane. It felt suffocating, like a bag over the head. I could see nothing. I wondered whether Mateaux, looking from the farther side of the cellar toward the ramp, could make me out in that meagre illumination from above. Best take no risks. I eased myself away from the ramp as carefully and quietly as I could, but the floor was gritty, and my feet made a faint crunch as I moved.

Now I froze into stillness and waited, like a hunted animal. Despite the chill I had felt outside, as soon as I left the shelter of the shared cloak, I was sweating, but, deprived of sight, I found my hearing sharpened. Mateaux could no more move silently than I could. His feet, too, crunched on the grit of the floor. He was drawing nearer. Yet, although he had had more time than I for his eyes to adjust, the darkness was nearly impenetrable, and the cellar must be filled with barrels, making any movement difficult.

I tried to visualise where I was, under the enclave. The cellar must extend from the line of the wall, out under the storehouses which backed on to it. Mateaux might know where the steps lay, but I had no idea. They might be at this end of the cellar, leading up into the back of one of the storehouses, or they might lie at the far end, emerging directly into the courtyard. I could not recall ever having noticed them, but it was unlikely that I would have done, if the opening into the enclave lay under a trapdoor, like the opening into the street, or behind a door in one of the storehouses. As far as I could judge, Mateaux was over at that far end of the cellar. Either he knew in advance that was where the steps were, or else he had already had time to feel his way around the walls.

Would the door or hatch at the top of the steps be

kept locked? Unless Mateaux had had a key to open the trap in the street, it seemed the opening to the chute was not locked, but that was only to be expected. Men delivering barrels of ale needed access, and no one would be likely to steal ale by dragging it *up* the ramp. The value of a barrel of ale would not be worth the trouble. However, if the canons had ever realised that the cellar provided a way into the enclave, there might be a locked door at the top of the steps out of the cellar.

Yet, if that were the case, Belancer would not have told Mateaux that this was a way into the priory. Unless he had given Mateaux a key. Nay, Belancer would never have had access to a key. He would have known about the chute from the street, for since the loss of his French wines, he had been obliged to deal in the better qualities of ale as well as his lesser wines. He would have used the chute to deliver his own barrels of ale.

Perhaps, I thought, almost with a gasp of foolish laughter, Mateaux and I were now both trapped in a locked cellar, the only way out being back up that precipitous ramp. It was not a pleasant thought.

And then I heard his steps approaching. Aware that some of that dim light from above might still reveal my position I stepped further back. And collided with an empty barrel, which fell over with a sound like a mighty drum, and rolled away – where, I could not tell.

I could hear the man breathing now, short breaths, not as if he were alarmed, but with the quick short breaths of excitement you will hear, when a hunter is stalking a dangerous beast. I had thrown myself down that ramp in pursuit of Mateaux. Now the tables were turned. I was the prey being pursued.

The empty barrel continued to roll across the floor and under the noise it made I felt my way behind the ramp to its far side, until I hoped that it lay between me and my pursuer. My eyes were growing more accustomed to this greater darkness now, and although I could not see him, I could detect a shifting of the dark as he searched the place where I had been.

What would he do next? Would he continue to search for me? Or would he make for the stairs, hoping to shake me off? From what Alice had said, this was a man who would coolly cut my throat, then move on without hesitation to carry out his true mission, which I was convinced was an attack on the prince. He must have deliberately timed his entry to the priory while the canons were celebrating Vespers. He could not afford to delay. His intention must be to escape again before the service was ended. Over the wall, perhaps, into the deserted fairground. Whatever he intended, dealing with me would delay him. I kept very still, scarcely daring to breathe. If he decided to forego his search and climb the stairs, I could follow him, and tackle him in the open air of the enclave, where there would be light enough to see him.

How I supposed I could tackle an armed and experienced killer, I did not allow myself to think.

Just how long we both waited there in stillness, straining our ears to detect when the other moved, I could not tell. The time seemed to drag out unbearably, although it was probably no more than a minute or two. Then he moved.

He no longer tried to be silent, but ran across to the far side of the cellar, where he had been before, knocking into barrels and sending some of them crashing and rolling across the floor. I wondered that he was not a-feared he might be heard from the courtyard, but perhaps he reckoned we were too far below ground. He must already have found the stair, before he was halted by my noisy descent down the ramp, for I could now hear distinctly the sound of shoes on stone steps.

I began to feel my way after him, making my way merely by the noise which he was not bothering to conceal. Several times I collided with the tumbling barrels, and was knocked once, painfully, to my knees. By the time I was on my feet again, I could hear him wrestling with a trap door. As he pushed it aside, a strip of pale light slid down over the man I was following and showed me the clear way to the stair. I began to run.

By the time I reached the bottom of the steps, he was through the opening and trying to thrust the trap door back into place, but something must have prevented, or else he feared he was running out of time, for it only covered half the space, leaving enough light for me to grope my way to the top of the steps and shove aside the cover, a heavy lid of wood this time.

As I suspected, Mateaux was already running in the direction of the guesthouse as I climbed up into the courtyard. It suddenly occurred to me that the prince might be attending Vespers, in which case he was in no danger, but I thrust that thought away. Mateaux would not have risked everything on such a gamble. He would have found a way to ascertain in advance that the prince did not attend the early evening service.

Again, I began to run.

Mateaux gave one glance over his shoulder, and hesitated.

I do not know what he saw. Not one of Walden's armed soldiers, certainly, which might have driven him at once to flight, or to a desperate attempt on the prince's life before he could be taken. Instead, the greater light in the court must had revealed the battered figure of an unremarkable townsman, unarmed and empty-handed, even lacking the bodily bulk of a notable brawler.

Instead of going on, he turned to face me, and I saw the unmistakable glint of steel in his hand.

I had no weapon but the small knife I used to cut my meat at table, and I have never been a man of my fists, but I could not slink away now, like some pitiful coward. And I was suddenly angry. This quiet priory, dedicated to our Oxford saint, and founded by her long ago, had already, within the last few days, suffered one evil attack. Now this enemy of England, this Frenchman who had already committed murder in our town, was bent on killing our prince, the glorious son of a glorious father.

With a wordless prayer to Saint Frideswide, and incandescent with that anger, I hurled myself at the man. Head down, I threw myself at his legs. As we collided and fell together, I felt the sting of his blade on the back of my shoulder.

The unconventional nature of my attack had clearly taken him by surprise. I had gripped him now, about the thighs, and I clung to him, knowing that my life depended on preventing him from reaching any vulnerable part of my body with his blade. I punched my head into his stomach and had the satisfaction of hearing the whoop of his breath. Then we were rolling about the dusty cobbles of the courtyard, locked together like lovers. I could feel the strength in my arms weakening, but as long as I could keep my hold, he could not free himself enough to take a deep thrust at me, though I felt the slash of his dagger repeatedly across my back. With a kind of wild inner laughter, I was glad I had not donned my best cotte, after all, This one would be cut to ribbons.

He was stronger than I, and more skilled. I could feel that at any moment he would wrench himself free. And that would finish me. All my senses were concentrated on this man, this hated enemy, but other sounds began to filter through to my brain. And surely there was more light?

I heard shouts, then a known voice calling, 'Nicholas!'

What was Emma doing here? I had told her to fetch Walden. If she came too close, Mateaux might choose to strike out at her instead of me. I swore aloud, shouting at her to keep away. And I became aware that Mateaux was swearing too, though in words I did not understand. Only the viciousness of his tone gave them meaning.

He had me down on my back at last. I was suffocating, with the weight of his body pressing down on my head. I would need to break free, or I would die from lack of air, but as soon as I did so, he would have me. I sensed that his dagger was raised, ready to slit my throat.

Then, miraculously, his weight was lifted half off me,

and I drew in great gasping gulps of air. I still had him clutched about the thighs, but an unknown voice said, with authority, 'Let him go now. I have him.'

I let my arms drop. They were shaking from the unaccustomed effort. Mateaux was dragged off me and I rolled over. I managed to get to my knees, but I felt weak and dizzy. A strong hand took me by the elbow and hauled me to my feet.

The buildings of the enclave swam a little as I stood upright, and I found myself face to face with the Prince of Wales.

'Your Grace!' I said, trying to bow, but spoiling the effect by staggering.

He still had me by one elbow, his other hand gripping Mateaux by the neck of his cotte.

'You have taken some slashes to your back,' he said cheerfully, 'but I believe you will live. The lady tells me this fellow was bent on assassination.'

The lady in question was close by, looking defiant.

'I told you to fetch the sheriff,' I said, ungratefully.

'There was no time,' she said. 'I told the gatekeeper what was afoot, and he fetched His Grace, and Walden's two men from outside the prior's house.'

The courtyard suddenly began to fill up, as the canons emerged from the church and a crowd of wide-eyed servants poured from the kitchens. There was a confusion of voices and exclamations, Walden's men came forward, and the prince turned to hand over the man Mateaux to them.

He must have been awaiting this moment, standing slack and obedient in the prince's grip. Suddenly his twisted out of the prince's hold, punched one of the soldiers in the face, slashed at the other with his dagger, which somehow he still held, and then he was off, running like a hare pursued by huntsman, and like the hare zigzagging between the buildings of the enclave. In his visits to the priory he had clearly made himself very familiar with its entire plan.

And I was certain I knew where he was heading. Against the south wall, the portion of the town wall which here served to enclose the priory, there was a low shed. I believe the canons sometimes kept animals there. Mateaux could easily scramble on to its roof, and, from the roof, over the wall. Once in the meadow beyond it, he could lie low, or even escape by river, if he had a boat moored down by the jetty.

My legs seemed to belong to me again, and I began to run, not like the soldiers and the few priory servants who had their wits about them, all of whom were following the Frenchman's erratic course. Instead, I made straight for the shed. I thought I heard one set of running feet behind me, but I did not look round.

There it was. I had been quick, but Mateaux had been quicker, spurred on by fear for his life. He was already scrambling on to the roof. I made a grab for his leg, but he kicked me in the face, then he was across the roof and reaching up for a projecting spur of stone just below the top of the wall.

I went up that roof like a cat escaping a dog, ripping my hose and nearly sliding back again. Someone gave me a shove from behind to stop me slipping, then I reached the wall just as Mateaux went over it. I reached for the same handhold, dragged myself up until I had my stomach on the wall, then swung my feet round and dropped to the ground. Someone dropped, neatly and lightly beside me.

'He'll make for the river,' I said.

'Aye.' A cheerful cry. 'Come! After the deer!'

We began to run. The clouds had started to clear, and I suppose at some point it had stopped raining. Enough of the moon had broken through that we could make out the fleeing figure before us.

And at last, Mateaux' luck ran out. He stumbled, as though he had put his foot in rabbit hole, then he went on, but limping. Together, the other man and I put on a spurt and overtook him. This time I had the good sense to grip his right arm, for somehow he still retained possession of his dagger. My companion twisted his wrist until he dropped the dagger with a yelp. Between us, we threw him to the ground, and the other man tied his legs together with his girdle, which glinted in the moonlight. With the more modest cord from around the waist of my own cotte, I bound the Frenchman's hands. Then we both sat on him.

'A good hunting,' my companion said, 'and a fine catch, Master Elyot.'

'Aye,' I said, 'Your Grace.'

Chapter Eleven

Edward of Woodstock made himself more comfortable on the Frenchman's back, after stuffing a handkerchief in the man's mouth to suppress his swearing. He clasped his hands about his up drawn knees as if he were settling himself for pleasant picnic in the sun of a summer's day, here in the Oxford meadow, instead of pinning down an intended assassin in the dark, with a cold autumn wind chilling us, now that our mad scramble after the man was over.

'So, Master Elyot,' he said, 'that was an unusual fighting manoeuvre you performed, there in the priory court. I have never seen it used before.'

'I had no weapon,' I said apologetically. 'I could not think what else to do.'

'Well, it proved effective. More effective, I confess, than my clumsiness in allowing him to slip out of my hold.'

'He is known as a skilled criminal in France, it seems. So Alice Walsea has told me. Yet never before have they succeeded in catching him. I suspect he has wriggled out of even more secure holds before now.'

'Ah, so Mistress Walsea is here.'

'She was. She left for Westminster yesterday, by boat.'

'My father will be sorry to have missed the excitement,' he said, twisting round in order to see my back. 'I fear you are bleeding rather freely.'

'I do not think any of the cuts are very deep.' I tried

to sound casual, although my back was beginning to throb painfully. I had barely had time to be aware of it before.

'How did you come to be there in the courtyard?' he said. 'You appeared out of the ground like the devil in a mystery play.'

'He found his way in through the ale cellar, and I followed him.'

I explained, as briefly as I could, the events of the last few days, and the chance that I had seen Mateaux in the lane, disappearing down the chute for ale barrels.

'You were escorting the lady home?'

'Aye. And I told her to fetch the sheriff.'

'As well she did not, or this fellow might have slain you first and me afterwards.' He thumped Mateaux on the head, though not particularly hard.

'What I do not understand,' he said, 'is how you knew he was coming for me.'

'I did not *know*. It was but instinct. What else could a notorious French killer want in St Frideswide's Priory but to kill the man most feared in France?'

'Then I am thankful for your instinct.'

I saw his teeth gleam in the moonlight as he grinned.

'After such a battle, I feel you have earned a knighthood.'

I laughed. 'Nay, Your Grace, I think not. I should not be able to maintain a knight's fee.'

'Then I must think of some other way to reward you.'

It was my turn to grin. 'I believe Your Grace is a lover of books. I keep a very fine bookshop here in Oxford. We can produce any book you may desire.'

'Any book? Indeed, I must give it some thought. But now, I fear, we are about to be interrupted. Or reinforced.'

He was right. A party of men was emerging from the priory's postern gate, carrying many torches. I thought I could make out the figure of Cedric Walden amongst them. Someone must have sent to the castle after all.

We both stood up, and the prince poked the Frenchman with the toe of his boot, then rolled him over.

'How did you know my name?' I asked. 'I did not think that my fame had reached the king's court.'

'The lady told me. "Nicholas Elyot," she said, "will be killed, trying to save you from that assassin's knife if you do not go to his aid." How could I refuse?'

'Indeed,' I said, 'it is difficult to refuse the Lady Emma Thorgold if she makes up her mind to something.'

'Thorgold?' he said.

'Granddaughter to Sir Anthony Thorgold.'

He nodded, as if he knew the name, but there was no time for further talk, for the party from the priory was almost upon us. It had been a strange interlude, there in the dark, as though we were no more than any two young men together, recovering after successfully capturing a villain, and somewhat pleased with ourselves. Should I ever meet the prince again, I was sure it would be on quite other terms.

The next hour or two seemed interminable, for I needed to give a full explanation of the events of the evening to Walden, with interjections from Emma and the prince, as we sat in the parlour of the guest house. Mateaux had been carried off to the castle under guard, and fortunately someone had thought to retrieve our girdles and replace them with rope, tying Mateaux on to a horse to convey him more swiftly out of the sight of the crowds still in the streets after the fair. The prince's girdle, I saw, was woven with gold thread and studded with semi-precious stones. I doubt any criminal has ever been secured with so costly a bond.

It was while I was knotting my own modest cord about my waist that another fit of giddiness overtook me. Canon Aubery, who was with us, speaking for the priory, caught me before I slumped to the ground, but Emma was beside him at once.

'You are badly hurt, Nicholas! Why have you kept silent?'

I suppose, in the dark, no one had noticed the state of

my back, and here in the lighted parlour I had kept it turned away from the company, for I was conscious of the disreputable state of my garments.

The canon and Emma bore me away to the infirmary, despite my protests, where I was stripped of cotte and shirt – what was left of them – laid on my face, and subjected to the application of some stinging salve. The wounds had almost been preferable.

Canon Aubery returned to the guesthouse, but Emma stayed to oversee the torture.

'Jesu!' I said, wincing, as more of the salve was smeared on. 'That stings like the devil. And I have just remembered. Our families will be beside themselves with worry. They will think we have fallen foul of the cup-shotten youths of Oxford.'

'They will not,' she said crisply. 'Some of us are able to keep our wits about us. I sent one of the lay servants, more than an hour since, to my aunt and your sister. Someone must look to these small matters, while the men perform their heroics.'

But, squinting up sideways from my prone position, I saw that she was smiling.

At last I was permitted by the infirmarian to sit up and to don a loose shirt he had found for me.

'Best not wear anything to rub that back,' he said, 'for the next day or two.'

Most of the inhabitants of the infirmary were asleep, but I caught the gaze of the cellarer, Canon Basing, on me.

'So it *was* the French vintner that you asked about,' he said. 'Mateaux?'

'Aye,' I said. 'Not simply a vintner. An assassin sent to attack our prince.'

'Master Elyot saved his life,' Emma said.

'More likely he saved mine,' I said.

She laughed. She might mock me, but I think she had truly been concerned for my life. And although I had shouted at her, afraid that she would be caught up in the Frenchman's violence, she had shown greater sense than I, seeking the nearest help to hand, rather than sending all the way to the castle. It would, indeed, have come too late.

At long last, we were able to go home, when the bell summoned the canons to Matins. Sheriff Walden insisted upon seeing us both all the way, supported by four of his men. He lifted Emma on to his horse, while he and I walked. I was glad of the dark, which concealed my beggarly appearance. With the state of my back, and the bruises I had acquired both falling in the cellar and rolling on the cobbles gripped to Mateaux, I was beginning to stiffen up, so I was glad when we had delivered Emma safely to her aunt's house and Walden walked with me the remaining distance down the High Street.

'You will not forget our meeting with Master Winchingham?' I said, unable to stifle a yawn. 'Midday, at the Mitre?'

'I have not forgotten,' he said, catching my yawn and laughing wryly. 'If either of us wakes early enough to leave our beds! I shall ask Master Winchingham to come to the castle beforehand. It will improve our case against the Frenchman if he can be identified as the rogue who was with Hamo Belancer shortly before he was murdered, and who struck down the merchant in the alleyway.'

'God give you goodnight, then, Cedric.' I fumbled for my key. Margaret would have locked the door on this rowdy night, but I hoped she had not also barred it. I had worn only my small linen scrip this past evening, buckled to the belt of my hose, but I had a moment of alarm that the key might have dropped out of it during my fight with Mateaux. To my relief, it was still there and, bowing to Walden, I let myself into the shop as quietly as I might.

There was a candle lantern burning in the kitchen, but so low that I replaced the candle at once, lest I find myself plunged in darkness. By its light, I saw that Margaret was not abed, but deep asleep in her chair. A dilemma indeed! It seemed cruel to wake her, yet, if I left her here, in the morning she would be as stiff as I was already.

I was saved the trouble of making a decision when

Margaret opened her eyes, shaded them with her hand, and complained. 'Move that lamp aside, Nicholas, you are blinding me.'

Hurriedly, I moved it away, but now her eyes widened in horror at the state of my clothes. Emma had made my shirt and cotte into a bundle, which I had brought with me from the priory, though I feared they were past mending. I stood before Margaret in the priory shirt, which had been made for some canon of ample girth, and what remained of my hose, ripped into holes large enough for a cat to jump through.

'Nicholas!' It seemed she was incapable of further speech.

'Never fret, Meg,' I said, giving her a hand out of the low chair. 'I was caught up in a tussle with the Frenchman we have been seeking, but he is safely locked up in the castle, and the sheriff has just seen both Emma and me home. We should be done with alarums at last, and may rest secure in our beds. I know I am ready for mine, and clearly so are you.'

I was determined she should not catch sight of my back tonight, or I should be subjected to more painful ministrations. What we both needed was to sleep for what little was left of the night.

Once in my bedchamber, I kicked off my shoes and stripped off my tattered hose, which fell into even great holes as I did so. The vast shirt would served as well as a night shift, I reckoned, as I blew out my candle and lay down carefully on my front. I would not be able to lie on my back yet awhile.

It was not surprising that I slept late the following morning, nor was it surprising that I was even stiffer than I had been the night before. I crawled about, slow as a slug, finding fresh hose and a loose cotte that was long enough to cover the long shirt. The infirmarian at the priory might advise me to wear nothing but the shirt, yet I could not walk about Oxford looking as though I were in my night shift. Loose as it was, the cotte caused some rubbing to my back, but I would simply need to endure it. The cloth of the shirt caught at the scabs as I lifted my arms to comb my hair and shave.

In the kitchen, Margaret was sorting out such of the leftover goods from the fair as had fallen to her share. She seemed a little tired, but more awake than I felt.

'How do you find yourself this morning?' I asked, pulling out a stool and sitting down at the table.

'I have known worse,' she said, wryly. 'I had some sleep before you came home. And you?'

'Slept like a child.' I said. 'And where *are* the children?'

'Rafe is over at the Bakers', and Alysoun has taken her new doll to show to Juliana.'

I smiled and raised my eyebrows. 'Is our madcap girl become a young lady?'

'That I doubt. But it is good to see her becoming friends with a girl like Juliana.'

I could not dispute that. Juliana was not a scamp of a boy like Jonathan, but she was still lively, and intelligent – and she loved books.

'Is there anything for breakfast?' I said hungrily. 'You are busy, I can fetch it for myself.' I half rose from my stool.

'Stay where you are. I have had Emma here already this morning, asking how you fared, and I have learned what happened last night.'

She smiled mischievously. 'We cannot have the close companion of our future king making his own breakfast.'

I laughed. 'Hardly that. But he is a fine man, prince or not.'

So Emma had come early, asking for me.

'And there is no need for you to smirk,' Margaret said, with her back to me.

'Nay, indeed, Meg,' I said meekly.

She gave me a royal breakfast of two coddled eggs with some of her new bread, then more bread with pats of

Mary's golden butter, topped with blackberry preserve. I even managed a large slab of Mary's best aged cheese, rich and full of flavour.

'Now I feel fit to deal with the business of the day,' I said.

'Aye, Roger and Walter have been busy in the shop these four hours and more.'

Stupidly, I had quite forgot that we reopened today, the fair being over. We would have a steady stream of students and masters, wanting everything from quills to *peciae*. Perhaps even a secondhand text or two.

'I must be at the Mitre before midday,' I said, and explained the plan to expose the fraudulent seller of the priory's books. 'I hope he has not been frightened away by all the troubles at the priory. If he was working for Prior de Hungerford – which is what we suspect – then he may decide that a wise discretion demands that he duck away from anything that might link him to it.'

'He may not have heard that de Hungerford is being held confined,' she said, 'until the bishop decides what is to be done with him.' She began to clear away my dishes.

'Aye, he may not. And even if he has, he may hope to bluff his way through the sale to Peter Winchingham, and pocket the price of the books for himself.'

'You had best be on your way, then. It cannot be more than half an hour till midday. You slept very late. I hope we will have no more of these broken nights.'

'I am sure this will be the last of it,' I said.

In the shop I found my two scriveners busy with both masters and students, now that the morning lectures were over. It felt strange to have lost half the day already. Assuring them that I would be back to lend my assistance in the afternoon, and nodding to several of the masters, I let myself out of the shop and walked swiftly up the High Street. It was essential that I should reach the Mitre before the unsuspecting fly entered our spider's web.

The clouds of the previous evening had been swept away by a brisk autumn wind. Beneath my feet the cobbles, washed clean by the rain, shone in the sun, with here and there a glint like gemstones, where a fragment of quartz caught the light. Despite the aching bruises and the stinging slashes across my back, I felt more light-hearted than I had done for days. The remembrance of sitting with the prince in the meadow would stay with me, long after my injuries had healed.

At the Mitre, the innkeeper showed me into one of the small private parlours. As Master Winchingham had observed, the building was indeed a very coney warren. The merchant was sitting comfortably in a cushioned chair, nursing a cup of wine, and Sheriff Walden was already with him.

'I have been to the castle this morning,' Winchingham said, as he gestured me to a chair and poured me a cup of wine. 'The sheriff asked if I would view the prisoner you captured last night.'

'I had some royal assistance,' I said. The wine was excellent.

'So I am told. The man Mateaux was led past a window while I watched. I am in no doubt. He is the man who attacked me.'

'Will that be evidence enough?' I turned to Walden.

'We also have a number of witnesses who saw him break into the priory, and attack you. His Grace himself will bear witness to that.'

'I suppose he might claim that I attacked him first,' I said doubtfully.

He shook his head. 'He was coming for you with his dagger before you grabbed him. They will all swear to that. And should that not seem enough, I believe we can persuade him to admit to the murder of Belancer and the intent to murder the prince.'

I did not like the sound of that. 'You would use torture?' My voice shook.

'If we must. I like it no more than you, Nicholas, but this was a foreign assassin, bent on killing the Prince of Wales. In any case, the *threat* of torture is usually enough to persuade men to talk, without ever the need to use it. Indeed, if he confesses readily, we can promise him a slightly easier death, for there is no doubt. He *will* hang.'

'It is nearly midday,' Winchingham said. 'Best if you conceal yourselves.' He gestured toward a screen which had been set up in front of one wall.

Walden and I stood up, taking our wine cups with us, as Winchingham drew the priory's Bible and book of hours out of his leather scrip and laid them on the table at his elbow. We found that two stools had been placed behind the screen, so we settled ourselves to wait, Walden on the outside, in case he should need to move swiftly to make an arrest.

We had only been in position a few minutes, when we heard the comfortable tones of the innkeeper approaching the door of the parlour. I realised that he must have been told of the plan, for he was being particularly affable.

'Aye,' he said, 'here is the merchant, Master Winchingham, awaiting you as he promised. You have enough wine, Master Winchingham? And you, sir, can I fetch you something to eat, for 'tis near dinner time? We have some excellent mutton collops, or perhaps a helping of veal pie? With roasted cabbage and parsnips?'

I could not hear the words of the man's reply, but the tone sounded negative.

We heard the door close at the innkeeper withdrew.

'Ah, Master Ford,' Winchingham said, 'let me pour you a glass of wine, and then – to business! I always feel that business is more happily conducted over a cup of good wine.' There was the clink of the flagon against the wine cup and the splash of liquid. 'Your good health, sir, and to our successful conclusion of this business.'

Peter Winchingham sounded relaxed and affable. I thought he was a better player than those we had seen at the fair, but then I considered that dealing as he did in many countries, with so many shrewd strangers, and with considerable amounts of coin, he was probably accustomed to drawing the men with whom he dealt into a state of genial accord.

I suppose the man Ford – I had not heard his name before – had accepted the wine and taken a seat.

'Now,' said Winchingham (and I could imagine him rubbing his hands together in satisfaction), 'let us to business. I am minded to buy both books. And in that case, I am looking for a slight lowering of the price. If I am prepared to take both.'

I felt Walden stir impatiently beside me. I knew he was eager to catch the fellow with the coins in his hands, and could not understand the delay. I shook my head at him. Ford would be less suspicious of any trap if Winchingham indulged in the usual bargaining between seller and customer. I could not hear the man's response to this, for he spoke in a low, mumbling voice. For several minutes they must have had their heads together, negotiating the price, then there was the scrape of a stool.

'And you say that the gentleman has no more books from his library for sale?' the merchant asked. 'I am disappointed to hear that. I might have been interested to purchase further volumes.'

There was a mumbled reply.

'Ah, well, that is my misfortune.'

There was the clink of metal as coins were counted out on the table, then gathered up. The fellow would be storing them for safety in his purse.

'Let us shake hands on it, then,' Winchingham said, 'before you leave.'

It was the signal.

Walden leapt out from behind the screen and seized the man around the neck and body. At the same time, three of his men burst through the door, coming to his assistance, although he hardly needed it. Ford was a miserable little man, pale and weedy, as Winchingham had described him. He barely struggled, but merely sagged resignedly in the sheriff's grasp.

His punishment, I suspected, would not be serious.

He could claim that he was merely the messenger, acting for another – certainly de Hungerford – and since the books came from the priory library, he would be believed. If he had decided, after all that had happened, to indulge in a little private business of his own, that would be difficult to prove. I could tell from Walden's expression that he recognised the man, perhaps under some different name. One of the petty villains of the town, hardly of account after Mateaux.

'Give us your purse, fellow,' Walden said, handing the man over to one of his officers. 'Master Winchingham, you had best retrieve your coin.'

Winchingham did so, and looked with some compassion at the man, drooping in the officer's hold, his face a study in hopeless misery.

'Poor fellow,' he said, 'he had but a groat and two pennies of his own.' He handed the purse back to the sheriff.

'Never fear,' Walden said cheerfully, 'he shall have free food and board for a while with us.' He turned to his men. 'Take him back to the castle. I will deal with him later.'

When they were gone, he beamed at us both. 'Neatly and quietly done, my friends. You will return the books to the priory yourself, Master Winchingham?'

'Nay, I shall leave that to Master Elyot,' he said. 'He knows their *librarius*.'

'In that case,' Walden said, 'I hope you will both now be my guests for the best dinner the Mitre can serve us.'

I returned to the shop rather later than I had intended, with the two books belonging to the priory in my scrip and fortified by the excellent dinner provided by the Mitre. The abundance of the food and the quality of the wine accompanying it had rendered me somewhat sleepy, but I managed to keep my wits about me for long enough to be of some use in the shop for the rest of the afternoon. Roger was able to return to his work on the second copy of his collection of tales, since I had sold the first to Peter Winchingham.

As soon as the shop became a little less busy, I went through to the kitchen to speak to Margaret.

'I have asked Peter Winchingham to take supper with us tonight. Nay, do not give me that look. After the dinner at the Mitre which Cedric Walden treated us to, neither of us will expect more than a simple family supper. You know him now, Meg. He does not stand on ceremony. He will be leaving in a day or two and I should like to have more speech with him before he goes.'

'Very well,' she conceded, 'but I wish you had given me fair warning.'

'There has been no time. Besides, he is not one of your pretentious new-made London merchants, like Gilbert Mordon. He is shrewd, and no doubt wealthy, but makes no parade of it.'

She grumbled a little, but it was mostly for show.

Perhaps it was no more than fatigue, but I seemed to go about the ordinary tasks of the shop that afternoon in a sort of dream. After the anxiety and fear of recent days, this tranquil – nay, boring – routine seemed unreal. I was truly glad that life was returning to its normal course, but, I regret to say, it felt somewhat flat.

As soon as it was time to close the shop, I told Margaret that I would return the two books at once to the priory before supper.

'I have no wish to keep them in my care,' I said. 'I will be glad to hand them over to Canon Aubery, who can place them in safety with the rest of the books from the library. Sheriff Walden tells me that his men have found the missing church silver in the prior's house, hidden under the floorboards in his bedchamber.'

She clicked her tongue. 'Do you tell me so! How came it about that such a man was ever admitted to the Church, and then rose to be a prior?'

I shook my head. 'How do any great men rise? Some through merit, no doubt, but others through bribery or trickery or the influence of powerful friends.'

'You are become a cynic, Nicholas.'

'Nay, I hope not. But these late happenings have left the taste of bile in my mouth. I never liked Hamo Belancer, but I did not strongly *dislike* him. Yet he has been proved a traitor, who connived at the murder of Prince Edward.'

'Mayhap,' she said, 'he did not know what the man Mateaux intended.'

I shrugged. 'You may have the right of it, but somehow . . . why should he have allied himself with Mateaux at all? That was his French blood speaking, I believe.'

'Well, he has paid for it.'

'Aye, he has. And he did not deserve to die like that. Though I suppose, had he not, he would have been discovered in his treason and would have hanged for it.'

I sighed. 'That reminds me. I meant to discover what has become of Belancer's old dog, poor fellow. He was distressed at his master's death.'

'We are not taking in another dog,' she warned.

'Nay, never fear! I will call in at the cobbler's shop on my way to the priory.'

As I let myself out of the shop, I saw Jordain approaching from the direction of St Mary's.

'I was coming to see how you fared,' he said, linking his arm with mine. 'It is all over Oxford, how you tackled a French assassin, armed to the teeth, with nothing but your bare hands, then went chasing after him in company with the Prince of Wales.'

'Who told you that?' Praise from a few friends was heart warming, but I had no wish to be pointed at by every gawping townsman in Oxford.

'One of my students. He had it from one of the sheriff's men he met in the Swindlestock tavern.'

I shook my head sorrowfully. 'You are failing in your duty, as one *in loco parentis*,' I said. 'You know the students are not allowed to drink in the town taverns, and most especially not in the Swindlestock.'

He laughed. 'And you and I never did, when we were students? I am blind to the occasional visit, but if it becomes a habit, and their studies suffer, I am ruthless.'

Jordain had never in his life been ruthless.

'Well,' I said, 'I have some errands. Are you on your way back to Hart Hall, or will you come with me?'

'I need not go back yet. What are your errands?'

I told him, as we crossed the street to the cobbler's shop. I noticed that someone had cleared the alleyway lying between it and Belancer's shop of the worst of the rubbish. The vintner's shop remained sealed and silent.

It was Goodwife Brinley who answered my knock.

'The old dog, Master Elyot? We have decided to keep him. He's no trouble, and he's gentle with the children. In these fierce times, 'tis as well to have a guard dog.'

I smiled. The old fellow might have been a great hunter, and even a guard dog, in his day, but not now. Still, I was glad he had found a safe haven.

As Jordain and I walked down to St Frideswide's Priory, I gave him an exact account of what had happened the night before.

'You could have been killed,' he said, 'throwing yourself recklessly down an ale chute into the dark. And what if he had caught you there, armed as he was?'

'The thought came to me,' I admitted, 'about halfway down the ramp, but by then it was too late to turn back.'

'I suppose it was,' he said. 'But you need not have tackled him in the courtyard of the priory.'

'Oh, I think by then I had no choice. There was no way out of the cellar but up the steps, and once I was in the courtyard, which was lit by torches, he saw me and came for me. What could I do? I am no heroic Arthurian knight, like those in the king's entertainments, but I could hardly stand there and wait to be killed.'

'I suppose not.' He thumped me on the back, and I winced. 'Well, I am glad you were not killed, and I am sure the prince is glad you prevented the Frenchman's plan. The rumour has it that you and he caught the assassin together.'

'We did. I liked him. Were he not royal, he would be a good friend.'

At this mild remark, he burst out laughing and no protest of mine could stop him. I foresaw, gloomily, that I should have to endure a deal more teasing.

Once we reached the priory, we found Canon Aubery in the prior's office, putting away the account books with relief.

'I am going to visit our patients in the infirmary before Vespers,' he said. 'Shall our infirmarian look to your back again, Nicholas?'

I shuddered. 'I thank you, but no. I have been sent by Master Winchingham to return these to you. I do not believe they have come to any harm.'

I laid the book of hours and the Bible on his desk. He smiled his delight and ran caressing fingers over them.

'Aye, no harm done, I think. The thief is taken, then?'

'The thief's messenger,' I said. 'He has confessed nothing yet, but the sheriff has him in hold. I am sure he will be in haste to name the true thief, to save his own neck.'

'Aye, you probably have the right of it. Have you heard that the missing church silver has been found?'

'I have.'

We walked with him as far as the door to the infirmary, but I refused again, politely, to benefit from any more of the priory's salves, and we headed back into town.

'I have not heard how that matter of the books ended,' Jordain said.

'You were too busy mocking my remarks about the prince, or I should have told you.'

'Tell me now.'

So as we made our way back to the High and along to my shop, I told him of how Sheriff Walden and I had waited, concealed, while Peter Winchingham concluded the purchase with the man Ford, and how he was then arrested.

'In the end,' I said, 'I think we were all sorry for him. Walden knows him of old. He told us over dinner.

Orphaned in the first month of the Pestilence, while still a boy. Keeping alive by petty crime ever since. He is barely twenty now. I think the sheriff will not impose too great a penalty. All that he needs is some honest work. For all that we know, he may have thought this *was* honest, employed as he was by a senior churchman.'

'Poor fellow.' Jordain shook his head. 'Surely there must be some way for him to earn his bread here in Oxford. He does not sound a very terrible villain.'

'Nay, he is not.'

'I'll turn up here,' Jordain said, as we reached Catte Street.

'Nay,' I said, 'we have hardly seen you these last weeks. Come you in to supper. Peter Winchingham is to join us, and Margaret is scolding me for giving her so little warning. You can help me to soothe her.'

My worries proved unnecessary. Emma was with Margaret in the kitchen, helping her to prepare the food, and they were both laughing as we came in.

'I have invited myself to supper,' Emma said. 'I wanted to assure myself that you had neither fainted away from loss of blood nor decided to run away and become a courtier.'

'Neither, I am glad to say.' I smiled at them both, flushed and bright eyed in the warmth of the kitchen after the autumnal feel in the streets. 'I am once again a humble Oxford bookseller, and glad to be done with the high drama of foreign spies and assassins, not forgetting rogue priors and stolen treasure. And see, I have brought Jordain to eat with us. Without your good meals from time to time, Meg, he has been starving on Hart Hall's pig swill.'

'What you need,' Emma said, laying out pewter dishes and spoons, while Alysoun followed behind with the ale cups, 'what you need, Jordain, is a wealthy patron with a great love of scholarship, and a loathing of boiled cabbage.'

'Cabbage is very nutritious,' Jordain said bravely. Then he spoiled the effect by adding wistfully, 'but a wealthy patron would be very welcome.'

There was a knock on the street door of the shop, and Rafe ran to open it, with Rowan jumping excitedly up at our guest.

'You must teach that dog not to jump on everyone, my pet,' I said to Alysoun. 'Someday she may knock some poor old lady over in the street, and think how sorry you will be.'

'She is only a puppy,' Alysoun objected, 'and she doesn't understand. She is always so glad to see everyone.'

Before we could pursue this further, Peter Winchingham was in the kitchen, bowing to Margaret and Emma, and throwing Rafe into the air so that he squealed with delight. I caught Margaret's eye and smiled.

We sat down, as I had hoped, to a family meal in the kitchen, and the merchant, beseeched by Alysoun, was soon describing the town of Bruges to us, with its network of rivers and canals, where it seemed he moved most of his goods about by boat.

'We have lots of rivers too,' Alysoun pointed out, 'here in Oxford.'

'You do, but you do not make the most of them.'

'They do not run through the middle of the town,' Jordain said mildly, 'for which we are grateful. We have enough trouble with flooding as it is. And they *are* used for moving goods, as your rivers and canals in Bruges are. We have excellent river transport to London, and upriver too.'

That reminded me. I turned to Winchingham. 'Has your barge returned from Westminster yet?'

'Aye, this evening. It is tied up near Trill Mill again. And Mistress Walsea has returned with a party from the king's court, not long before I came out. She stopped at the Mitre to speak to me before they went to the sheriff at the castle. I told her they came too late, that you had throttled the French assassin with your bare hands. Or so the story goes about the town, as I was told by one of the inn's pot boys.'

I found myself flushing. 'As you know, I did no such

thing. The Lady Emma was there, and can bear witness.'

'Indeed,' she said, her eyes sparkling, 'I was there and so saw a most wondrous battle. David again Goliath. The unarmed hero against the sword wielding villain.'

'It was a dagger,' I said dryly, 'and he would have slit my throat, had the prince not come to my rescue.'

To put a stop to this teasing, I thought of something I had meant to ask Peter Winchingham over our dinner at the Mitre, though the opportunity never came.

'When you first called on me,' I said, turning to him, 'you said you planned to come back to England, now that the king and Parliament have decided to move the wool Staple here.'

He nodded. 'I do.'

'You also said that you intended to buy a manor with enough land to rear a small flock of sheep of your own.'

'Aye, I did. And I want to set up my own spinners and weavers. I shall need to buy in far more fleeces than I can produce myself, but when I was a boy I used to spend time on my grandfather's farm, my mother's father. It was over in the Welsh Marches, Herefordshire, but that can be a troublesome area, when the Welsh are restless. The Cotswolds are more peaceful. Not so likely to be raided by a party of wild Welshmen.'

I smiled, thinking of Dafydd Hewlyn, the parchment maker. I wondered whether his forebears were wild, raiding Welshmen, harrying Winchingham's grandfather's farm.

'You have never said whether the manor you went to see near Burford suited you.'

Margaret lifted the ale jug and smiled at him.

'Aye, I thank you, mistress.'

When she had filled his cup he drank deep. 'Excellent ale, Mistress Makepeace. Your own?'

'It is.'

I could see that by now she was quite won over.

'I saw the manor, Master Elyot,' he said. 'It was well enough, but somewhat smaller than I had in mind. I was disappointed, for I want to be near Oxford – for your excellent route to London.' He bowed at Jordain. 'And also near Witney, where the weaving of woollen cloth is beginning to increase, ever since it declined here in Oxford.'

He shook his head.

'Your university has been driving the weavers out of town.'

Jordain opened his mouth to protest, but I shook my head.

'So, the manor I went to see was too small, and too far on the other side of Burford. Had it been larger, I might have considered it, even with the greater distance, but, nay, it would not do.'

'So you have not yet found a manor?' Emma said. 'Nicholas told me that you were storing your goods at the Mitre. I thought that you had decided to stay.'

'Indeed I have.' He smiled at her. 'I was about to leave my inn – I was staying in Burford – when the innkeeper told me of a manor about which there had been some trouble. It had been in the king's hands, then it was not, then the king had it again and wanted to sell. As ever, he needs finance for the French wars, and he cannot always persuade Parliament to raise all that he needs from taxes. This manor is large enough, and nearer to Witney and Oxford. I rode over there just before I returned to Oxford.'

Margaret and I stared at each other, both struck with the same thought.

'You will purchase it?' I said.

'Aye. I have already sent instructions to my man of law in London. It seems the business should not take long, for it is of no use to the king, whereas the value in money will be welcome. As I mentioned before, Master Elyot, I must return to Bruges, but I want to bring my daughter and my younger son over to England before winter sets in.'

'And what is the name of the manor?' I said. 'You will remember that my sister and I come from those parts.'

'It is rightly called King's Leighton,' he said, 'but it is mostly known as Leighton Manor. Close by a village called Leighton-under-Wychwood.'

Chapter Twelve

At the outburst of laughter and exclamations, the merchant looked bemused. It was some time before the noise died away, and it was Alysoun who said, 'But Master Winchingham, Leighton is *our* village!'

'Your village, my maid?'

'Aye, that is where our farm is, and our cousins. We were there, helping with the harvest. And I went to a hunt at the manor. And there was a roast swan.'

I came to Winchingham's rescue.

'What Alysoun means,' I said, 'is that our ancestors have been yeoman farmers at Leighton-under-Wychwood for generations. Margaret and I grew up there, on our father's farm. It is my cousin Edmond who holds the land now. And indeed most of us here, with other friends, spent several weeks there, helping with the harvest.'

He smiled at Alysoun. 'Do you tell me? And you went to a hunt at the manor? I know that the privileges of the manor include the right to venery in parts of Wychwood.'

'I did not *exactly* hunt,' Alysoun admitted. 'But we went to the hunt breakfast in the wood. Papa rode to the hunt. And I found an arrow with peacock feathers.'

'And there was a roast swan? That was very grand!'

'It was very rotten,' Margaret said, wrinkling her nose. 'I have no time for such dishes, naught but folly and expense.'

'I will tell you the full story some other time,' I said

hastily. I did not want the subject of the arrow with the peacock feathers to be explored. 'But we shall be glad indeed to have you and your family at the manor. The de Veres, who had been lords there since the Normans came, have been sore missed. There will be a great welcome for you amongst the villagers. And I know that my cousin will also be glad of your coming. Indeed, there are rights of venery and rights of warren, but of greater interest to you will be the good grazing land for sheep. It is not extensive, but I know you do not plan for a large flock. The demesne contains excellent mixed agricultural land as well, plenty of arable and a dairy herd. Burford is the nearest town, but as you know, you will be within easy reach of Witney.'

I knew that the others realised that I was trying to divert him from Alysoun's arrow, so they soon joined in, praising the pleasant situation of the village and the manor.

'I am sure you will be happy there,' Margaret said. 'It is a fine house, now that the neglect of recent years has been repaired, and if you take on the former servants of the de Veres, you will be well served.'

'Most of the customary service of the villeins,' I said, 'has been converted to rents in coin, but you will be able to hire plenty of day labourers in lieu. And there is a very fine cellar, laid down by Yves de Vere. You must consult the cellarer, Warin Hodgate about it. I think he is personally acquainted with every barrel.'

'Well!' Peter Winchingham laughed. 'It seems a very fortunate accident indeed that the first manor I viewed was a disappointment. I must have been guided by some kindly saint to Leighton Manor. And you have the right of it, Master Elyot. I have no plans for a large flock. 'Tis but a fancy of mine to own a few sheep of my own. All my life I have worked with wool, from the clip to the finished cloth, but never owned the creatures from which we all benefit. It is time.'

I smiled. 'The present flock there is small, but you might wish to buy in a good ram. The de Veres' old shepherd died this year past, and since then the care of the sheep has fallen to any servant and none. If you decide to hire a skilled man, you should speak to our shepherd, old Godfrid. There is no man knows more about the beasts. He will be able to tell you where you may find a good man.'

'I see that I have bought not only a manor,' he said, 'but a wealth of good will as well.'

'Your own good will in helping Cedric Walden secure his man has done you credit here in Oxford,' I said, 'though you suffered for it in that stinking alley. And I would you should call me Nicholas. We stand on no ceremony in this household.'

He half rose from his stool and bowed. 'I should be honoured, and hope that all here will call me Peter.'

'We too should be honoured,' Margaret said with dignity.

Alysoun opened her eyes wide. 'And me?'

'Master Winchingham to you, my pet,' I said, 'until you are a lady grown.'

She slid down from her stool and climbed on to my lap. 'And when will that be, Papa?'

'Not for years and years,' I said, 'until you are an old lady like Emma.'

She frowned. 'I do not think she is so *very* old.'

Emma laughed. 'Quite old enough to take you up to bed. Will you come with me? I know a very good story about some sheep who decided to climb a mountain.'

Rafe hopped down and seized her hand. 'Will you tell me, too?'

'I will, if you get quickly into your night shift.'

They climbed the stairs, the children still chattering. Margaret, I saw, was watching them thoughtfully.

I hoped that no one would mention the unhappy events that had taken place recently at Leighton Manor. Later, I would tell Peter Winchingham the full story, but I was sure that our merchant from Bruges, with his son and daughter, would cast a new and cleansing light over the place, bringing back the happy atmosphere that had existed there in my youth. Sire Raymond, I was certain, would enjoy his company, two booklovers who could share their passion.

Our talk turned to the dreadful events of recent days, the death of Hamo Belancer, the prior's attack on his own church, and the intended assassination of the prince, until Margaret put an end to it, saying it was not a fit subject for a tranquil evening. When our guests began to stir and talk of leaving, she said firmly that she would brew up some spiced ale.

'For it is turning colder now. It will warm you from within, before you venture outside.'

Emma had joined us quietly after settling the children.

'I will escort you home,' I said. 'There may still be some of the town rowdies about the streets after the fair.'

'Nay,' she said, shaking her head. 'There is no need. Peter goes back to the Mitre and we may walk together, and with Jordain too, most of the way, but you would need to return alone. Your back must still trouble you. I know that you have had many broken nights of late. Get you to bed and let your body heal itself.'

There was no shaking her from this, so perforce I must yield.

'Will you be at home tomorrow?' I asked. 'I should like to discuss your next book with you. Walter is most pleased that you will make the book of his mother's stories, but he tells me that he has several more still to write down.'

'Is there nothing else?' She looked wistful. 'I have had enough of cooking and selling at the fair to last me a year. I long to return to inks and parchment!'

Margaret began to ladle out the hot spiced ale. 'Have a care!' she warned. ''Tis hot enough to burn your lips. Leave it a while.'

'Aye,' I said. 'I had almost forgot. The Lady Amilia has ordered another book, which she demands must be made by the same scribe and illuminator, and bound to match her book of hours. Perhaps in time she will require an entire library!'

I saw that the merchant was listening with interest, with enquiry in his eyes, but not spoken. There was little need to keep silence when everyone else here knew what was intended to be a secret.

'Emma worked in the scriptorium when she was a novice at Godstow,' I explained.

At this his eyebrows went up, but he was too polite to exclaim at this unexpected revelation.

'Another time,' I said. 'Emma herself may tell you all her story when there is more leisure, but she never took her final vows. Let me show you.'

I fetched that first book of hours which had opened my eyes to Emma's skills and laid it before him. He turned the pages delicately, stopping from time to time to exclaim, or to laugh at the sly jests she had slipped into the pictures. When he laid it down, he looked at her with a new respect.

'You made this, mistress?'

She nodded, colouring.

'She has made another book of hours,' I said, 'for this Lady Amilia – a wealthy customer of mine. Demanding, but not as learned as she would have us suppose. And now she has ordered another book.'

'But, Nicholas,' Emma said, cautiously sipping her spiced ale, 'you have not said what this new book is to be.'

I looked at her, glumly.

'She wants an entire book of troubadour songs, words and music both, and fully illuminated. I hardly know where to begin. I think I know the gist of one song. I know the tune at least, but I am not sure if I have the words aright. The true troubadour songs are all in the *langue d'Oc*. How we are to make a whole book of them, I cannot imagine.'

'Does the lady understand the *langue d'Oc*?' Peter asked.

I shrugged. 'I find it doubtful. It will be some notion she has acquired. She and her husband were at court a few months ago. Perhaps it is the new fashion there.'

'My daughter has a great fondness for music,' he said, 'though I do not know whether she knows any songs of the troubadours. I shall ask her when I return to Bruges.'

'I thank you,' I said. 'My journeyman Walter said bluntly that we need a troubadour.'

'Not easy to find in Oxford,' Emma said.

'Exactly what I said to Walter. I thought at first that there might be some scholar in the university who could prove of help, but I have decided since then that it is too frivolous a subject. What do you say, Jordain?'

He had been listening, without comment, and now shook his head.

'I can think of no one, and you are right, Nicholas. Anything as lovely and light-hearted as the songs of the troubadours would probably be beneath the notice of our scholars.'

'Not always light-hearted,' Emma objected. 'I think many tell of lost loves and broken hearts. I remember when I was young and impressionable, a troubadour came to my grandfather's house and sang such songs, though I cannot remember them now, only their melancholy. He was very handsome, that troubadour, in a soulful way.' She grinned at me. 'I was quite in love with him for months.'

Peter laughed. 'I think you will like my daughter, mistress.'

'Well,' I said, 'lacking a troubadour, I look to you all for help in filling this book as the Lady Amilia requires. Without the songs, there will be nothing for Emma to work with.'

Soon after this Emma, Jordain, and Peter took their leave. I went with them into the street, and watched them head up the High, Emma between the two men, an arm slipped through each of theirs. I regretted losing a little more time with her, but I knew she had the right of it. Sitting for so long on a stool had set my back aching. I could feel where some of the slashes had bled and the priory shirt had stuck to the drying blood. It would be a painful business removing the shirt, but I had promised Margaret that she might salve my back tonight. She had little faith in whatever the priory infirmarian had applied before.

When I came back into the kitchen, she was stacking the dirty plates and already had a pot of water heating on the fire to wash them. I took hold of her arm and firmly pulled her away from the table.

'Leave them, Meg. They will wait till the morning. And leave the bread dough, just for this one night. We are both so tired we can barely stand.'

'I cannot bear to see this,' she said.

'Shut your eyes, and you will not see it.'

'At least I need not worry about the bread. Emma made up the dough before you came in with Jordain.'

'That was good of her,' I said, feeling quite inordinately pleased.

'Aye, she is a good girl.' She sighed. 'Very well,' she capitulated. 'I will leave these dirty things, but I have not forgotten your back.'

'That may be left as well,' I said, in hope.

'Nay, it may not. That blade was certainly dirty, and the cuts may fester. Go you up to your bedchamber and take off that dreadful shirt. Then you may lie on your face and I will salve your back. Off with you.'

I saw that the only way to ensure that she left the kitchen untouched was to do as she bid. Removing the shirt was an unpleasant business, and started more of the cuts bleeding, which I could feel, though not see. Indeed, I was not even sure how many cuts there were.

I lay down on my bed and despite the pain I was nearly asleep before Margaret came in with a bright candle lantern and a pot of her own salve.

'How many slashes are there?' I asked, this being still in my mind.

'A perfect net of them,' she said. 'Six or eight at least. Now lie still while I spread this on them.'

Margaret's salve was blessedly cool and soothing, unlike the stinging potion applied by the infirmarian. I had expected it to hurt, but, to my surprise, my back even felt better after she had done with me.

'I wish you might leave your back open to the air all night,' she said, 'but you will be cold.'

'I will leave it so, as long as I may,' I said. 'At least I may have the bedclothes up to my waist.'

Face down as I was, I had to grope around behind me to find the edge of the feather bed. Margaret took hold of it and drew it up, tucking it in firmly.

'That will do for now,' she said. 'Once the salve has soaked in you will need the warmth, so you may pull it up to your neck. Do not catch a chill.'

She tousled my hair affectionately, as if I were no older than Rafe, and bore the lantern off to her own chamber.

I fell asleep almost at once.

Although I woke once or twice during the night, experiencing more pain than I had done straight after the fight, my back felt considerably better in the morning. At the bottom of my clothes coffer I found an old shirt, softened with much washing, which I drew on carefully over my head. Although it was not as loose as the priory shirt, that one had been of much coarser cloth. I donned a warm cotte over the top, for there was no denying that my bedchamber was cold this morning. I shivered, thinking of the bitter days ahead. Although Oxford lies in a hollow formed by its two river valleys, those same rivers make the winters damp. And although we are spared the worst of the winds one meets on the hills of the Cotswolds, the months of winter here can be brutally cold. I must remember to order more logs from the forester who works on Shotover Hill, and charcoal for the brazier I keep lit in the shop during the winter months, for scriveners cannot work if their hands are cold.

When I reached the kitchen, Margaret had nearly finished clearing away the remains of last night's meal, and even the children were helping. Rowan had discovered some spills under the table, and was making herself useful by clearing those away.

Ashamed that everyone in the family except me was hard at work, I laid out our usual simple morning fare.

'Aunt Margaret says we may have honey this morning,' Rafe said, wrapping his arms about my leg. 'Is that man really going to live in Leighton?'

'Master Winchingham, not "that man",' I said, disentangling myself. 'Aye, he has bought the manor. We shall see him next time we go to the farm, though I think he will come to Oxford quite often as well.'

'I like him. He gave me my monkey.'

'He did indeed. Now, sit you down, my little man. Here is some of your aunt's bread. She is a wonder, making it fresh every morning.'

He sat down readily, but saw no wonder in the arrival of fresh bread on the table every morning. It had always been so.

'Papa,' Alysoun said, when we were all seated and I had spoken the blessing. 'How long is it until Christmas?'

Margaret laughed. 'Two months yet, Alysoun. The fair is just over, and the students newly come to Oxford.'

Like everyone else in the town, we reckoned our seasons by the coming and going of the students.

Alysoun sighed. 'I wish it was Christmas. Now the fair is over, there is nothing to do.'

'You have hardly done your lessons with Papa,' Margaret said, 'since before we went to the farm. That will give you plenty to do. And did you not say that Juliana promised to help you make clothes for your doll?'

Alysoun's face had not exactly fallen at the mention of lessons, for she enjoyed them, but she brightened at the mention of making clothes with Juliana.

'May I go this morning?' she said.

'It is too far for you to go alone,' Margaret said, mindful that the town would not have settled yet after the fair.

'I can take you to St Mildred Street,' I said. 'I have some business in Fish Street this morning, and it is on the way. You will need a warm cloak.'

As soon as we had eaten, she ran off to fetch her doll and her cloak.

'But what can I do?' Rafe said mournfully.

'You and I,' Margaret said, 'are going to make gingerbread. You remember that you had gingerbread at the fair? Well, we can make some every bit as good.'

'And I shall be glad,' she said, turning to me with a smile, 'to be back in the peace of my own kitchen. Alysoun may miss the excitement of the fair, but I am not sorry it is over. What have you to do in Fish Street?'

'Oh,' I said evasively. 'I needs must see John Shippan, the carpenter. And I will also ask him to put in an order for us with the forester for more logs. I noticed last week that we have not enough in store for the winter.'

If she realised that I had not answered her question, she did not persist. I could tell from the abstracted look in her eye that she was busy taking the reins of the household into her hands again. Like me, she was happily returning to a tranquil life.

Alysoun chattered all the way up the High Street, and at the turn by the Mitre she slipped her hand from mine and ran ahead to the Farringdons' house.

'May Alysoun stay with Juliana this morning?' I asked Maud, when I had caught up. 'It seems Juliana made an unwise offer to help her with her sewing.'

Maud laughed. 'They will enjoy themselves. Will you step in, Nicholas?'

'Nay, not now, but I shall be coming back later. I wonder whether I might draw you into a small conspiracy with me?'

She looked surprised, but listened while I explained what I wanted her to do.

'Certainly,' she said. 'That will not be difficult. We shall see you later, then.'

I went on my way, pleased that I had managed to speak to her alone.

Before I reached Carfax, I met Walden riding toward me. He reined in his horse.

'I was coming to see you, Nicholas. You have saved me the length of the street.'

He leapt from his horse, to speak to me more easily.

'The Frenchman, Claude Mateaux, has made a clean confession of everything. You will be glad that the application of torture was unnecessary.'

'I am indeed glad. I have no very kindly feelings toward the fellow, after the way he etched my back with his dagger, but I do not feel torture is a Christian practice.'

'Neither are murder or assassination,' he said grimly.

I bowed my acquiescence.

'However, the mere suggestion that we would resort to torture unless he made a clean breast of his crimes was enough to loosen his tongue.'

'He admitted to killing Hamo Belancer?' I said.

'He did. And your guess was correct. Their meeting here was not accidental. It seems they have been in correspondence for some months. They were acquainted in France and it was someone's idea that the bribe of restoring Belancer's estates would be enough to secure his alliance.'

'His treason, rather,' I said.

'Mateaux said "someone" had the idea?'

'Aye,' Walden said. 'He claimed not to know who, and I believe him. The French king will have his own intelligencers just as our king does. However it was, Belancer was offered the restoration of his French property if he agreed to help Mateaux to reach Prince Edward.'

'He was an unpleasant man, but I would never have expected him to be a traitor.'

'He was obsessed with the loss of his lands, but more than that, it seems he bore a grudge against the prince himself, blaming his campaigns in France for the French reprisals which brought about the loss of his vineyards. According to Mateaux, Belancer had come to regard the prince as personally responsible.'

'Not the belief of a rational man,' I said, 'but I suppose we had come to see his obsession as irrational, though none could have believed it would go so far.' I paused. 'I remember now that the last time I spoke to him, he seemed to be clutching to himself some exciting and vengeful secret, but I would never have guessed what it was. Yet even so, he did not deserve to die like that.'

'From what Mateaux has said, there was never any intention of restoring his land. Once he had served his purpose, he was disposed of, being of no further use.'

'What I do not understand,' I said, 'is how they could have known in France – weeks ago, I suppose – that the prince would be staying at the priory now. I doubt whether the prince himself would have known it then.'

'That was not the original plan,' Walden said. 'It was believed Prince Edward would be in residence at the Palace of Woodstock. Belancer had a regular order to deliver ale to the palace once a month. Mateaux was to meet him in Oxford, then travel with him to deliver the ale, posing as his servant. Once inside the palace, it would be up to him to find and kill the prince.'

'Only when he arrived in Oxford,' I said, 'under the guise of the fair, he discovered that the prince was at the priory.'

'Exactly. It became necessary to devise a new plan. That was what they were about when Master Winchingham stumbled upon their meeting at Belancer's house. And once Mateaux learned there was a secret way into the priory, which he could use without drawing attention to himself, he decided quite coldly to rid himself of the man who could point the finger at him. His intention was to kill the prince, slip away from the priory, and then resume his role as a merchant attending the fair. Afterwards, he could return to France undiscovered. It seems he really is a merchant vintner. It is an excellent role for a man who needs an unexceptionable reason for frequent travel. Ironically, he was awarded a part of Belancer's vineyards as payment for some previous task he had undertaken for the French crown.'

'It seems,' I said soberly, 'that Peter Winchingham was mighty lucky to escape with his life.'

'Indeed. Mateaux thought he had killed him, although he could not be sure in the dark. Winchingham must have a particularly thick skull.'

'So he says himself.'

'As it happens,' Walden said, 'it seems that you and Jordain Brinkylsworth are also lucky to have escaped with your lives.'

'What do you mean?'

'After Mateaux had dealt – so he thought – with the merchant, he went back into the house to finish the wine they were drinking and to lull Belancer into a state of slightly muzzy confidence. He had just killed him when you and Brinkylsworth came blundering up the alleyway and fell over Winchingham. Mateaux could have gone for you, two innocents, unarmed, caught up in rescuing the merchant. Instead, he decided to lie low, put out the candle, and waited until you were gone.'

'I *thought* I saw a light go out. So he was still there when we picked up Peter Winchingham! That makes it all clear, what happened to Hamo Belancer, and also why. What of Prince Edward?'

'Mateaux was quite calm and unrepentant about that. To him it was merely another task, for which he would be paid. He does not even seem to have the normal Frenchman's hatred of our prince. He would have cut him down as indifferently as he killed Belancer, or as he would slaughter a pig at Michaelmas.'

I shuddered. I was sure the sheriff was speaking no more than the truth, but the thought of such a human creature, without human feelings, sickened me.

'So there you have it all,' Walden said, drawing his horse near and straightening his stirrup leather.

'He will hang?'

'Oh, aye, he will hang. But I gave him a promise. Since he made a clean confession of all, he will not suffer all the other penalties such an act of treason should entail.'

I knew quite well what he meant. As children we were told the grim story of Roger Mortimer's death, traitor to the present king's father. Though whether Mateaux's acts could count as treason in law, I was not sure. He was a subject not of the English king, but of the French king. He had not succeeded in his intention of killing the prince. On French soil, when the temporary truce expired, it might have counted as just one more act of war. Well, it was not for me to make such fine distinctions. He had, undoubtedly, murdered Hamo Belancer.

Walden and I parted at Carfax, in sombre mood, but as I made my way to John Shippan's workshop, I put all thoughts of Mateaux and Belancer behind me, feeling suddenly cheered by the scent of new cut wood and wax polish which wafted out from the courtyard.

Saving up the pleasure of seeing the desk until last, I found Shippan's senior journeyman first, and arranged for him to include my request for firewood with the workshop's next order for timber from the forester. This was my usual method of buying logs, for it saved me paying a carrier, even if it meant waiting until Shippan required more green timber.

'Aye,' the journeyman said. 'I'll be sending an order in two-three weeks, not more. You should have your logs by the end of November, before the worst of the weather sets in, never fear.'

Satisfied with this, I asked him to included a sack of charcoal in my order, for the forester worked with a group of charcoal burners in the Shotover woods.

Then, at last, I went to seek out John Shippan, and Emma's desk.

He was in the main workshop, overseeing one of the apprentices who was turning a bedpost on a lathe – somewhat nervously, I thought, working under the master's eye. I stayed quiet until he finished, not wanting to cause his chisel to slip by interrupting.

'Fair enough,' Shippan said, as he examined the work, 'though there is too much thickness here.' He pointed to one spot, which, to my own untrained eye, seemed the same as the rest. 'Rest your eyes for now, lad.

When you come back to it, you will see.'

He turned and caught sight of me.

'Master Elyot, you have come for your desk.'

'I have.'

'Two of the lads will bring it down for you, and load it on a handcart. You are sure you do not want me to deliver it? I can do so tomorrow.'

Tomorrow would be far too long to wait.

'Nay, I shall take it today.'

While the apprentice who had been working on the lathe and another lad climbed the steps to fetch down the desk, I paid Master Shippan, one eye nervously on those treacherous steps. However, the boys reached the ground safely, then wrapped the desk in sacking for protection and laid it in a handcart.

'I'll send Will with you,' Shippan said. 'He can save you bringing the cart back. And he can help you carry in the desk.'

I was grateful for this. Having seen that two strong lads had some difficulty bringing the desk down Shippan's steps, I thought I would be unable to manhandle it up the stairs in the Farringdons' house. I doubted whether Juliana would have been strong enough to help me.

Will was the apprentice who had been turning the bedpost, and I suspected he was glad to escape from under his master's scrutiny for a time. Shippan was the finest carpenter in Oxford, and to be trained by him was a privilege, but I expected that his standards of craftsmanship were demanding.

'How far are we to go, Master Elyot?' the boy asked, as we pushed the handcart over the cobbles outside the Guildhall. Here they were kept in good repair, better than in some other streets.

'Not far. Just along St Mildred Street.'

'No distance then,' he said cheerfully.

'How long are you into your apprenticeship?'

'Two years. A little more. I have learned to know all the woods, and I can make most joints, though nothing like so well as the master. Master Godwin says that will come with practice.'

Master Godwin was the journeyman with whom I had placed my order for firewood.

'I am sure it will. Was that your first bedpost?'

'Aye, and we are not allowed to use callipers. We must judge it all by eye.'

'I am sure that will come with practice, too. If you used callipers, I suppose you would not develop the eye.'

'Probably not.' He grinned. 'Still, I'm glad of a change.'

When we reached St Mildred Street, I asked him to wait for a moment, past the first few houses, and went on ahead to the Farringdons' home. Juliana answered my knock. She smiled and looked over my shoulder.

'Mother has taken Emma to the bottom of the garden, to collect the apples from that old tree. There are quite a few, so you are safe yet a while. Where is this mysterious object?'

I turned and waved to Will to bring the cart the rest of the way.

'It is a scrivener's desk,' I said, 'to replace that wobbly table. Can you move the table, before we carry the desk upstairs?'

'Aye, there will not be room for both.'

She pushed the door as wide as it would go, and ran through to the stairs leading up from the kitchen.

I was mighty relieved to have Will's help. Solid oak, the desk was, and it seemed somehow much larger here in this small cottage than it had looked in Shippan's workshop. And it was heavy! We were both panting by the time we had manoeuvred it, with some difficulty, up the narrow stairs and into the girls' bedchamber. For one bad moment I feared it would not pass through the door, but Will removed the swivelling shelf, and then we were through. As he fixed it in place again, he glanced about with interest.

'I thought you would want this in your shop, Master

Elyot.'

'Nay,' I said, 'this scrivener works from home.'

Once we had the desk in place where the light from the window would flow over from Emma's left, illuminating her work without interruption, I saw that it would fit neatly into the room. It was larger than the table, but mainly in height.

'My thanks to you, Will,' I said, pressing a groat into his hand. 'Have a cup of ale on your way back. It was thirsty work.'

He grinned. 'Thought we'd never have it up those stairs, Master Elyot.'

And he went off, whistling.

Alysoun had come to peer through the door. She seemed amazed at the sight of the desk, and wanted, at once, to play with all its devices.

'Not now,' Juliana said. 'We will go and fetch Emma. Mind, you are not to spoil the surprise! We will simply tell her we want to show her something in the bedchamber. We might pretend to be somewhat worried. Do you think you could do that?'

'Aye.' Alysoun's eyes shone at being part of a conspiracy, and they ran off down the stairs together.

I went to the window to watch, but kept to one side, lest Emma look up and catch sight of me.

Juliana and Alysoun walked down the unkempt garden together, along the path which had been cleared through the long grass and nettles. Come the winter, we must clear the rest. Juliana was strolling casually, holding back Alysoun, who was skipping excitedly. I saw Juliana lean down and say something to her. Alysoun nodded and stopped her skipping. They disappeared behind a row of rampant gooseberry bushes.

It seemed a long time before they reappeared with Emma and Maud, but I suppose Juliana had been careful not to seem in a hurry, which might have alerted Emma that something was afoot. As it was, she was strolling slowly, carrying a large basket of apples. The four of them came back to the house – though I saw that Alysoun could not refrain from the occasional skip – then they disappeared from my sight as they entered the kitchen.

'Can you come up to our bedchamber, Emma?' Juliana's voice floated up the stairs. 'There has been a rather odd delivery.'

'For me?' Emma sounded puzzled. 'Is it something from my grandfather?'

'You had best come and see.'

I could hear their feet on the stairs. It sounded as though all four were coming, and Maysant as well. This was not quite what I had planned. I drew back into the corner, but kept the sight of the open door in my view. I wanted to see her face.

Then she was there, shading her eyes with her hand from the sunlight flowing in from the window. She stood quite still. I had a moment of panic. Would she be offended? Perhaps she had liked the little table. What had possessed me to make such an extravagant gesture? Well, if she did not like it, I could always take it away for my own use. I thought wryly of trying to get it through the door and down the stairs again.

For a moment she went quite white, and then colour began to rise from her neck and flood her face. She took one step into the room, and then two.

I heard Maud say, 'Come away girls.'

They must have retreated back down the stairs, but I was not listening.

Emma took two more steps into the room. Then she saw me.

To my astonishment and alarm, I saw that there were tears in her eyes.

'Oh, I beg you, Emma,' I blurted out, 'do not cry. I can take it away. I should not have interfered.'

She shook her head. She ran her fingers over the carved vines along the frame, and caressed the silken smoothness of the writing slope. I began to hope again.

'Nicholas,' she said softly, 'oh, Nicholas, you read

me as surely as any book.'

I came towards her and laid my hand beside hers on the desk.

And she put her arms around me.

Historical Note

The great town fairs of the Middle Ages were the centres of commerce for centuries, attracting both those who came to sell and those who came to buy. Merchants would travel from country to country with their wares, under conditions which would seem daunting to us today. They used strings of pack-ponies or mules, sea-going ships, and river barges. There were dangers along the way, not only from poor roads, precipitous mountain passes, storm-tossed sea crossings, and dirty inns, but also from gangs of robbers, out to steal both goods and money, who would not hesitate to kill. In many cases this meant employing an armed guard to protect the safety of both goods and men. Yet somehow the merchants managed it, carrying along with their goods news of far flung parts of Europe and the Mediterranean.

There could be danger, too, from wars between the countries of Europe. In 1353 there was a brief truce between England and France in the long conflict which has come to be known as the Hundred Years War. Given the characters of the two kings and the importance to England of the crown's French possessions, the resumption of the war was only a matter of time.

The most famous medieval fairs were the great fairs of Champagne, but by Nicholas's time, these were beginning to decline, to the benefit of lesser fairs, like St Frideswide's Fair in Oxford. The charter to hold a fair and benefit from all the tolls and rents was granted to the Priory of St Frideswide by Henry I in the early twelfth century. Initially it was held in the summer, but in 1228 the date was shifted to six days (some accounts say a week) starting on the Feast of St Frideswide on 19 October. During the days of the fair, all the shops in Oxford must remain closed, although the inns could provide for their guests.

The loss of their own income and the substantial monies accruing to the priory were long resented by the townspeople of Oxford, particularly the traders. Matters would perhaps not have been quite so acrimonious had the priory had a better reputation, but the canons repeatedly attracted criticism for their behaviour from the bishop (at that time the Bishop of Lincoln). A number of conflicts appear in the record, including that of 1336 mentioned in the story, when the prior and canons were kidnapped and intimidated by a group of townsmen.

I have taken one liberty with time. The attack by Prior de Hungerford, accompanied by a group of secular thugs from the town, on the sub-prior and canons, during Matins (the midnight service), actually took place about eight months later – I hope I'll be forgiven for bringing it forward. Prior de Hungerford was an out-and-out scoundrel!

The priory grange, mentioned in the story, appears to have stood on part of the ground now occupied by the university Botanic Garden, at some distance from the main enclave.

When I wrote *The Bookseller's Tale*, I made a brief mention of St Frideswide's Fair, assuming that it was held on the obvious open area of St Giles, where later fairs were located, and where St Giles Fair still takes place every autumn, although it is a very different kind of fair nowadays. Further research revealed that St Frideswide's Fair was held close to the priory, which was natural enough, making it easier to control. The fairground seems to have been the northwest portion of what is now Christ Church Meadow, just outside the town wall which formed the southern boundary of the priory enclave, and just past the South Gate for those coming from the town.

Time passed. The monastic institutions were dissolved and their property seized by Henry VIII, St Frideswide's being suppressed even earlier (by Cardinal Wolsey) in April 1524. The fair was handed over to the town and held around the Guildhall, but the town never made a success of it, so that it eventually died. The priory buildings, income, and property were 'acquired' by Wolsey, who planned to create on the site his huge Cardinal College. The wonderful church had the three bays at the west end of the nave demolished to make way for what is now Tom Quad, but mercifully the plan to destroy the rest of the medieval church was never carried out and it later became Christ Church Cathedral, with its own bishop. I was confirmed there when I was a student – and long before I knew anything about St Frideswide's Fair.

Wolsey too fell, in 1530, to the capricious jealousy of Henry VIII, who took over the college project in 1532, completing it as Christ Church College, familiarly known now as The House. If Nicholas were to stand in the church today, with his back to the truncated west end of the nave, he would recognise it, though it would probably look a little bare to him.

Thanks to the efforts of many concerned members of the university and citizens of Oxford, the wonderful meadows stretching south, down from the town wall to the rivers, still remain beautiful and unsullied, a large piece of the country in the middle of the town. These meadows used to be rougher, with several streams wandering across them, streams which are now culverted, but walking there it is not difficult to imagine Nicholas and Emma sitting by the river, with the merchants' barges coming upstream and the busy hum of the fair at their backs.

A final thought. Many people do not realise how far back in the past the use of spectacles occurs, but in fact they appear in portraits of the fourteenth century. When they were first developed, they would have been expensive. However, by early in the following century they were so common that

hawkers were selling them in the streets of London, alongside the pedlars of hot pies and other delights. Read the fifteenth century poem *London Lickpenny* and you will see them mentioned:
> *'Master, what will you copen or buy?*
> *Fine felt hats, or spectacles to read?'*

The poem is worth reading in any case for its ironic refrain 'For lack of money I might not speed'.

Nothing ever changes!

The Author

Ann Swinfen spent her childhood partly in England and partly on the east coast of America. She was educated at Somerville College, Oxford, where she read Classics and Mathematics and married a fellow undergraduate, the historian David Swinfen. While bringing up their five children and studying for a postgraduate MSc in Mathematics and a BA and PhD in English Literature, she had a variety of jobs, including university lecturer, translator, freelance journalist and software designer. She served for nine years on the governing council of the Open University and for five years worked as a manager and editor in the technical author division of an international computer company, but gave up her full-time job to concentrate on her writing, while continuing part-time university teaching in English Literature. In 1995 she founded Dundee Book Events, a voluntary organisation promoting books and authors to the general public.

She is the author of the highly acclaimed series, *The Chronicles of Christoval Alvarez*. Set in the late sixteenth century, it features a young Marrano physician recruited as a code-breaker and spy in Walsingham's secret service. In order, the books are: **The Secret World of Christoval Alvarez**, **The Enterprise of England**, **The Portuguese Affair**, **Bartholomew Fair**, **Suffer the Little Children**, **Voyage to Muscovy**, **The Play's the Thing,** and **That Time May Cease**.

Her *Fenland Series* takes place in East Anglia during the seventeenth century. In the first book, **Flood**, both men and women fight desperately to save their land from greedy and unscrupulous speculators. The second, **Betrayal**, continues the story of the dangerous search for legal redress and security for the embattled villagers, at a time when few could be trusted.

Her latest series, the bestselling *Oxford Medieval Mysteries*, is set in the fourteenth century and features bookseller Nicholas Elyot, a young widower with two small children, and his university friend Jordain Brinkylsworth, who are faced with crime in the troubled world following the Black Death. In order, the books are: **The Bookseller's Tale**, **The Novice's Tale**, The

Huntsman's Tale and *The Merchant's Tale.* Both this series and the Christoval Alvarez series are being recorded as unabridged audiobooks.

She has also written two standalone historical novels. ***The Testament of Mariam***, set in the first century, recounts, from an unusual perspective, one of the most famous and yet ambiguous stories in human history, while exploring life under a foreign occupying force, in lands still torn by conflict to this day. ***This Rough Ocean*** is based on the real-life experiences of the Swinfen family during the 1640s, at the time of the English Civil War, when John Swynfen was imprisoned for opposing the killing of the king, and his wife Anne had to fight for the survival of her children and dependents.

Ann Swinfen now lives on the northeast coast of Scotland, with her husband, formerly vice-principal of the University of Dundee, a rescue cat called Maxi, and a cocker spaniel called Suki.

You can receive notifications of new books and audios by signing up to the mailing list at www.annswinfen.com/sign-up/ Learn more at her website www.annswinfen.com

Printed in Great Britain
by Amazon